ZON

by
M.B. Smith

I0564627

Justice M. Hill Publishing
Ashburn, VA

M.B. Smith

Artwork courtesy of Brian Tarallo
www.LizardBrainSolutions.com

ISBN: 978-1-304-28352-8

ZON

Other books by M.B. Smith:

Chancy, Queen of Ashes
Love, or a Safe, Sterile Life
System of Secrets
Purity
The Children of Kalothia
The Secret of Hawk's Talon

Main Characters:

High Prince Aden Cade: Heir to Kealt's throne.
High Princess Sia Selarney: Aden's wife and the daughter of King Ivege and Queen Sarin.
Abby Watanabe: Earth Alliance officer and Aden's former lover.
General Lucien Brawn: Leader of Kealt's military coup.
Major Aija Vilas: Brawn's chief aide.
Colonel Frune Jasper: Leader of the resistance.
Bang: Leader of the Taal Prime Council.
The taal: Telepathic rulers of Seti.
Glyn and Gris Haberat: Aden's half sister and brother in law.
High Princess Celesta Selarney: Aden's full sister, who is married to Sia's brother Polis.
High Prince Polis Selarney: Heir to the Ardalan throne.
Queen Sarin Selarney: Queen of Ardala.
Howard Gross: Chief representative of the Outer Space Exploration Corporation (OSEC).
The Laima System: Located in the Poseidon Galaxy, home to Kealt, Ardala, and Seti.
The zon: Blood-thirsty, insect-like creatures who were obliterated by the Earth Alliance.
The Earth Alliance: A political and military organization of human worlds in the Milky Way.

To my family, who patiently tolerate and support my poorly compensated, but highly labor-intensive hobby.

M.B. Smith

Prologue

Adrift in space for weeks, with just hours left before his life support failed, a desperate traitor held an energy weapon to his head. He was trying to muster the nerve to kill himself before his ship's systems failed and he suffered a much more painful death.

Months earlier, following the end of the Zon War, he had fled the Laima System in a zon short-range reconnaissance ship. He had chosen the wrong side in the war, and doubted the victors would be in a forgiving mood. He survived for a time by living off the largess of his few remaining friends on distant colonies, but could never stay long for fear of being betrayed, something he knew much about.

He was a bureaucrat, not an engineer. He had no idea how to maintain a ship, let alone a vessel built with alien technology. To make matters worse, the zon ship was never meant for the rigors he subjected it to, and, over time, its systems began to fail.

Three weeks before, he had gotten into a skirmish with qrell pirates. While he succeeded in fending them off, he overtaxed his engines in the process and they soon failed. With the ship's replication system exhausted and his stores virtually gone, he rationed what he had left and sent out a general distress call. However, he was in an isolated region of space and wasn't surprised when no one immediately answered.

While he waited, his mind frequently drifted back to his former life, full of comforts, power, and servants to do his bidding. Desperate to maintain his lifestyle, he sided with the zon when their war with the Earth Alliance drove them back to the Laima System in the Poseidon Galaxy. When he was eventually exposed as a traitor, he fled the system with no clear plan and embarked on a precarious existence.

Now he was dirty and tired. He hadn't eaten for a week, or had any water for three days. Soon he wouldn't even have enough power to send out a distress call. Not long after that, life support would fail and he would die, from either suffocation or hypothermia, both of which promised to be painful and unpleasant.

He pressed his eyelids together and slowly pulled the trigger. Just as he had finally reconciled himself to his fate, alarm bells went off. It was the ship's proximity sensors warning him that a collision was imminent. He activated the still functioning vidscreen and saw a vessel that was so large he had to reduce magnification several times to see it in its entirety. It was obviously a warship, but unlike anything he had ever seen. The vessel hailed him, but he no longer had the power to respond. As he was in a zon ship, he was concerned that whomever was trying to hail him would shoot first and sort the rest out later. Instead, the cabin began to shimmer, and he found himself transported to a holding cell on the alien vessel.

A youngish human, well dressed and handsome, greeted him. "Welcome aboard the *Halifax*," he said. I'm dying to hear your explanation for being the only occupant of a short range zon vessel drifting helplessly in the middle of nowhere!"

The fugitive began to stutter, as he always did when he was nervous. When he explained that he was a former senior bureaucrat on a planet the man was familiar with, the man tried unsuccessfully to hide his excitement. "That's very interesting," he said, "but you still haven't told me how a man in such a prestigious position manages to find himself on a broken-down zon vessel way out here."

The fugitive told his version of the truth as best he could, in a way he hoped wouldn't result in his immediate death, but the man wasn't really listening. He was much more interested in his understanding of the inner circles of his planet's politics and society. It didn't take him long to conclude that his "guest" could be a very useful tool in his grand plan, and would do anything to live another day—especially if that day promised to return him to his previous exalted position, which he eventually promised him. Of course, they were just words—the man would have agreed to anything to secure the fugitive's cooperation.

The man began to put together the outlines of a plan that would net him a fortune sufficient to retire on the pleasure planet Dionysus. In fact, he thought, if things went right, he might be able to buy the entire planet…

Chapter I

Abby's dream didn't come as often as it once did, but it was always the same: She walks down a long hallway and enters a room that is dark except for the dim illumination of a single, small candle sitting on top of a cake. In the shadows she can make out vague figures fighting to keep from laughing. She smiles and turns to flip on the light. When she turns back, all that remains is a smashed cake and several bloodless husks...

Jolted awake, Earth Alliance officer and senior xenobiologist Abigail Watanabe shot up in bed shaking from her nightmare. No matter how many times she had it, it always seemed real. She felt her bedclothes, which were soaked with sweat. Tears now forming in her eyes, she glanced at the clock. She didn't have to get up for another half hour, but, too afraid to lie back down she decided to take a shower.

Today she was going to meet her good friend, Admiral John Trent. Trent, who was the Earth Alliance ambassador to the Laima System, had asked her to come to his office in the Kealt palace complex to brief him personally on the results of the archaeological dig she was leading on Seti.

Along with Kealt and Ardala, Seti was one of three habitable planets in Laima. Ruled by an enigmatic, telepathic species called taals, Seti was resource rich and dangerous. It also was where the original pilgrims from Earth made landfall in Laima many thousands of years earlier.

After she stepped out of the shower, she dried herself and brushed out her thick, shoulder length, black hair. When she was finished, she put on a bra and panties and pulled on her black, red trimmed, one-piece uniform. Looking in the mirror, a dusky, elegant face with black, almond shaped eyes and fine features looked back at her. She thought a little makeup would do her good. She smiled wryly, wondering if she would remember how to put it on if she even had any.

When she entered Trent's office later that morning, he jumped up from behind his desk and embraced her heartily. When he released her, he held her at arm's length, looked her up and down, and remarked that nearly a year in the jungle hadn't hurt her a bit. He pointed to two overstuffed chairs and asked her to have a seat. Then he grabbed a data crystal that was sitting on his desk and sat down in the chair across from her.

He laid the crystal on the small table between them, leaned back, and with his hand on his chin said with a smile, "This is remarkable work, Abby. In just about a year, you and your team have pushed back our knowledge of Earth history by thousands of years. Art, literature, music, politics, anthropology…hell, even sports and entertainment. I could go on and on. It's all here. It'll take us decades to make sense of all this; truly remarkable!"

The data crystal Trent was referring to was part of Abby's report on the ancient generational ship discovered in the jungles of Seti the previous year. "Discovered" wasn't the proper term—the inscrutable taal had revealed the ship's existence to High Prince Aden Cade of Kealt and his now-wife, High Princess Sia Selarney of Ardala, after they caused the royals to crash on the planet.

The wreck was once part of a fleet of generational ships sent out from an overburdened Earth to find and seed other habitable planets. Most of the ships ultimately failed in their quest, but against all odds, one made it to the Laima System in the Poseidon Galaxy. Although the ship had originally made landfall on Seti, within a few generations, with the subconscious coaxing of the telepathic taal, most humans had migrated to Kealt and Ardala, which were far more hospitable planets. As Laima's human population grew and thrived, they eventually forgot how they had reached the system, and their origin became shrouded in myths and legends.

Several years earlier, when a voracious, insect-like species called the zon sought to migrate to the Milky Way in search of human blood, their ensuing war with the Earth Alliance led them both back to Laima. Out of desperation, the long forgotten taal revealed themselves and the generational ship to Aden and Sia. They hoped its significance would unite the royals' fractious subjects and that they in turn would protect Seti, the galaxy's single known source of abundant xanide, a crystal essential to the humans' technology.

After the EA—as the Earth Alliance was more commonly known—annihilated the zon, the taal asked Abby to lead the team that would excavate the wreck. Kealt and Ardala had different versions of their early history, and both agreed it would be best for a neutral observer to lead the project. In addition, Abby had saved Aden's life, endearing her to Bang, the leader of the taal.

"Well," Abby replied, "it wasn't that hard. The generational ship was in surprisingly good condition, considering it's been laying on the surface of Seti for 10,000 years. Whoever built it, built it to last. Before it was abandoned, its last caretakers meticulously downloaded all its databases into crystals that will literally last forever. They left the crystals well protected in a place where they would be easy to find. Then they left us a 'road map' for the ship itself. The difficult thing is going through such a huge ship inch by inch, and ensuring everything is cataloged and tagged. *That* could take decades."

"You're being far too modest," insisted Trent. "You're working under horrendous conditions on one of the most inhospitable, supposedly habitable, planets in the universe. And you have to work fast, because once you opened that ship, stuff is decaying at an accelerated rate. I know the stress you're under trying preserve what's important before it's gone again, this time forever."

"All true Admiral," Abby agreed with a grin. "With that in mind, do I have your permission to depart for Seti tomorrow—I wouldn't want my team to think I've abandoned them."

"Permission granted," replied Trent. "Oh, I almost forgot to ask: How are our friends the taal?"

"I don't know," answered Abby. "I haven't seen one since the dig began, but they must be nearby. I can't think of any other reason the local fauna have left us unmolested for so long."

"You know, in a few weeks the Kealts are throwing one of their famous parties to initiate a new museum and academic center they're dedicating to your generational ship. They've asked me to extend an invitation to you."

Abby grimaced. "Yes, well, I'm sure the invitation was merely a formality. I seriously doubt the Cade family actually wants me there."

"To the contrary!" he insisted. "The invitation came from King Edris himself. I can assure you, he's quite taken with you! Besides that, the Kealts are actually very grateful for everything you've done."

"Maybe," she replied sheepishly, "but there was this little affair I had with the high prince...Sia might try to rip my heart out if I get too close to him."

Trent guffawed. "Ha! I'd forgotten about that! Still, that was before they were married. I'm sure she'd be willing to let bygones be bygones…"

The affable and voluble Trent liked Abby and he liked to talk. It was past noon when she finally stood up to leave. Before she reached the door, he said, "Happy birthday! You didn't think I'd forgotten, did you?"

When she merely smiled in reply, he asked her if she had plans to commemorate it. She said, "Well, nothing very extravagant. There's a little pub I like not far from here. It should be open by now. I think I could use a drink. Would you like to join me?"

"Why, yes, I think I would."

Just then his secretary came in and advised that Aden and Sia themselves were there to see him.

"Damn, I'd forgotten all about them! I'm sorry Abby."

"It's all right—I wouldn't be very good company anyway."

After she left, Trent took a moment to gather himself, then ushered the royals into his office. Embarrassed he'd forgotten their appointment, he apologized profusely. "It's bad form forgetting a meeting with a future king and queen!" he noted.

"Quite all right ambassador," replied Aden. "What can we do for you?"

After some brief small talk, Sia asked, "Was that Abby I saw leaving as we came in? By the time I realized it was her, she was gone before I could say 'hi.'"

"It was. She was reporting on the results of her dig—quite remarkable. She's going back tomorrow."

"Did you convince her to come to the celebration?"

"No, I'm afraid not."

Sia frowned. "Do you know where she's going? I'd like to invite her personally."

"Well," replied Trent, "it's her birthday. She said she was going for a drink, but I didn't ask where."

Sia looked knowingly at Aden. "Perhaps I can track her down, if you two would excuse me?"

Aden looked at Trent, who said, "Of course."

After she departed, Trent said, "Thanks for coming here, Aden, especially on such short notice. I know it's not proper protocol, but I needed to be sure we wouldn't be overheard. Unfortunately, I'm afraid here is the only place I can be sure no one's listening."

"Well that's quite a buildup."

"Yes, I'm sorry for being so dramatic. I explained what I'm about to tell you to your father earlier, and he suggested I speak to you directly. I need to warn you: OSEC has drawn a bead on your solar system."

"OSEC?" replied Aden, furrowing his brow.

"The *Outer Space Exploration Corporation*. They're a massive business entity that isn't purely government or private, but combines the worst aspects of both. OSEC is manipulative, conniving, and ruthless, and has tremendous military and economic resources at their disposal. They are most interested in Laima, primarily because of Seti."

"Xanide," replied Aden knowingly.

"Exactly. Please, I've been rude again, have a seat." He pointed to the two chairs he and Abby had recently vacated. "Would you like a drink? Have you ever had a spirit we call bourbon?"

"I have not, but I think I would."

Trent walked over to a small console laden with various alcoholic beverages, picked up a bottle and filled two glasses. He carried them over to where Aden was sitting, handed him one, and sat down across from him. After he took a sip, he said, "Well, what do you think?"

"I have to admit, I prefer wine and ale to spirits, but this is not bad. Perhaps I could trade some Kag wine for a bottle or two?"

"It's from a place called Kentucky in our American Province. If you promise not to let it sit around, I'll give you a bottle before you leave."

After Aden assured him that wouldn't be a problem, Trent frowned. "Where do I start?" he asked rhetorically. He took a sip of his own whiskey, put down his glass and leaned back in the chair. After a brief pause, he launched into the history of OSEC...

Three hundred years earlier, it began as a small corporation whose specialty was solving difficult technical issues for government and private entities. It quickly grew in stature, taking on bigger and more complex contracts, until, for a time, it became the Earth Alliance's prime military contractor. As it grew, it spread throughout the Milky Way, finding and settling resource rich worlds, and literally buying others. Over time, it became more powerful than many governments.

When it eventually attempted to take over Earth itself, first economically and then militarily, the EA stepped in and evicted them from all EA worlds. OSEC never again took them on directly, but worked diligently behind the scenes to erode relationships between EA worlds. OSEC focused on creating their own alliances, which, while not yet as powerful as the EA, were now second only to it in scope and influence in the Milky Way.

During the zon war, OSEC sat on the sidelines hoping the zon would weaken the EA so severely they would finally be in a position to confront it militarily. Unfortunately for them, the war actually led to a resurgent EA, one that was now so powerful, OSEC was worried about its own continued existence. The EA's organic ships, which it had never allowed OSEC to build, were unmatched in the universe, and now there were more of them than ever before. While OSEC's conventional ships were impressive, they couldn't hope to compete with the EA's warships, organic or conventional, until they discovered xanide.

According to Trent, OSEC believed if they were able to dominate the only known abundant source of the crystal in the universe—Seti— even the EA would not be able to compete with the new generation of xanide-powered ships they would build.

When Trent paused to pour them more whiskey, Aden asked, "Why do you think they're coming here now?"

"We have very good sources. We know they've already initiated contact with both your governments. You need to be ready Aden. They are smart, patient, and ruthless. They'll probe your worlds for weaknesses; they'll try to play you off against one another; and when they need to, they'll kill. I can assure you, they have no compunctions about destroying the entire Laima System if that's what it would take for them to get at the xanide."

"If you don't mind, ambassador, I'd like another glass of…bourbon, is it?"

After leaving Trent, Abby headed to her favorite place on Kealt, a small walk-down bar called the Public Inn. People who were unfamiliar with the sprawling palace complex rarely stumbled upon it. She had learned about it from Aden, back when she first caught his eye by pretending to be a dopy refugee named Drusa Prine.

When she reached it, she was pleased to see its doors were open. The handful of patrons who were already enjoying its comforts took little notice of her when she settled into a well-used booth away from the door.

The ancient inn was small, cozy, and, this time of day, brightly lit from the sun streaming in through its narrow, street-level windows. The interior was framed in thick, dark timbers, which, along with its uneven stone floor, gave it a feeling of substance and permanence. It was also worn, rustic, and private, which was why Aden liked it so much. While the large stone fireplace that covered the pub's rear wall was now dormant, Abby fondly recalled colder days in times past when it roared with the intensity of a small sun.

She ordered a bottle of French wine, which had quickly become wildly popular on both Kealt and Ardala, partly because it was good, but also because it was novel and very expensive. After her server poured the first glass and left, she held it high in a toast and said to the air, "I love you. I miss you. See you soon."

"Thank you, I appreciate the sentiment!"

Abby was startled to see Sia standing next to the table.

"I'm sorry high princess," she replied with an embarrassed look. "I didn't see you standing there! I was toasting…friends of mine…that I lost during the war."

"Well then, please accept my heartfelt apologies for interrupting; and please, you know me well enough to call me Sia." She placed her hands on her burgeoning belly. "I would ask to join you in honoring their memories, but that will have to wait a few more weeks I'm afraid." When Abby merely stared at her mutely, she added, "I'm sorry for being so rude. Would you mind if I sat with you for a moment?"

Apprehensive over the Ardalan high princess's unexpected interest in her, Abby hesitantly replied, "Ah, no, of course not. Please, have a seat." She had to pull the table closer to her so Sia could fit onto the bench across from her.

Once seated, Sia said, "I know you're leaving soon, so I wanted to invite you personally to the dedication ceremony for our new generational ship memorial."

"Thank you," answered Abby. "That is very kind of you. Unfortunately, the rainy season is coming to the dig on Seti and we're going to need all hands to secure the exposed sites around the ship."

"That place has a rainy season?" asked Sia. "When we were there, it rained almost every day!"

Abby took a long drink of wine. When she put her glass down, she said, "It does—hard and harder." Both women laughed.

Sia asked the server to bring her back a glass. She picked up the wine bottle and said, "On second thought, would you mind? I love this stuff and I've been assured a sip now and then won't hurt the baby." When Abby gestured with her hand, Sia poured a small amount into her glass and held it high. "Here's to you and your departed friends."

"Thank you," replied Abby, lifting her own glass, "and to yours as well. I know you've also lost people close to you."

Sia took a small sip. "If this place France is anything like the wine it produces, I would surely like to visit it one day."

"Earth went through a bleak period when much of our ecosystem was severely degraded," noted Abby. "We've worked hard to restore it, with great success. France would indeed be a wonderful place to visit. How did you know I was here?"

"Trent wanted to talk to us about something, and when we got there, you had just left. He said you might have gone for a drink, so I took a guess you'd be here. I can't imagine anyone could know Aden for very long without getting dragged to this dungeon, which for some reason remains his favorite getaway."

"Very intuitive; it is quiet and off the beaten path."

"Abby, how long are you going to hide away in your jungle redoubt?"

"Excuse me?" she replied, after nearly choking on her wine at the directness of her question.

"I know most of your original team have already rotated out. You are very talented, of that I have no doubt, but I'm equally sure there are others who could ably take your place. What is it that could possibly keep such a young, beautiful, vivacious woman like you captive for so long?"

"Sia, I'm sorry," she sputtered, "but we don't really know each other that well."

"Perhaps not," she agreed, "but when Aden and I were lost in the jungles of that place, we literally lived moment to moment. I realized then, if we always waited for the perfect time to say what should be said, that time might never come. After what you did for us, and this entire solar system, I feel that I have to say this: You have a lot to offer. Don't waste your life laboring in a jungle that has already given up its most important secrets."

"I appreciate you're trying to be kind to me. I don't mean to be rude, but this is my own business."

"One would almost think you have a broken heart."

"I can assure you, I'm not a pining, 'spurned lover,' if that's what you think."

"No, it goes much deeper than that," answered Sia. "You lost something precious during the war with the zon. I don't know what it was, but you do it no honor by rotting away in the jungle. Get out of there. Live your life!"

Abby filled her glass, poured some into Sia's, and held hers aloft in another toast. "Here's to you and the safe birth of your child!" When she put her glass down, she added, "I have to say, I've underestimated you. You're a good person. Aden did well marrying you."

"Thank you, Abby, that means a lot to me," replied Sia. "I'm sorry for whatever it is you've lost. Thank you for the wine."

With that, she stood up to leave. When Abby also stood up, Sia surprised her by taking her hand and placing it on her belly. While Abby felt the life stirring in her womb, Sia said, "You saved Aden's life multiple times. Without you, this would not have been possible. In fact, if it weren't for you, we might all be dead, plowed under in the EA's genocidal war with the zon."

Sia let go her hand, then kissed her on the cheek and turned to leave. "Oh," she said suddenly, "I just remembered: Happy birthday! Hopefully we'll see you again at the dedication!"

Chapter II

"Sia, I've never seen you more radiant!" said Aden, watching her standing before their bedroom mirror, carefully putting the finishing touches on her makeup. "Motherhood certainly flatters you!"

"No, it is you who flatters, my husband," replied Sia. "I'm fat as a cow, bloated, and gassy; but thank you anyway."

"Well, you are certainly the most attractive cow I've ever seen!"

Sia turned and slapped him playfully. "You are an awful man! I don't know what I see in you!"

"Neither do I," he answered. Then he hugged her tightly and added, "But I thank God you do!"

"Oh, you're messing up my hair!" she complained. "If it's not perfect, you know what the media will do to me."

"I do. I think we'll both be happy when the dedication is over. I understand they want to give us a medal for befriending the taal and finding that generational ship."

Satisfied she looked as good as she was going to, Sia took Aden's arm, and together they walked out of their quarters and into the courtyard. There a hover car was waiting to take them to the ceremony. Once they were on their way, she smiled teasingly at the now daydreaming high prince. "What has you so mesmerized?" she asked. "The hope of seeing Abby again?"

"What? Oh, no. You know it's unlikely she'll be there. She's gone native. She only comes out of the jungle when Trent requires a report."

Sia tapped him on the knee. "Tell the truth, you miss her sometimes."

"The truth is, I never knew her. When we were seeing each other, she was pretending to be someone else. I've barely said two words to her since she dropped her act."

"I've been thinking about that," said Sia. "Did it ever occur to you it wasn't an act? That part of whom you saw was the real Abby, the one she's hidden away from everyone? Perhaps her Drusa 'persona' gave her the freedom to be herself."

"Maybe," he conceded. "If that's what she needed to be herself, I pity her."

"I think she needs your prayers more than your pity."

Aden put his hand on Sia's thigh. "Why this sudden interest in someone we both barely know?"

"I don't know," she replied. "After what she did for us, I wish there were some way we could help her find her way out of that damn jungle."

Before Aden could answer, the car came to a stop at the steps of the generational ship memorial. The front of the memorial was a scale replica of the bow of the generational ship itself, with its name, *The New Mayflower*, stenciled across it. The rest of the building resembled a part of the ship's fuselage. As Aden helped Sia out of the car, event personnel met them and escorted them past the frenzied media into the building.

They had received a VIP tour of the facility the week before, but that didn't temper their awe as they were led through the exhibit to the reception hall, where they would wait with other dedication officials until the event was ready to begin.

"Amazing," said Aden, as they walked past glass-covered displays of artifacts recovered from the ship. "You know, they also left behind DNA records of every voyager on the ship. Before long, it will be possible for every human in this galaxy to trace their origin directly to the original travelers. It is truly mind boggling."

"Perhaps to you!" answered Sia with a smile. "Exploration and adventure are your interests. I'm much more looking forward to listening to 10,000-year-old music and wearing new fashions that are just as old. Imagine all the new recipes!"

"Even older," corrected Aden. "They landed 10,000 years ago, but they carried records thousands of years older than that. It will take a long time to go through all that."

"You know Ardala is building its own memorial."

"Yes. We share these artifacts with them, and possession will rotate between us. Their memorial isn't yet finished, but knowing Ardalans as well as I do, I have no doubt they will make every effort to outdo ours."

"Ours, theirs, we, they…isn't it supposed to be just 'us,' now?"

"Well, we're getting there," responded Aden ruefully. "We have a good deal of our own history we still need to work through."

Sia squeezed Aden's arm. "Who knew all this and more was in that ancient wreck when Bang led us it? To think we were the first humans to see that ship in 100 centuries. It is certainly humbling."

"Indeed," he agreed.

They had stopped in front of an exhibit on the animals carried on *The New Mayflower* when an aide came up to them. "Your Highnesses," he said, "please forgive the interruption, but the festivities will begin shortly. If you would follow me…"

In the reception area aides flitted about frantically, ensuring that the participants in the day's events understood how they would unfold. Seeing Aden's father, King Edris, beset by more than his share of them, Aden and Sia went over to rescue him.

Edris beamed at them as they approached. "My children!" he exclaimed. "Perhaps you can help free me of these gnats who seem to think I'm incapable of following a few basic instructions. I so miss that traitor Tock on occasions like this. I haven't had a proper aide since he disappeared. It's almost gotten to the point where I'd eagerly grant him amnesty if he'd return!"

Tock Horat had been Edris's chief aide prior to the Zon War. Afraid his stature would suffer if Edris succeeded in democratizing Kealt, he sided with High Prince Kux Mar, who was collaborating with the zon in an unsuccessful attempt to overthrow the government of Kealt. After the war ended, Kux was killed during a coup attempt, and his uncle, Abeg Mar was eventually elected to lead the Council of Commons. Tock disappeared before he could be arrested, and hadn't been seen since.

Getting the hint, the aides left to deal with other issues. After exchanging backbreaking hugs, Aden said, "I thought Gris and Glyn would be here?"

"I'm afraid not, son. Gris is tending to important matters elsewhere in the galaxy, of which you are aware. And last I knew, Glyn was on her way to join him. Our good friend Admiral…that is…Ambassador Trent is here somewhere, representing the Earth Alliance. I was so hoping Abby would be with him. She is rather pleasing to the eye, wouldn't you agree?" Suddenly remembering Sia was there, he quickly added, "Although she is not nearly as beautiful as you my dear!"

"Nice try, father!" replied Sia, in mock offense. "I don't suppose the taal responded to our invitation?"

"No," answered Edris contemplatively. "Officially no one has seen or heard from them since the xanide negotiations ended months ago. I have heard rumors that our governments have been in contact, but since I'm not in the government anymore, I'm not privy to that information."

"If that were true," said Aden, "surely your new friend Abeg would have let on!"

"You underestimate him; that man can keep a secret. He also has a sense of honor, believe it or not. Ever since his nephew Kux tried to sell us out to the zon, he's been a model citizen."

"If you say so!" responded Aden doubtfully. "I've heard rumors myself that the Earth Alliance is rather irritated by the outcome of the xanide negotiations. They have made no secret of the fact that they would very much like to procure some crystals for their ships, although I don't know how they could be more formidable than they are already." He nodded his head and looked behind Edris. "Speak of the EA, here he comes now."

"Your Highnesses, nice to see you all again," said Ambassador Trent, who was wearing an uncharacteristically dour expression.

"The same to you," replied Edris, bowing slightly. "Ambassador, you look rather grim for such a joyous occasion. I hope everything's all right?"

"Edris, as I've explained to you and Aden, OSEC is beginning to establish a presence in your galaxy. It has developed a taste for xanide, some of which they've managed to salvage from debris you've left floating around after many of your battles with the zon. The EA plays rough, but fair. We want xanide as well, but we would never try to take it by force. OSEC has no boundaries. They're a lot like the zon—they prefer to work from the inside out, but in the end, they'll do whatever they have to, to get what they want.

"Fortunately the selkie—the life forms that cover our organic ships—have a moral component that limits OSEC's ability to use them. That's one reason they're so interested in xanide. With enough of it, their conventional ships could potentially threaten our own."

"Aden told me about them," replied Sia.

"Then you know they're a huge, multi-planet conglomerate. Anything they can make money doing, they do. When we're watching, they play it straight, but we can't be everywhere at once. The EA is powerful, but we're stretched thin from the zon war, which, ironically, further enriched OSEC—they helped build some of our conventional ships. Right now, we're not capable of keeping an eye on them in Poseidon.

"You said they manipulate governments?" replied Sia.

"Yes, and they're very good at it. It's much cleaner than a straightforward military conquest, but they're capable of that as well. The EA tries to keep OSEC in check, but it's grown so large and powerful, it's impossible for us to monitor all of their activities. And with the demands on our resources from our Milky Way allies, our presence here will be severely limited for the foreseeable future."

Suddenly realizing the drag he was putting on what was supposed to be a celebration, Trent raised the glass of Kag wine he was carrying in a toast. "Please accept my apologies for being so grim on such a fine day. Here's to Kealt and Ardala."

"Well, so much for small talk!" joked Sia, touching his glass with hers.

"Indeed," replied Edris. "It seems peace will always be a challenge. We've been through this ambassador, why bring it up again now?"

"We have reason to believe they are going to make a move soon, although we don't know what it is. I'll say this though, it will be big— that's how they operate."

The conversation continued awkwardly until Trent excused himself a few minutes later.

"So father," asked Aden, happy to change the subject, "how are you finding life as a civilian?"

He was referring to Edris's formal transfer of ruling authority to Kealt's Council of Commons months earlier.

"Very easy, thank you. I could ask you the same question. I was surprised when you resigned your rank as prime admiral. Why did you do that?"

"With a new, democratic government I thought it best that, as a relic of the old royal system, I should step aside. If I stayed, I'd likely become an issue for some political party to rally around or against."

"You say you don't like politics, but you are certainly an astute practitioner. Are you sure that one day you won't run for office yourself?"

Aden smiled. "I would never say 'never' about anything, after all that we've been through."

"A wise answer. Now we must go—it appears we're being summoned to get things started."

Guests were beginning to file into the vast auditorium that would host the ceremony. Aden escorted Sia to their seats in the front row with the other dignitaries, including members of the Council of Commons, the democratically elected rulers of Kealt.

On cue, King Edris stepped up to the podium and delivered stirring opening remarks. He was followed by a series of politicians, scientists, and celebrities, as well as audio and visual presentations involving different aspects of the generational ship and the data recovered from it. Aden was right, near the end of the evening he and Sia received a medal in recognition of their role in finding the ship.

With Sia by his side, he stepped up to the podium and received a raucous ovation. The audience went silent, as they raptly followed his account of their shipwreck on Seti, their struggle to survive, and their salvation at the hands of the taal. When he concluded with a strong defense of initiatives intended to draw Kealt and Ardala closer to each other, he received a standing ovation, something that would have been unheard of just a year earlier. As they walked away from the podium, he stopped and shook his father's hand.

"Excellent work son," Edris said above the din. "May I borrow your lovely wife? We have no Ardalan representatives here, and I would appreciate it if she would help me with the closing remarks."

"Father, she's hardly prepared!"

"It's fine, Aden," she assured him, taking Edris's arm. "I would be proud to stand by you."

Aden smiled, bowed, and walked away as Sia and Edris continued on to the podium. He never felt the explosions that rocked the auditorium.

Upon hearing of the attack, Sarin Selarney, the Queen of Ardala, immediately left Ardala to be with her severely injured daughter. By the time she reached Kealt, the military had taken over the government and blame for the bombing was beginning to focus on Ardala. Her ship was allowed to land, but almost immediately ordered to depart. Just after breaking orbit, she was killed when a plasma conduit exploded in her quarters. Peace was among the many casualties of those events.

Chapter III

Sweat dripping into her eyes, Abby carefully sifted dirt that had been covering an ancient refuse heap discovered near the generational ship. After two months of careful digging, they had barely made dent in it. While it was just trash, it could teach them much about human life on Seti 10,000 years ago.

She had been at it for five hours and was about to stop for the day, when a small object began to take shape as the soil around it escaped through the screen she was using to sift the debris. It was crusted and bent, but the shape was familiar. She picked it up and used a small brush to clean it. Her efforts slowly revealed a piece of gold jewelry that was unmistakably a cross, a symbol of a religion that persisted to the present day on human worlds everywhere.

Seeing something had caught Abby's attention, another archaeologist came over to see what she had found. When he realized what it was, he whistled in amazement. "Not that we needed any proof that Christianity came with *The New Mayflower*, but this nails it."

"It does indeed," she agreed, as she stood up to get a better look at it. "This has been buried in the ground for thousands of years. What are the odds we'd stumble across it?"

"Oh, I'd say probably about the same as three taals wandering onto our dig site."

"Now that wouldn't be luck, that would be a miracle!" answered Abby, as she resumed her efforts to clean the artifact.

"Then I believe in miracles."

"What?"

"There are three of them standing behind you."

Abby turned and was shocked to see that three taals had indeed entered the site and were watching her. She carefully placed the cross in her breast pocket, and walked over to them. She had only seen a taal once before, and that was at a first contact ceremony in Kuste, the main settlement on Seti. She didn't know if any of these were among that group, but they were magnificent nonetheless. Huge, long limbed, and fur-covered, with massive, blocky, mane-ringed heads that reminded her of a tiger, they were the most impressive and intimidating creatures she'd ever seen.

"This is certainly an honor," said Abby, not knowing what else to say. "To what act of divine providence should we attribute this much appreciated visit?"

One of the taals' thoughts registered in her brain. He said, "Kealt and Ardala have been attacked. As the sovereign rulers of this planet, and for your own safety, we demand that all humans leave immediately. A ship will be coming for you this time tomorrow. It will take you to the spaceport, where other ships will be waiting to evacuate you."

"It will take us weeks to secure all of our sites!" protested Abby. "We can't leave now!"

"You will have one day to make the necessary preparations to preserve what you can. We will watch over the rest."

With that, the taal said no more and left the site. Abby and her team of ten scientists worked frantically to move as much of their gear and artifacts into the relative safety of the generational ship as they could. As the taal promised, a ship promptly appeared 24 hours later.

With a short window before the ambient xanide radiation drained enough of the ship's reserves to make liftoff impossible, Abby and her team hurried to put the more perishable artifacts in the cargo hold.

It was a Kealt shuttle that had come for them. Abby noticed that the pilot and copilot were armed, and on edge. When they lifted off, she asked to speak to the pilot. Reluctantly, he opened the hatch to the cockpit. She stepped through it under the watchful eye of the copilot, who had his weapon trained on the hatchway.

"What is it you want to see me about?" asked the pilot gruffly.

"For one thing, I would like to know what the hell is going on!"

The pilot took note of the EA insignia on Abby's blouse. "You're Earth Alliance?"

"Yes."

"How many of your team are Ardalans?"

"What? What difference does it make? We're a joint team excavating the generational ship."

"I know that, I need to know who we can trust."

"I can assure you," insisted Abby, "you can trust us all."

Seeing Abby's intense expression, the pilot relaxed. "Look," he said, "I'm sorry. Things are a little tight right now. Did the taal, or anyone else, tell you what's happened?"

"The taal said only that Kealt and Ardala had been attacked, nothing more."

"Two weeks ago, someone set off a bomb during the dedication ceremony for Kealt's new generational ship memorial. Not long after, Queen Sarin was killed in an accident onboard her ship. She had come to Kealt to see High Princess Sia, who was injured in the attack, but General Brawn kicked her off. They say it was an accident, but everyone thinks it was the Ku Assa. Each side is blaming the other. We're on the edge of war, which is why the taal have asked everyone to get the hell off their planet— they don't want to get caught up in it."

"Two weeks ago?" asked Abby. "And we're just learning of this now?"

"You're a little off the beaten path," said the pilot, "and the damned xanide blocks communications. I think for a while people forgot you were out here."

Afraid to know the answer, Abby asked, "Other than the queen, were there any… casualties?"

"Hell yes! King Edris, almost the entire Council of Commons, your ambassador—Trent, is it?—and a lot of others. High Princess Sia is in bad shape and neither she nor the baby are expected to live."

"Oh my God!" she exclaimed. "What about Aden? Was he injured?"

"Last I heard, he's in a coma."

"Who did it?"

"Good question," replied the pilot. "As I said, Ardala and Kealt are blaming each other and both planets are on the verge of war. Kealt is under martial law, and High Princess Celesta is under house arrest."

"Why?"

"She's from Kealt and a Ku Assa to boot. I mean, all of Ardala watched her save Sia by killing dozens of zon and the intelligence minister's men with just a sword. Would you want that little killing machine running free on your planet if you were on the verge of war with her planet? Not likely. Now, if I've answered all your questions, would you mind returning to the cargo hold?"

When they arrived at the spaceport, Abby realized that, with Trent dead, she was now the EA's ambassador to the Laima System. Unsure what to do, she boarded a ship for Kealt.

En route, she learned that Kealt was under the rule of General Lucien Brawn, who had replaced Aden when he resigned as Kealt's ultimate military authority. Kealt and Ardala had both mobilized their militaries, each concerned the other was behind the attacks, and would try to take advantage of the resulting instability.

As her shock wore off, Abby wept for Trent, who had been a father figure to her. She had never been a religious person, but she touched the old cross she was still carrying and prayed for him, Aden, Sia, and their families.

Chapter IV

Aden was standing in a vast field of green grass. It was a warm day, with just a hint of a breeze. Off in the distance he could see something coming towards him. It was a horse, and it was moving fast. As it approached, he saw it was wearing a saddle. When the horse reached him, he grabbed it by the reins.

"Red Mike, old boy!" he exclaimed, while heartily patting his thick neck. "It's been a long time! I really miss our rides together. What brings you here?"

The horse whinnied and bobbed his head, as he did whenever he wanted Aden to ride him.

"Why not?" he replied, in response to his entreaty. "Let's see where you want to go."

As soon as Aden was astride the big horse, he took off. He galloped across the field until the field ended, then he continued through the cold and dark land that bordered it. He maintained his breakneck pace for an impossibly long time. Eventually the blackness receded, the sun came back, and he was galloping through a jungle.

Aden realized they weren't on Kealt anymore, but Seti.

Just when he wondered if the horse planned to run forever, he slowed down as he entered a clearing. It was where he and Sia had once been shipwrecked. In fact, the ship was still there, although the local flora had virtually swallowed it. On the far side of the clearing, he noted the bolba tree that had almost been the end of him still stood.

Aden dismounted Red Mike and tied him securely to a tree limb. When he turned around, he saw the bolba tree was glowing. It grew brighter in intensity, until it disgorged the light in the form of a person. While Aden couldn't see her features, he could tell it was a woman, and she was carrying something. As she approached the light began to fade, and her features slowly came into focus. It was Sia, and she was holding a child!

"Hello Aden."

"Sia, are we…dead?"

"No, but I'm afraid we'll have to leave you soon. Fortunately you have powerful, wonderful friends who have made it possible for us to see each other one last time."

"The taal."

"Yes. It took several of them to bring us here. They tell me they've never done anything like this before—it's very stressful on them."

"Is that our son?"

"Yes. He's beautiful." She held him out to him. "Here, hold him."

Aden took him from her and cradled him gently. "You're right, he is beautiful." He looked up and asked, "What happened? Why are we here?"

Sia's face took on a melancholy expression. "Aden, this is going to be hard on you."

"What happened?" he repeated. When Sia brought him up to speed on the events that had shaken Kealt and Ardala, he asked if the taal knew who was responsible.

"If they do," she said, "they won't tell me."

"This makes no sense! Ardala and Kealt are still rebuilding our forces after the Zon War. Neither side has the stomach for more conflict."

"Nonetheless, both sides are gathering for battle. The smallest provocation could lead to all-out war."

"Sia," replied Aden, who had suddenly lost all interest in anything but her, "what happened to us?"

"We were both injured in the bombing of the Generational Ship Museum. My time is almost up. You are badly injured, but you're strong, you will survive."

"No!" bellowed Aden. "I won't let you go!"

Sia smiled wanly. "You have no choice my dear husband, and neither do I. The taal who spoke to me before bringing us here wanted me to give you this warning: Things are not always what they seem. Trust your heart."

"You have my heart!"

"I'm sorry, my love," she replied sadly, while embracing him with the baby between them. She kissed him and added, "Time for us to go. We have stayed long enough."

Reluctantly he allowed her to take back their son. Then she turned and walked toward the bolba tree. When he tried to follow her, she looked over her shoulder and said, "My journey is not yours. For now, you must stay behind. You know whom you can trust. Trust them." As she reached the bolba tree, she began to glow. Then she stepped into it and was gone.

Not knowing what to do, Aden stood staring after her, his feet rooted to the ground. After a while he felt something tugging at his vest. It was Red Mike. Aden put one foot in the stirrup, stepped up and threw his other leg over the horse's broad back. Then he took off, retracing the path they took to get there. When they reached the field where the trip began, he dismounted and the big horse galloped off, leaving him alone.

As the horse disappeared over a hill, he felt someone take hold of his hand. Suddenly his eyes fluttered open and he was lying in a hospital bed. It was Abby.

"Dru…Abby…what are you doing here?" he croaked, after taking his hand back and roughly pulling a tube out of his throat.

When he started to pull out other tubes, she said, "Aden, please don't do that, you could hurt yourself! The doctor will be here in a moment." When he struggled to sit up, she raised his bed to help him. "Don't strain yourself. You have been badly injured."

"How long have I been here?"

"About a month. You were injured in an attack on the Generational Ship Museum. You've been in a coma since then."

"Are we still under martial law?"

"Yes," she replied. "How could you know that?"

"Was the entire Council of Commons killed?"

"Abeg Mar is still alive, although he was grievously injured. The rest are dead." She frowned before continuing. "Aden, you're not ready for this, but you'll know soon enough and you should hear it from a friend. Others were also injured in the bomb blast. Sia…"

"…I know. When did she die?"

Abby looked away and sniffed. "Two days ago," she answered.

"Our son?"

"I'm sorry Aden."

"Have they buried them?"

"Yes. General Brawn did it quickly and without ceremony."

"Sarin is gone too?"

"Yes. She came to be with Sia, but when Brawn realized she was here, he sent her back without allowing her off the ship. She later died in an accident in her quarters."

"Brawn is running Kealt?"

"Yes, do you know him?"

"Well. That is not good news for Kealt or Ardala."

Against her advice, he again began yanking himself free from his tethers.

"Stop it!" she demanded while standing up and trying to restrain him. "You're not healed! You have serious injuries!"

While she protested, he swung his legs over the edge of the bed, tried to stand up, and promptly collapsed. "Help!" called Abby. "Help!"

Several doctors and a couple of burly orderlies immediately appeared and as gently as they could, considering Aden's massive bulk, helped him back onto the bed.

The senior doctor said, "Your Highness, it's good to see you're awake. I'm afraid you're going to have to stay at least a few more days. Your fractures have begun to heal, as have your internal injuries, but your body's weak from being inactive for so long. Now that you're up, we'll begin your therapy immediately. I know this is tough and you've been through a lot…"

He paused while the other doctors and attendants left, then looked around nervously to insure no one else was in earshot besides Abby. When he was sure they were alone, he said in a low voice, "Much has happened since you were injured, high prince, none of it good. Kealt needs you. Please, take care of yourself." With that, he shook his hand and left.

When the room was empty, Abby resumed her seat next to the bed and asked, "How do you know so much about what's happened?"

Not willing to expose the taals' role to her, especially since, in Trent's place, she was now the EA ambassador, he mumbled something about having had a dream brought on by things people said when he was unconscious. When he asked her how long she'd been with him, she told him two weeks.

"The whole time?"

"Yes," she said, smiling wanly. I came as soon as I could. They wouldn't let me see Sia. Aden, I'm truly sorry about her. She was a remarkable woman."

"Why?"

"Why what?"

"Why are you here? Tell the truth, did you hope to glean something of intelligence value from us? Or were you hoping that when Sia died you could find a way back into my heart?"

"That is cruel," she replied angrily. "I've never betrayed you and never will—to anyone. Surely I've earned at least that much faith?" When Aden merely turned away, she stood up abruptly and walked toward the door. She paused before leaving, and while fighting back tears said, "You are the one not being honest—I was *never* in your heart."

Three days later the doctors deemed Aden fit enough to go home. One of his servants had brought him some proper clothing, and he was changing into it when he heard a knock on the doorframe. Without waiting for an invitation, a young woman in a black, old-style Kealt Imperial Guard uniform stepped into the room. Tall and lean, with long, naturally wavy auburn hair, pale green eyes and angular features she was stunning, even by Aden's standards.

"Yes?" he said, as she crossed her arms and smiled at him condescendingly. "Can I help you?"

"Well, the great, legendary, High Prince Aden Cade awakes. You know, there was a pool going as to whether you'd ever snap out of it. I lost, and not an inconsiderable sum."

"I'm sorry," he replied evenly, "have we met?"

"I am Major Aija Vilas, prime adjunct to General Lucien Brawn, who now runs this place…this place being Kealt. He sent me to ensure that you understood your situation in the new order."

"The new order?"

"With the Council of Commons essentially destroyed and your father dead, there was a power vacuum. Since nature abhors a vacuum, General Brawn stepped in to bring order until we can restore a proper government. He and he alone will decide what that government will be. If you try to interfere…well, I understand you're not just a marble statue, but intelligent as well."

Aden cinched his belt, then sat down in a chair and began to pull on his boots. "A threat, major? If you knew anything about me you wouldn't have bothered."

"I'm not a fool. An army couldn't cow you. I'm simply setting the record straight."

Aden yanked the laces tight on his boots and stood up. "Why is your 'new order' so concerned about me? I'm just another citizen. I've never had political aspirations."

"Perhaps not," she agreed. "Yet somehow they find you. The Council of Elders was going to crown you king before the general intervened. They are cowards after all."

"What? How could you know that?" When she merely smirked in reply, the answer became obvious: "You bugged their chambers!"

"I'm not going to mince words with you, Cade. If you cross us, you'll be joining your father and beloved wife sooner rather than later. That's not a threat, but a promise. And we'll also be keeping close tabs on your old EA girlfriend. One wrong step from either of you and you'll be watching the world through a small grate barely large enough for a food bowl to pass through."

Aden raised himself to his full height and loomed over Aija. With his steel-gray eyes, long, unruly black hair, scruffy face, scarred cheek, square jaw, strong cheekbones, and massive frame he was a fearsome sight, but Aija didn't flinch. "Careful major," he cautioned, "you shouldn't make promises you can't keep." With that, he forced his way past her and into the hallway.

Chapter V

Ironically, former High Prince Abeg Mar, the only member of the Council of Commons to survive the bombing, also was the only member who wasn't a commoner. While he had fought for years to prevent King Edris from democratizing Kealt, the Zon War made him realize the risks in having absolute power tied up in one person. Not only did he embrace democracy, he ran for the Council of Commons and was elected its first president. At Aden's request, he agreed to meet him in the royal gardens.

Aden was sitting on a bench in his father's favorite place under the massive goliathan tree when Abeg found him. He had a patch over one eye and held a cane in his one remaining arm. Aden stood up as he limped toward the bench.

When they sat down, Aden said, "Prince Abeg, it seems democracy has been hard on you."

Abeg laughed sardonically. "I was expecting you to accuse *me* of planting the bomb!"

"I wouldn't put it past you," he admitted, "but only an idiot would get blown up by his own bomb. You're many things, but 'idiot' isn't among them!"

After they were both done laughing, Abeg said, "It's good we can find humor in something, because these are certainly unhappy times. I am most sorry about Edris and your wife. I miss them both dearly, despite our nascent friendship. I understand Brawn cowed the Council of Elders into rethinking their decision to crown you king. Shame, you would have made a good one, even if it doesn't mean what it once did."

"Abeg," said Aden, "we cannot allow this dictatorship to take hold."

"I agree. Do you have a plan?"

"I wish I did."

"Can Gris help?"

Aden frowned. "You know he's not ready. Regardless, I'd rather find another way."

"I'm not sure how else you can dislodge a tick like Brawn. He's already dug in deeply."

"Surely his support is not universal?"

"No," agreed Abeg, "but he has plenty of it. He's using the threat of war with Ardala to consolidate his forces, and he's pandering to clans that traditionally have not been well regarded. Unfortunately the threat is real, and most don't want to change horses under such circumstances."

Aden rubbed his broad chin thoughtfully. "Do you think it was he who planted the bomb?"

"It's possible. Apparently it was beamed into a void in the lectern, which was made of carbanite."

"Our beaming technology can't penetrate carbanite. Neither can Ardala's."

"No, but the zons' can, and so can the EA's."

"The zon are gone," noted Aden, "and why would the EA commit an act of war?"

"The zon left a lot of their toys lying around. As you know, we're already incorporating some of their more advanced technologies into our own ships. As for the EA, they've made no headway negotiating with the taal for a consistent supply of xanide. With Kealt and Ardala on the verge of war, they could be counting on the taal needing a more reliable ally."

Aden shook his head. "That makes no sense! The blast also killed Trent! At any rate, they couldn't keep such a secret from the taal."

"Who knows what the taals' limits are? Perhaps we give them too much credit. The EA also could have sent negotiators who knew nothing of it. As for Trent, they've suffered hideous loses during their war with the zon. One more death in pursuit of such a glittering prize might be a small price to pay."

"Do you think…Abby…had anything to do with this?"

"Ah, Doctor/Captain/Ambassador Watanabe," replied Abeg slyly. "A most beautiful and impressive young woman, who, conveniently, wasn't there when the rest of us got, quite literally, blown to hell. No, I don't. I've seen the way she looks at you. She'd rather go to bed with you than kill you."

Ignoring his crude comment, Aden said, "Just before the explosion, Trent told me OSEC was about to make a move. They also have the necessary technology, the motive, and, according to Trent, no moral compass to deal with."

"I wondered when you'd get around to them. It's quite possible, based on the council's dealings with them, but I wouldn't jump to conclusions quite yet. Whomever did it must have had an intricate understanding of Kealt protocol and society to know when and where to plant the bomb, and how to hurt us most. I doubt they would have such detailed information about how we work. Of course, they could have had help…"

"A spy?" replied Aden, aghast at the thought. "What Kealt would do such a thing?"

Abeg snickered. "Why the shocked look? It's not like we've never had them before." He pulled out a cigar, and with Aden's consent, lit it.

As a billowy cloud of smoke lifted skyward, Aden asked, "Does Brawn know about our contingency plan?"

"Your father appears to have been prescient, insisting that we move our eggs to different baskets like that. Of course, at the time he did it because he didn't trust the EA, not because of Brawn or OSEC. In answer to your question, as far as I know, Brawn isn't aware of our little sleight of hand, although it could be just a matter of time. We've hidden our trail very carefully, but there is a trail nonetheless, and a large one."

"Hopefully we'll be ready before that."

"Hopefully," agreed Abeg. "The shipment of the key ingredient is already en route; however, with Kealt and Ardala's stepped up patrols, we'll be lucky if it finds its way out of the solar system."

"I thought it was being carried on a cloaked ship? With its transponder deactivated, even a Dipsa class warship couldn't find it."

Abeg paused while he took another pull on his cigar. After exhaling leisurely, he said, "Unfortunately that's not possible now. We're having to ship it in 'plain sight,' so to speak. While that may sound good in theory, I've always believed that things are best hidden when they're best hidden!"

Aden smiled grimly. "You are quite the pessimist, but I have to admit, I agree with you!"

Abeg stood up. When Aden followed suit, he said, "I'm an old man. No one will miss me when I'm gone. You, on the other hand, may be the only person who can pull this planet together again. Take care of yourself, high prince."

Over the next few months, Aden bided his time. Relations between Kealt and Ardala were growing increasingly strained, with armed skirmishes becoming more frequent and closer to home. The only thing preventing all-out war was the fact that, after the grievous loses sustained during the Zon War, neither planet was confident they had the forces to win one. However, Aden knew that wouldn't always be the case.

He needed to reach his sister Celesta, but planet-to-planet communications, except for official business, were blocked. And with the solar system swarming with military patrols operating on a hair trigger, flying to Ardala was out of the question.

Swallowing his pride, he went to the EA ambassador's residence. An aide he'd never seen before admitted him and made him wait in the atrium. When an hour went by with no sign of Abby, he was about to leave when another aide came out and ushered him inside. He knocked on the large wooden doors that marked the entrance to her office, and when she bid him enter, the aide departed.

"So," she said, without getting up from behind her massive desk, "what could bring the mighty High Prince Aden Cade to my lowly dwelling?"

"Abby, I'm sorry—I've been an ass to you."

"Yes, but now that you need something from me, you've decided to apologize."

"I need to know if my sister's all right."

"Why do you need me to do that?"

"Interplanetary communications except over official channels is prohibited by both sides. However, as the EA ambassador to both worlds, you're free to contact anyone you want. Even if you weren't, I suspect you have the technology to overcome any technical obstacles."

"Whether or not that's true, months have gone by since communications between Kealt and Ardala were proscribed. You've never asked for my help before. What is so important you need to talk to Celesta now?"

"I'm not going to lie to you," he answered, "but I can't tell you the truth either."

"Of course not!" she replied with a sarcastic smile. She leaned back in her chair, put her hands behind her head and her feet up on the desk. "I just need to trust you, right?"

Exasperated, Aden said, "OK, I deserve this! I'm sorry I bothered you." Then he turned and stomped toward the door.

"Aden, wait!" answered Abby. When he froze where he was, she said, "I know it took a lot for you to ask for my help. I'm sure you'd rather chew your own arm off. But if you want me to trust you, you're going to have to trust me."

"I don't want to put you in danger."

"That's very touching," she replied, as she stood up and walked over to him, "but a lie."

He grinned at her and said, "Only partly. You will be in danger."

"I'm a big girl."

"You are indeed," he replied, "but I still can't tell you."

"Very well, high prince," she said, while she pushed buttons on a console on her desk. Seconds later, a hologram of a very pregnant Celesta appeared before him.

"What is this?" she gasped. "What am I doing here?"

"Hello Celesta. I've missed you."

"Aden," she exclaimed. "Thank God you're all right! How did I get here?"

Abby stepped into her line of sight and said, "You're still on Ardala. What you're seeing is a hologram of this room, as well as Aden and I. We're seeing a hologram of you."

"Why are you working with her?" asked Celesta.

"You can trust her," he replied.

"If you say so. My brother, I'm very sorry about Sia and your son."

"And I, Sarin."

"Would it be possible for me to sit down? This has been a fairly challenging pregnancy and I'm supposed to stay off my feet."

Aden looked at Abby. "Can she?"

Abby said nothing, but pulled a chair over to Celesta's hologram and waived for her to sit.

"Thank you, this is much better," she said, cautiously settling onto the chair, skeptical that it would hold her.

"Why are you under house arrest?"

"Really Aden," she replied humorously, "have you forgotten that the entire planet saw me kill all those zon on a public vidcast? After seeing that, would you want *me* running around *your* planet unsupervised?" When he didn't answer, she added, "That's a joke! I'm free to go wherever I want; although I think it's best to keep a low profile for now."

"How are things on Ardala?"

"Ivege's trying hard to step back and figure things out rationally. He doesn't want to react rashly or emotionally and play into the hands of whomever is behind this, but Sia and Sarin's deaths have devastated him. He's gathering our forces—he's concerned that your General Brawn is aching for a fight. He always was a thorn in father's side. He never supported his overtures to Ardala, and when he essentially gave them half of Seti, that was more than he and many others could take. They would very much like to go back to the ways things were."

"As it turns out, it wasn't ours to give anyway," he reminded her, referring to the re-emergence of the taal to reclaim their world after a millennia-long absence.

"Regardless, the sentiment remains."

"Fortunately for all of us," he replied, "I've been told Kealt is taking longer than anticipated to rebuild its fleet. And now, with the taal-imposed moratorium on mining, xanide is in short supply, especially the stuff that's military grade. Moreover, without those new Dipsa class ships at full capacity, Brawn won't be picking a fight any time soon. Besides, he hasn't consolidated power on Kealt yet. Fighting has broken out in a number of southern and western provinces that have refused to accept his sovereignty. Harma and Pador have been especially restive."

"Aden I was born in Pador. You have to stop him!"

"I know. Celesta, did you remember to send Gris a birthday present?"

Abby furrowed her brow. This was a strange thing to ask, considering the weighty subjects that preceded it.

"Forget my own father's birthday?" she replied brightly. "Of course not! However, I have run into a little snag."

"Oh?"

"The delivery service has gone out of business."

"I see."

"We're looking for another company. Any ideas?"

"I'll have to get back to you on that. Celesta, I have to go. I don't know how this is going to end, but however it does, I love you."

"And I you."

"Congratulations Celesta," said a smiling Abby. "Children are a beautiful, miraculous thing. Now, please stand up or you'll find yourself on the floor when this transmission ends."

When Celesta was gone, Abby turned to Aden. "Congratulations are also in order for you. You'll soon be an uncle again!"

"Yes," he replied. He bowed slightly and added, "I've intruded on your hospitality enough. With your permission, I'll take my leave."

"I assume from your cryptic exchange that you need to go to Ardala to pick up this 'birthday present.' Have you a plan?"

"No, not yet," he admitted.

Abby touched his arm. "Remember who your friends are."

"I know who they are," he answered, "even if I forget from time to time."

Chapter VI

While Kealt and Ardala technically had not been at war for two centuries, they had rarely enjoyed peaceful relations, at least as most societies would define them. Low-level armed conflicts broke out frequently over control of key shipping lanes, access to commercial or strategically valuable planets, treaties with alien species and other reasons, some petty, some not. Despite the absence of a formal war, thousands on both sides had lost their lives in these conflicts.

Under King Edris and King Ivege they put aside their rivalry, albeit grudgingly by many on both planets. Edris, who himself had fought in many battles with Ardala, had lost two sons to it in a misunderstanding over access to Seti. Despite this, he had spent most of his life working to bring true peace to these otherwise enlightened societies.

With Ivege's equal determination to coexist peacefully, Kealt and Ardala had been enjoying their best relations in their long history. General

Brawn, chief of the military coup that now ruled Kealt, was determined to change that.

Tall, broad shouldered, craggy, white-haired, and serious minded, Brawn had come up through the ranks the hard way, despite his membership in the influential Sarfas clan. The Sarfas' constituted one of Kealt's four high houses, along with the Hebrids, the Cades, and the Mars. Once they were among the most politically powerful clans on Kealt; however, their fortunes had waned over the centuries. The Council of Elders, which selected Kealt's kings, had grown weary of their extreme chauvinism, propensity for warlike and violent behavior, and their conniving nature. While still a force on Kealt, especially in the military and economically, it had been five kings since a Sarfas had sat on the throne.

Despite belonging to such a prestigious clan, Brawn's path through life had been a hard one. Orphaned at an early age, and with no other close relatives, he was raised in an orphanage where older children frequently abused him. Later, while many of his contemporaries joined Kealt's officer corps, without a sponsor all that was available to him was an assignment as a lowly kareivis 3rd class, a rank usually reserved for members of the poorer houses, such as the Low House of Sokk.

However, Brawn took advantage of his opportunities, and before long his natural intelligence and leadership abilities asserted themselves. He made his way quickly up the ranks, eventually earning a commission. By the time the bomb that changed the Kealt political landscape ignited, he had taken Admiral Cade's place atop the Kealt military hierarchy.

His rapid ascent did not surprise anyone who knew him. After all, his family had a long, illustrious military tradition. They had served Kealt well and faithfully for many generations, and fought and died for it. Over the decades, Brawn had lost his father, two brothers, several uncles, and many friends to Ardala. However, it was the loss of his beloved wife, Dandria, that gnawed at his already sparse soul like fylfly larvae. It nibbled at it a little piece at a time, imperceptibly, until one day he woke to find it had completely consumed it. Absent even the smallest remaining shred of his humanity, only one thing drove him: The desire to destroy Ardala completely and utterly.

While his position was extreme even among his fellow clansmen, the destruction of virtually the entire Kealt Government had raised possibilities he could not have imagined. Even though the perpetrators of the crime still had not been identified, there was little doubt in most people's minds—and certainly none in his—that Ardala was behind it.

When Queen Sarin was killed in a supposed 'accident' a week later, most people, even on Kealt, believed the Ku Assa, the shadowy, implacable, and feared protectors of Kealt royalty were behind it. With these events, the seeds were sown for Brawn's long hungered for revenge.

He chafed at the chance to provoke a weakened Ardala into a military confrontation, but moved cautiously because it was taking longer than anyone anticipated for Kealt to rebuild its own zon-decimated forces. However, he was confident that when their five new Dipsa class warships came on line, Ardala would be no match for Kealt regardless of the state of their own fleet.

The first four Dipsa prototypes had entered duty prematurely near the end of the Zon War. Only one, the *Edris*, survived, due primarily to the technical intervention of an EA engineer sent onboard to spy. Based on the performance of the *Edris*, even the EA respected this new, revolutionary class of ship. It was by far the largest warship ever built by Kealt or Ardala that had cloaking capability. When fully operational, it could fire its main weapons while cloaked, and was armed with enhanced versions of Ardala's dreaded fusion cannons. In addition, they were capable of carrying dozens of tactical spacecraft of various sizes and configurations. They were juggernauts, capable of razing a planet to its mantle.

Unfortunately for Brawn, the technical flaws that led to the destruction of three of the Dipsa prototypes proved difficult to overcome. Specifically, when multiple power-intensive systems were used together, such as when firing the main guns while cloaked or shielded, the xanide matrix became unstable, risking an explosion on the order of a small star. While an EA engineer had found a way around these limitations, he only implemented his solution on the *Edris*. When the conflict ended, the engineer disappeared along with his solution.

Today Brawn paced in front of his desk, frequently glancing at his chronometer. He was expecting an update on the Dipsa project from Samuel Thems, the project's senior engineer, and he was late. When he finally appeared a half hour past the appointed time, Brawn was not in a good mood. It would soon worsen.

When the chief engineer finished his report, Brawn exclaimed, "So you're telling me it will be months more before these ships will be fully operational? They're already a year behind schedule! It's taking longer to build these ships than the prototypes!"

"I'm sorry sir," responded Thems nervously, "but, as you know, most of the key engineers on the original Dipsa project were killed when the zon destroyed three of the prototypes. Many of the rest left the project after that, and aren't even on Kealt anymore."

"Any more excuses Thems?"

"The truth is, sir, without the EA technology that fixed the problems on the *Edris*, these ships may never be fully operational, especially if we can't get our hands on a sufficient quantity of military grade xanide. Even so they are formidable, far superior to anything the Ardalans currently have in their inventory."

Brawn disagreed. "Without the ability to operate multiple systems simultaneously they're just big, heavily armed ships," he countered. "They'll be vulnerable to Ardalan weapon systems, which are at least as capable as ours. Hell, they gave them to us! And what's this about xanide? I issued orders to take it from civilian systems if we had to."

"Sir," said Major Vilas, who had just entered the room, "that would be unwise. Not only would we risk further destabilizing our already restless civilian populations, it wouldn't work. The civilian sector gets the bulk of its xanide from depleted, recycled crystals no longer of military value. The rest of it was never mil-grade to begin with."

Brawn smashed his fist on the desk. "Then dig it out of the ground!"

"We're trying sir, but there is very little native xanide left on Kealt. The few mines still in operation that we have access to are mostly exhausted. It's doubtful they contain enough of the right crystals to meet our needs. The only viable mines are deep in Pador Province, in the heart of the resistance."

"Then send ships to Seti and take it from the damn taal by force!"

"We've tried that too. The ships we sent vanished."

Brawn was about to launch into a tirade when his intercom buzzed. "Yes?" he replied impatiently.

"Sir, Howard Gross from OSEC is here. He says he has an appointment."

"Yes, yes he does," he answered gruffly. "Just a moment." He muted the intercom. "We're not finished with this, major! I want xanide and I don't care where you get it! Chief Engineer, if you and your men don't solve the problems with the Dipsa class ships soon, you'll never have to worry about anything again! Now, both of you, get out of here!" Before they reached the door, he changed his mind and told Major Vilas to stay. "I think you'll find my guest interesting," he said, as Thems left.

Once Thems was gone, his secretary escorted the OSEC visitor into the room. "Ah," exclaimed Brawn, forcing himself to sound pleasant, "very good to see you again, Mr. Gross."

Howard Gross, a handsome, confident, well-dressed man in his mid-30s, smiled condescendingly. "General Brawn, I can assure you the pleasure is all mine. May we sit down?"

"Yes of course," Brawn replied, pointing to a pair of overstuffed chairs off to the side of his office. Suddenly remembering that Aija was still there, he added, "This is Major Vilas, my chief aide. I hope you don't mind that I've asked her to stay?"

"Certainly not," replied Gross evenly, as he got comfortable. "Thanks for seeing me general; I know you're a busy man."

"Yes. I understand you have a proposition for me that will make it worth the trouble for both of us."

"Perhaps," replied Gross with a grin. "As you're doubtlessly aware, there is a great deal of interest in xanide in the Milky Way. Unfortunately, it seems the only place in the universe that has it in abundance is Seti. Neither the EA nor OSEC has had much luck negotiating with the taal, a most elusive and inscrutable species."

"They are indeed," replied Brawn, "and now they've kicked us off Seti altogether; as of now, we don't have access to xanide either. So, what is your proposition?"

Gross looked down while tapping his fingers together. When he lifted his head he said, "We understand Ardala is responsible for the vicious attack on your government. We also know your impressive new ships aren't ready and won't be for some time. We can help you finish them, correctly, but you're thinking too small."

"Oh?"

"If you're interested, and if you agree to do your part, we have the means to turn Ardala into an asteroid belt without them."

"An interesting proposition indeed; what's in this for you?"

"Once the Ardalans are defeated, there would be no one to stop you from conquering Seti, and gaining access to enough xanide for both of us."

"What's to stop you from making the same offer to them?" asked Brawn.

"They are a stubborn bunch," observed Gross, "intent on sticking to the treaty they negotiated with the taal and Kealt. Of course, they can be more selective in whom they negotiate with; their fleet is virtually replenished and *they* have an adequate supply of xanide."

"So you have and they said no!"

"More crudely put than it needed to be, but, in a word, they said 'No.' A most shortsighted approach on their part, I must add—one that you could benefit from at their expense."

"I see," replied Brawn. "Even if we do agree to help you—and your offer is most tempting— the taal are a formidable opponent. We have already lost a number of ships trying to extract xanide by force."

"Well, we have technology that blocks their telepathic abilities. We can also pinpoint them individually on the surface. We can destroy every one of them from space, if we need to."

"Then why do you need our help?"

"Ardala will not sit still for an attack on Seti. Our ships are powerful, but we don't have enough of them to take on an entire planet as advanced as they are. We need to eliminate them as a threat before moving on Seti."

"What about the EA?" asked Brawn. "They want xanide too. Are they just going to sit by and let you do this?"

"If they try to interfere, we have a nasty surprise for them. Regardless, they have many responsibilities and their forces are spread thinly throughout two galaxies. In this solar system, we have far more assets than they do. Besides, we won't attack Seti, you will, with technology we will provide."

"Even if we agreed to help," replied Brawn, "there is still the xanide problem—we barely have enough to power all of our ships."

"If I told you we might have a fix for that as well, would that seal the deal?"

Brawn looked at Aija, who had taken a seat on a small couch on the other side of the room. "What do you think, major?"

"I think Mr. Gross is making some pretty big claims. It's easy for him to *say* they can defeat the EA. I'd like to see some proof first."

"That's why I asked her to stay, Gross, she speaks the truth."

"And I appreciate that," he replied condescendingly. "On Earth we have an expression: 'Words are cheap.'" He stood up, reached inside his jacket, and pulled out a data crystal. "I think you'll find all the proof you want here." He waived it in Aija's direction. "Major, would you be kind enough to bring this up for us?"

At his request she came over and took the crystal, and while they waited for her, he added, "The vidcap you are about to see was made a week ago. It was taken by one of our allies during an encounter with an EA deep space exploration ship."

Aija brought up a 3D display, which hung above their heads like a globe. The three stood around it and watched as a vessel approached

the EA ship and opened fire. The EA ship
quickly returned fire, rocking the other vessel.
Then it released a single, small missile the EA
ship easily intercepted. During its destruction, it
released a bluish cloud that settled onto the EA
ship's shields. In seconds, silvery veins spread
out in all directions. The ship's shields crumbled
rapidly, and the cloud descended onto the ship
proper. In the same manner, it attacked its
organic hull, changing its hue from a mottled
green to black as it enveloped it. The EA ship
attempted to break off, but experienced a
catastrophic hull breach. One medium torpedo
from the other vessel finished it.

"Very impressive!" said Brawn, when the
vidcap ended. "What was that?"

"A bio weapon that attacks the hulls of the
EA's organic ships," replied Gross. "We
salvaged it from an abandoned zon base. At the
time of their destruction, they were very close to
finishing it. Another few weeks, and the war
might have gone a different way."

"Very impressive indeed," answered Brawn,
"but that was a civilian ship, presumably lightly
armed and shielded. How would your weapon
fare against a frontline EA warship?"

"Fair question. An EA warship is certainly
more robust, but they're built in essentially the
same manner and of the same raw materials.
They have more power to fight the infection, and

would take a little longer to defeat. However, we have every reason to believe the end result will be the same."

"Yet you're not willing to tackle the EA head on," noted Aija.

"Not to be rude," replied Gross, "but do you have any of that fine Kag wine? I find it much more full-bodied and enjoyable than that thin, unimaginative stuff they serve on Ardala."

Brawn nodded toward Aija, and while he and Gross resumed their seats, she produced a bottle from Brawn's small bar. She pulled the cork, brought the bottle to the table between them, and poured them both a glass. Gross held his aloft. "Here's to Kealt! May you finally take your proper place in this solar system!" They touched their glasses and, after taking a large swallow, Gross exclaimed, "This is magnificent! I must take some back with me!"

Brawn took a much smaller sip and placed his glass back on the table. "I think we can arrange that!" he replied impatiently. "Now, if you don't mind, Aija raised a good point."

"Where were we…oh, yes, I remember now! I agree with the general," answered Gross. "I like your bluntness major! You do indeed make a good point. The fact is, OSEC grows more powerful every day; however, the EA is a formidable opponent even without the advantage of their bio ships. We see no profit in provoking them directly."

"Won't they get involved when they become aware of your aid to us?" asked Aija.

"Possibly, but as I just explained, they're stretched thin. After the Zon War, their allies in the Milky Way are demanding a greater presence in their neighborhoods. We, on the other hand, are 'all in,' in Laima. We have over two hundred of our best ships already here, and more are en route.

"The EA is unlikely to get involved here, regardless of the outcome, if they believe your little war is organic in nature. And once, with our help, you prevail over Ardala, you will move on to Seti. With the technology we'll provide you, it should be an easy target. After you have apparently subdued both worlds on your own, we will come out of the shadows and help you consolidate your spoils as your guest."

"And all you want is some xanide?" asked Brawn.

Gross grinned sarcastically. "Well, more than some—I'd say a lot! We'll also need a substantial down payment of crystals and a small plot of land, hopefully with a mild climate, on which to base our ships in this solar system."

Brawn stood up and held out his hand. "Gross, your offer is a good one, but we'll need time to think about it."

Gross stood up as well and shook his hand. "I'm sure you'll make the right decision, general." He walked over to the door, but paused before pulling it open. "Oh, I understand one High Prince Aden Cade is still extant?"

"Unfortunately," replied Brawn, "the man has more lives than a horvis toad!"

"He is quite a capable man. If I were you, I'd see that he has an accident. Or perhaps I could deliver him to you?"

"How?"

"I'll be in contact with the major soon. I believe we'll need her assistance. Think about our deal, general, but don't think too long!"

After Gross left, Brawn turned to Aija, who was wearing a pensive expression. "So, major, what's on your mind?"

"We need to move cautiously, sir. We've seen the power of the EA. We also know what they're capable of when aroused. OSEC may be as powerful as Gross says, but they're still hesitant to take them head on. We need to be very careful before committing the future of this planet to them."

"I agree. The problem is, we're running out of time. Right now, most of the population is galvanized for a fight with Ardala. The longer this drags on, the more support for our little coup will begin to dry up, and demand for a return to civilian government will grow. Once that happens, the window to attack Ardala could quickly shut, regardless of the measures we apply. I can't wait for us to complete those ships on our own. Besides that, he seems to believe he can obtain xanide."

"Again, I'll believe it when those pale blue, beautiful crystals are lying at your feet."

"Yes," he replied. "You and me both. Aija, I assume you came here to update me on the uprising in the Pador Province?"

"I did. A large portion of the population has surrendered; however, many are holding out and have retreated to their major military bases and an area that is home to their xanide mines. They're putting up a strong fight, and we believe they're receiving assistance from the Ku Assa. They're never where our intelligence says they should be, and they know how to hit us where we're vulnerable.

"Despite our best efforts, their forces are holding fast. Unless we crush them soon, other provinces might join them. As you fear, some are already clamoring for new elections, or at least a new king. As your man Gross noted, High Prince Aden Cade is quite popular."

Brawn frowned. "The Hebrids and Cades always were a stiff necked, stubborn bunch. If they won't yield, use strategic xanide munitions. That should slow them down a bit."

"They're too close to the mines. We would risk detonating the xanide veins, some of which lead all the way back to Rilan! We all could be destroyed."

"I thought those veins were depleted?" replied a frowning Brawn.

"They are, but even the trace amounts that remain are more than sufficient to create a massive explosion."

"Then use conventional weapons, I don't care, we need to obliterate them before they succeed in exhorting others to join them!"

"It will be a challenge. As you know, Pador hosts two of our largest military bases. The rebels are extremely capable and well-armed."

"I'm sure a war with Ardala would end all this nonsense quickly! I need those ships to be fully operational!"

"Yes sir!"

"One more thing: I agree with Gross. We need to keep a close eye on Cade and his girlfriend, the acting EA ambassador. As much as I'd like to, we can't kill him yet. He's a symbol of stability, if nothing else. If he dies, I'm afraid hostility toward my regime will only intensify."

"Already done sir," she replied smartly.

"Then why are you still here! Dismissed!"

Chapter VII

As Aija left the Kealt Prime Command, she decided it was time to pay High Prince Aden Cade another visit. She ordered a hover car to take her to the Kealt Palace complex several kilometers away, after confirming his presence with another military aide assigned to the complex.

When her car passed a refugee settlement on its way to the palace, it reminded Aija of her humble beginnings. She had grown up poor, even by the modest standards of her downtrodden clan. Primarily located in the Klavan and Harma Provinces, the Sokks performed most of Kealt's menial and backbreaking jobs, when they even had jobs. Their society suffered from poor education, bad nutrition, and fractured families.

The military was one of the few avenues out of grinding poverty, and many Sokks took advantage of it. As a result, they were disproportionately represented in Kealt's armed forces, though few made it to the officer ranks. The Sokk were fierce fighters, and renowned for their courage and determination in battle. They died by the thousands in the war with the zon, and in periodic conflicts with Ardala.

King Edris had made uplifting Klavan, Harma, and other poor provinces a priority, but their peoples had suffered from benign neglect and, at times, blatant discrimination for so long, he faced the daunting task of rebuilding their spirit as well as their infrastructure. One of his more successful initiatives was breaking down the doors for capable Sokks to compete for positions in Kealt's officer corp. Aija herself was one of the beneficiaries of that effort.

Like Brawn, and like most Sokks, she had originally enlisted as a kareivis 3rd class. However, with the doors now open to Kealts of all stripes, she quickly rose through the ranks, won a commission, and was eventually assigned to Brawn's command by King Edris himself.

While Brawn was initially reluctant to embrace her, during the Zon War she impressed him by leading a small infantry squad that defeated a much larger zon force holding a strategically important asteroid. Despite the enmity that existed between their clans, Aija was fiercely loyal to Brawn, and followed his orders without question.

Brawn himself, as a member of the Sarfas clan, had no love for the Sokks; but, being politically astute as well as a strong military tactician, the alleged Ardalan bombing of the

Kealt Government made it easy for him to manipulate them into supporting what was effectively a military coup. While not all Kealts were in favor of his coup, most were inclined to go along with it, at least until the perceived Ardalan threat subsided.

The only provinces that still resisted him, Harma and Pador, couldn't have been more different from each other. Harma was backward and poor, while Pador was affluent and the seat of learning and culture on Kealt. Pador also was home to the Hebrid, Mar, and Cade Clans, and the ancestral birthplace of many of Kealt's great kings, including Edris himself.

As the hover car drew near the palace, Aija also thought about her much-loved half-brother, Ludis. He was older than she was, and had essentially raised her after her parents died when she was little more than a toddler. Ludis had died five years earlier, during a battle with a group of Ardalan civilians contesting Kealt's claim to a marginally habitable piece of rock in a sparsely settled region of space. She missed him and thought of him every day.

As the car drew to a halt in front of the entrance to the palace complex, she felt a familiar hatred bubbling to the surface, as she thought of the man responsible for his death. She would stop at nothing to exact her revenge, but knew she had to bide her time.

She got out of the car and showed her ID to a guard, who granted her entrance onto the grounds. The palace administrative offices, where Aden was supposed to be, were a long way from the entrance, but she was still seething when she reached them. Like all great bureaucracies, the ministries continued to hum along as though nothing had changed. And for them, not much had. General Brawn focused most of his energies on the military, and was content to leave the day-to-day running of things to others as long as they stayed out of his way. Understanding the price of maintaining the status quo; i.e., their comfortable jobs, they obliged him.

She found Aden in the large foyer of the building that housed the heads of various Kealt government ministries. Big, strong, and untamed, he had the roughhewn look of a warrior about him. He also was undeniably handsome despite the scar on his cheek he received from a youthful encounter with an angry taal; but Aija knew there was far more to him than good looks.

He was having an animated discussion with a group of silver-hued aliens belonging to a species she didn't recognize. When he saw her, he ended the meeting, shook their hands vigorously, and sent them on their way.

"Well Major…Vilas, is it? A pleasure to see you again. It's been a while. From our last conversation, I thought I'd be seeing more of you. Although I have to say, I'm not disappointed in your lack of attention. So, what brings the chief aide of the Kealt junta to this lowly place?"

"I didn't come to trade insults," she replied coolly. "Is there a place we can go that is more private?"

"Of course," he answered brightly. "If you'd be so kind, would your loveliness follow me?"

When he began to lead them to the exit she said, "That's the way out."

"I thought you said you wanted a private conversation?"

"I did," she replied, gesturing with an extended arm. "After you."

Aden led her into the courtyard, and from there she followed him to the royal gardens and the benches around the famous goliathan tree that had been King Edris' favorite retreat. After they sat down, he said, "My father loved this place, as much as any on Kealt. I too find it relaxing and good for clearing my head. Now, what is it you wanted to see me about?"

"Who were those aliens you were talking to? I've never seen that species before."

"They're called the vartek. We made first contact decades ago, but since then, we've had few encounters with them. They're a shy species, but peaceful."

"What brings them to Kealt now, and why are they speaking to you and not the government?"

"They were very unsettled by the Zon War and the appearance of two more powerful, potentially hostile parties, namely OESC and the EA. They're seeking a mutual defense pact with us in case things go bad. I don't think they have much to worry about though, since they're a poor race and have little of value that would spark the interest of either OSEC or the EA.

"As for why they were talking to me, your man Brawn has refused to meet with them. They were asking me to serve as their agent and get them an audience. Can you imagine anything so ridiculous? Regardless, you're a busy woman and I'm sure the vartek aren't why you're here."

"You've been good about keeping a low profile," answered Aija directly. "General Brawn wanted me to ensure that that you understood how important that was to the rest of your life."

"Are you threatening me again, major?"

"Apparently I'm not doing it well," she said dryly, "because each time you ask for clarification. I don't expect you'll listen to me, Cade, but this is fair warning." She leered at him and added, "You're such a handsome man, it would be a shame for something bad to happen to you."

"I've stayed out of Brawn's way!" he replied angrily. "I'm doing what I was doing before my wife, my unborn child, my father, and my friends were murdered: Working to help the people of Kealt, especially those who haven't always been treated well. In fact, that includes most of your clan! I'm also seeking to uncover the forces that perpetrated this heinous act. God help you if that trail leads back to you and Brawn!"

"Now *you're* threatening *me*? Everyone knows the Ardalans did this! If you want justice, you should join our side. The time will soon come when there will be no more Ardala."

Aden stood up abruptly, and for a moment, Aija thought he was going to strike her. Instead, he said, "My sister is on Ardala. I have many good friends there as well. If others from that world were behind this attack, they'll be rooted out and dealt with appropriately. Be certain of one thing: I won't sit by and watch twisted people like you and Brawn goad them into war. My father gave his life and that of his sons to preventing that, and now, perhaps, I've given my wife and a child I'll never know. Tell Brawn that if *he* knows what's good for *him*, *he'll* stay out of *my* way!" With that, he turned and stomped off.

A formidable opponent, Aija thought coolly, as he disappeared from view. She suspected that when this chapter of Kealt history eventually closed, it would be Aden standing, and she and Brawn nothing more than a bad memory.

A half hour later, she was in Abby's office. When she came out to greet her, Aija was impressed. Abby was as beautiful as she was, with an exotic look. Her file said she belonged to an ethnic group Earthers called "Asian," and more specifically, "Japanese," a group that was represented on *The New Mayflower* when it made landfall. However, 10,000 years later there was little trace of it, either on Kealt or Ardala. Most likely they were a smaller group and either died out or eventually assimilated into the greater gene pool.

"Hello major," said Abby with a polite smile. "I've seen you several times before, but we've never been formally introduced. What can I do for you?"

Maintaining the stern demeanor she wore when she walked in the door, Aija replied, "I'm here on behalf of the Kealt Provisional Government. We treasure our relationship with the EA. I understand you have a 'noninterference' policy regarding other cultures?"

"We do."

"Then please, follow it."

"Excuse me?"

"Not long ago we followed Aden Cade to your doorstep. Not long after that, we detected a neutrino carrier wave emanating from your facility…a most impressive technology by the way, impossible to jam. Regardless, communications between Kealt and Ardala are prohibited except with the express consent of General Brawn."

"Surely that doesn't apply to diplomatic communications? I'm also the EA's acting ambassador to Ardala."

Aija smiled at Abby the way she'd smiled at Aden. She said, "We certainly will not interfere with your legitimate diplomatic activities. Just be aware that Aden Cade is a known Ardalan sympathizer. He'll pay a high price for that, if his proclivities don't change. I know you're fond of him. Still, it would be best for you to keep your distance from him."

"Thanks for the advice, major," replied Abby with a forced smile. "Our relationship is no longer what it was. In fact, it's strained at best. Your 'advice' won't be hard to follow."

Abby didn't flinch as Aija walked up to her, leaned in, and blew in her ear seductively. "You're cute!" she said softly. "I like you. Behave yourself Miss Abby!"

Aija left Abby's office unconvinced her warning had any impact. She knew the effect

Aden had on people, and found it hard to believe any friend of his would be able to throw him over as easily as Abby seemed to. She also would require close watching.

With Brawn's obsession for xanide and willingness to give OSEC a foothold on Kealt to get it, Aija decided to personally visit the nearest front-line military outpost to get an update on the rebellion. She been receiving conflicting reports on how the war was going, and decided to see for herself. She commandeered a fast, near ground military transport and headed to Pador, which was hundreds of kilometers from the capital.

An aircraft would have taken less time, but since no cloaked ships were available it would be vulnerable to the resistance, which possessed state of the art air defense systems. While it was slower, the transport presented less of a target. It employed antigrav technology, similar to that used in hover cars, and hung seven meters off the ground as it sped along.

As she drew closer to the front line, she realized the reports she'd been receiving were grossly optimistic. Entire towns were leveled and uncollected bodies lay in the streets, some being eaten by opportunistic scavengers. Hundreds of thousands of people had once lived in these places and now, except for the occasional government checkpoint, there was no sign of anyone. She later learned that very few people had actually surrendered; those that weren't killed retreated with the rebels as government forces advanced.

The government's forces were headquartered in Pador's historic provincial capital, Juris. Once a place of crystal palaces, plush gardens, and art museums, it was now mostly rubble. The commander in charge of Brawn's forces made his headquarters in the Juris Museum of Fine Arts, the most renowned repository of Kealt art on the planet. He had chosen this location because he believed the rebels would not attack it. So far, he was right.

When he saw Aija, he greeted her with false enthusiasm. He knew the conflict wasn't going well, and the personal appearance of General Brawn's vicious aide seemed more like a visit from the Angel of Death.

"General Bendiks," said Aija grimly, "the reality on the ground is much different from the reports General Brawn has been receiving."

"Yes major," he replied deferentially, even though he was several grades her superior. "The rebels are a hardy bunch. They have access to our most advanced weapons and shielded bases, and they always seem to be one step ahead of us."

"Have you made any progress toward securing the xanide mines that ring this place?"

"Not much, our forces have been focused here, trying to capture the city."

"From the looks of it, it isn't worth capturing anymore," she replied, as she walked over to a large map hanging from the wall. She pointed out several locations. "I want you to redeploy your forces here, here, and here. We need those mines!"

"But major, those mines are small and not very productive," protested Bendiks.

"No, but they'll be lightly guarded. We need xanide, and they might still contain enough for our needs."

Against his better judgment, Bendiks later moved the bulk of his forces to the mines Aija had indicated. She was right: They were poorly protected and fell quickly. On her orders, most non-defensive combat operations ceased, and Bendiks' men focused on bringing the mines back on line.

It was an extremely labor-intensive endeavor. The rebels had destroyed much of the mines' infrastructure as they retreated, but under the best of circumstances, they were difficult to work due to their almost inaccessible location deep in steep mountainsides. Because the terrain around the mines also made them difficult to defend, Bendiks was forced to deploy the remainder of his men in a perimeter around them. It was now a war of attrition, with the rebels holding the upper hand. He desperately needed more resources, but Brawn was reserving most of his forces for the looming war with Ardala.

The old mines gave up their treasure grudgingly, and the yield was disappointing. However, while the xanide Bendiks' men scraped from them wasn't sufficient to power Brawn's war machine, it was enough to keep the lights on in Rilan. Aija considered that a victory.

Chapter VIII

"Hello Abeg, thanks for seeing me on such short notice," said Aden, as the old man settled into the booth across from him.

"Well, it's seldom anyone asks me to go anywhere these days," he replied. He touched the patch covering his empty eye socket. "Especially in my depleted state. I hope you don't mind if I take advantage of your hospitality and order an ale?"

"Too late," replied Aden, as a server set down two ales. "I already took the liberty."

Abeg threw his down in one gulp. "Well then, how about another?"

Aden pushed his across the table. "Here, have mine. I'm afraid I'm in need of a clear head."

Abeg paused before starting on his second ale. "Oh?"

"There's a problem with Gris's birthday present."

"His birth…oh yes. And what would that be?"

"The delivery service went out of business. No one goes to where he lives anymore."

"That is a problem. I assume you have an alternative solution, and that is why you need me?"

"It is indeed," answered Aden. He grabbed the server as he walked by and ordered two more ales. "I suppose one won't hurt," he said. Once the server was on his way, he added, "I'm going to deliver it personally."

"How are you going to do that? Brawn and his men are watching you. They'll never let you off this rock." He nodded to a spot behind Aden. "In fact, if I'm not mistaken two of them are right behind you enjoying a couple of steaks on the house. Edris never would have tolerated that. Speaking of which, I'm sorry it took us so long to put our differences behind us. He was a good man, Aden." He lifted a fresh ale. "Here's to Edris…and Sia."

Aden picked his up as well. "May we be worthy of their sacrifice."

"Indeed," replied Abeg, placing a half-empty glass back on the table. "So, what is it you want me to do?"

"Do you still meet with the EA ambassador from time to time?"

"As head of the Council of Commons, in fact, as the only remaining member of said council, I make it a point to see her comely persona at least monthly. In fact, I have an appointment with her later today. Is there something you'd like me to pass on to her?"

"Yes. For her sake, I think it's better if I keep my distance from her…at least on Kealt. Also, we're not on the best terms right now. That fact notwithstanding, we have an anniversary of sorts coming up. If she was interested, maybe we could get away for a few days. If not, tell her I understand. You can fill in the blanks for her when you're with her."

"Very well," replied Abeg, while he looked at his chronometer. "Oh, look what time it is!" He slugged down the remainder of his ale and stood up. "Sorry high prince, I've got to be on my way. One man doing the work of twelve, and all that! I'll pass on your request."

As he limped toward the door, Aden wasn't sure he understood what he was trying to tell him.

Two weeks later he was rising from bed when the room began to shimmer. Before he could catch his breath, he materialized on the bridge of a spaceship. The captain's chair swiveled around and Abby said, "Happy anniversary, Aden."

"You got the message! I wasn't sure Abeg understood me."

"He's a shrewd man, that one, and a bit of a letch. I'm not sure why you trust him. I gathered from his message you need transportation to Ardala, and it has to do with delivering Gris's 'birthday present.' Your reference to our anniversary stumped me for a while. Then I realized you must be referring to the night I met you at the ball your father threw for you and Sia, which happens to be this night."

Aden, who was wearing nothing but a pair of briefs, said, "Good work; I knew I could count on the both of you. Now, I hope you packed appropriate clothes for me. I'm sure we'll both be more comfortable."

"There was a time when neither of us would have cared," she replied wistfully. When he didn't answer, she said, "I anticipated you might need some supplies. If you go through the bulkhead behind you, your quarters are the second set on the left. I'm not sure how long this little 'vacation' is going to last, but I believe you'll find adequate accommodations." Before he reached the bulkhead, she added, "Oh, I'm going to be busy for a while, so you might want to make yourself at home. We're in orbit above Kealt and I'm waiting for final clearance to depart."

Aden found his cabin without incident. As she indicated, it was well stocked with everything he needed, including a set of black, insignia-less, military fatigues. When the ship cleared orbit, she went back and asked him if he was hungry. When he replied affirmatively, she led him to the ship's galley and made him breakfast.

She brought him a large plate full of eggs, bacon, potatoes, onions, toast, butter, and jelly. "I believe Kealt enjoys most of these foods," she noted. "In fact, they share the same names. I guess some things don't change." She also gave him a mug of a steaming, fragrant liquid he didn't recognize.

"You're right, we have most of these," he agreed, as he dug in, "but I'm not sure they've ever been this tasty!"

While he devoured his food, she said, "Your timing is good—I'm overdue to brief our new ambassador to Ardala. Trent always resisted having a dedicated ambassador for each planet, probably because he enjoyed being a celebrity on both worlds. Now that he's gone, we're doing what we should have done from the beginning.

"When I get back, I won't be long for this solar system, since my permanent replacement on Kealt also will be arriving soon. When he gets here—and since the Seti dig has been shut down indefinitely—I'll be reassigned, probably to somewhere back in the Milky Way."

"I'm sorry to hear that," he replied, pausing between bites. "It will truly be Laima's loss." After he finished the last of his bacon, he picked up his drink and gave it a good whiff before tasting it. After the first swallow slid warmly down his throat, he said, "This is delicious as well! What is it? It tastes as good as it smells!"

"It's a natural stimulant we call coffee. It's by far the most popular breakfast drink in the Milky Way. I can't believe it didn't find its way to Laima aboard *The New Mayflower*."

"Perhaps it did, but for some reason couldn't be cultivated," replied Aden, as he prepared to take another sip. "Either way, that is a shame."

Abby waited patiently for him to finish. When he pushed his plate away, she picked up his dirty dishes and placed them in a machine designed to clean them without water. Then she asked him if he'd ever been on a bio ship before. When he responded that he hadn't, she offered to give him a tour. He jumped at the opportunity. He'd been curious about the EA's living ships since he first encountered one on a mission to rescue some scientists just prior to the zon attack on Ardala.

He knew the organic portion of such ships was actually a life form the Earthers referred to as a "selkie." They had discovered the selkie centuries earlier, floating in a void between galaxies. Too perfect to be natural, they believed that a superior, though unknown intelligence had created them expressly to form the hulls of ships. They were tough, resilient, and fed off all forms of energy. When grown around the inorganic portions of a ship, they formed a matrix that was almost indestructible. During battle, they absorbed enemy weapons fire and used it to power their own systems. While all things had limits, they were practically invincible.

As they walked through the ship, Aden asked if he could touch the hull. When Abby agreed, he reached up and put his hand on it. It was a light, mottled green color. It appeared to be slimy and riddled with what looked like veins. To his surprise it felt dry and warm, and it pulsated.

"Very impressive," he said, as they left the engine room. "And I gather that one person is sufficient to pilot her?"

"Yes. This ship can support as many as two dozen crew and passengers, but the selkie manages all ship's functions, including maintenance of its nonorganic components. She uses ambient radiation to synthesize almost anything, including food."

"What is the range of this ship?"

"Almost infinite, as we measure such things," Abby replied.

"Can she fight?"

"Well, yes, to a degree. She's too lightly armed to be an effective front-line warship, but against most foes she can hold her own."

"I understand these ships bond to their captain?"

"Yes. This was Trent's personal ship when he was ambassador. This one was most upset when he died. It took her a while to accept me. Actually, I don't think she's fully bought in yet."

"Bought in?"

"Sorry, it's an Earth expression. It means as far she's concerned, the jury's still out on me. Oops! Sorry, another expression you probably don't know!"

"Well, I think I get the gist of it," he answered with a laugh. "Do these ships have a gender then?"

"Not as we think of it; but as they spend time around humans, most gravitate toward one or the other. This one decided to be female—a bitchy one at that."

"You don't say?"

"Yeah. She resents me for taking Trent's place. When I'm in the shower, sometimes she'll turn the water to ice. She hides my stuff. In general, she makes it known I'm not her favorite person."

"Are you…safe?"

"Yes!" she replied emphatically. "A selkie has never hurt a member of its crew, ever! They can be emotional creatures, but they're extremely loyal."

"When we first encountered the EA on that piece of rock Polis's relative was exploring, you and Trent were wearing suits made from the same organic material as this ship. How come I've not seen you wear it on this ship?"

"Those suits are standard equipment on military vessels, which tend to be larger and more complex. Since the *Hyperion* is considered a civilian ship, it isn't equipped with them."

She eventually led Aden back to the galley, which doubled as a bar, and asked him if he wanted a drink. Remembering how early it was, at least where he started, he asked her for more coffee instead. She brought their drinks over to a low table in front of a large, leather couch. After they both sat down, she said, "Well, we're on our way to Ardala. The trip will take a week in normal space, give or take. What happens when we get there?"

"I'll beam down to the planet, and you report to work."

"That's it? Don't I deserve more than that?"

"It's better for all of us if you don't know. That way, if something happens even the taal couldn't get it out of you."

"Your concern for me is touching."

"Abby, I appreciate your help. There is no one, and I mean no one, I trust more than you. Please trust me."

"I'm still an EA officer. If what you're doing has ramifications for us, I deserve to know regardless of your motivation for keeping this…whatever it is…to yourself."

"The risk to the EA is minimal, although its very presence in this solar system means there are potential ramifications. You know I would never do anything to put you in danger."

"Like ask me to smuggle you between planets on the verge of war?"

"I see your point."

"Aden Cade, I can't let you go through life thinking I'll mindlessly do whatever you ask."

When she said it, she smiled at him, a warm, open smile that reminded him of how beautiful she was, and what a willing lover she'd been a seeming lifetime ago. Considering that Sia had been dead less than a year, these feelings were not welcome and he quickly dismissed them. It was going to be a long week, made longer by his undeniable physical attraction to her.

As the trip went on, he felt his resolve weakening. While Abby didn't dress provocatively, her uniform accentuated her full breasts and clung tightly to her other exquisite curves. A soft caress, a gentle touch, a whisper, an unprovoked smile, she used them all to gain his attention. He went to bed dreaming about how she had smelled, tasted, and felt. He had no room for these feelings. With Sia still so fresh in his memory, he wasn't ready to move on, and didn't know if he ever could.

When Abby announced they would arrive on Ardala the next day, he said a prayer of relief. To celebrate, she prepared the best meal of the trip. She also produced a couple bottles of precious French wine, which were gone long before the meal concluded. Fortunately, she found two more. They talked about everything— everything that is, but for the two-ton taal in the room: Sia was out of bounds for both of them, each for their own reasons. When they finished the last bottle, Aden got up and thanked Abby for dinner. He went over to her, leaned down, and kissed her gently on the lips.

Later, when he was in the shower preparing for bed, he turned at the sound of the shower door sliding open. It was Abby. She was naked, but all he could see was her smile. It was a radiant, loving, inviting, seductive, paralyzing smile; one that threatened to devour him. Before he said anything, she stepped inside and gently pushed him out from under the hot water.

Dumfounded, he watched as she coated her hands with bath soap and scrubbed her body erotically. Before long she turned, put some soap on his chest, and seductively worked her way down his body. Just as he was about to explode, she laughed, stood up, and left the shower. She wrapped a towel around her, said good night, and walked to the door.

Before she could open it, Aden strode over to her, picked her up, and carried her to his bed while she pretended to struggle. Consumed by the release of so much pent up passion, they made love fiercely and without reservations.

Hours later, an alarm went off. "Oh no!" Abby exclaimed, bolting out of bed, "we've arrived! I've got to get up to the bridge!"

She ran to her quarters and threw on her uniform from the day before. She rubbed down her hair as best she could, put some lipstick on, and quickly made her way to the bridge. She paused before stepping onto it to take a deep breath and regain her composure. When she was ready, she walked calmly to her chair and opened a video link. Once she established her identification and received a landing permit and flight plan, the young officer on the other end said, "Ambassador, the high princess would like to talk to you. Can I put her on?"

When Abby agreed, he pushed a button and Celesta took his place on the vidscreen. "Well ambassador, rough night last night?"

"What?" replied Abby.

"Your hair's a mess; your lipstick looks like you put it on in a rollercoaster; your blouse is half open; and you're not wearing any underwear. I'm sure the young ensign who cleared you for landing enjoyed the show, but the rest of us would appreciate it if you would exercise a little more decorum. You are representing the EA, after all!"

"Oh…yes…I'm sorry!" Abby stuttered, as she struggled to secure her ample bosom.

With undisguised disgust, Celesta said, "The king desires a word with you and our new ambassador after you secure your ship. Please take the time to dress properly. We'll all be grateful."

When she signed off, Abby turned and saw Aden standing behind her laughing.

"What's so funny?"

"My dear sister takes a while getting used to. I apologize on her behalf."

"Aden, are you sure whatever you're up to is going to work?" asked Abby.

"I don't know," he replied grimly. "It better."

Chapter IX

A bby landed her ship without incident. When the Ardalans scanned it for contraband, as they always did, she frowned.

"What's the matter?" asked Aden "Is something wrong?"

"I don't know. They routinely scan all ships when they land. Their technology won't penetrate this ship's hull, but they do it anyway."

"OK…"

"This time they scanned me twice, the second time was much more powerful."

"Enough to get through your hull?"

"I don't know. I hope not."

In order protect Aden, who would be arrested on sight if discovered, Abby prepared to beam him directly to Celesta's quarters. As he waited, she went to him and said, "I don't know if we'll ever see each other again. Knowing you, whatever you're up to is dangerous. Besides that, I may be gone before you return. I'm…I'm sorry we didn't get to know each other better. I know I'll never forget you."

"Abby, what we did last night was wrong."

"I'm sorry…what?" she replied.

"Sia hasn't been gone a year. I dishonored her memory by having relations with another woman."

"*Relations with another woman*!" she spat back at him. "So that's all I am to you? Of course, you express your regret now, after I served as a convenient receptacle for your semen!"

"Abby, I…"

"Shut up!" she commanded. "I don't know why I'm disappointed. After all, this is how our relationship has always been—I give, you take! It's a shame, Aden. You're a better man than that!"

"Abby…" he said, reaching out to her, but before finished, he was standing in front of Celesta in her quarters.

"No," she answered gruffly, "she's gone, hopefully forever. What on Kealt do you see in her?"

"She's a lot like Sia—and you," he replied, as he regained his equilibrium.

"Well, she shouldn't be so obvious when she makes love to you. It's very unbecoming."

"What?"

"Never mind, give me a hug!"

As he wrapped his arms around her, he thought of Sia, who also was very pregnant the last time he hugged her. "Can I see my nephew?" he asked, when the embrace ended. "He must be getting big!"

"I'm sorry Aden, he and Polis are away for a couple of days, until our business is concluded. It was a good excuse to get the servants out of the way."

"I understand," he answered. "So, what happened?"

"The ship carrying father's 'present' is at the spaceport, loaded and ready to go. The problem is, our pilot is injured. We've been unable to find a replacement skilled enough and trustworthy enough to navigate the region of space where father is waiting. As you know, between the radiation, meteor belts, black holes, and any number of equally dangerous stellar phenomena, he's in one of the more difficult to reach regions in this galaxy. And then there's the fact that the route takes the ship through some of Kealt and Ardala's most heavily patrolled shipping corridors."

"We could go around those obstacles."

"Yeah, in about three years. We don't have that much time."

"So, what's the plan?"

Celesta walked over to the wall and swept her hand across it. The hologram simulating a portion of the wall vanished, revealing a gaping hole. She reached into it, pulled out a satchel, and reestablished the hologram. She handed the satchel to Aden and said, "Inside is a qrell ID, a certificate of passage, and an approved flight plan. The ID is perfect, in fact it's legitimate, but your picture is on it. I don't imagine there are many people in the entire universe who don't know what you look like by now."

"I don't look much like a qrell, either."

"No, but they're known for hiring human expats, especially for unpopular jobs, such as piloting a waste recycler."

"A waste recycler?"

"We intended to use a cloaked ship, but after everything that's happened, they've been in short supply. We had planned to move the cargo off Kealt the week of the bombing, but we waited too long. After Brawn took over, he locked down all cloak-capable ships. Leaving Kealt, let alone traveling across Ardalan space, became problematic.

"Through a cutout, the Ku Assa purchased a waste recycling franchise from the qrell and leased a ship. It's called the *Zazor*. It makes regular stops on Kealt and Ardala, and, since it carries toxic waste, it was easy to smuggle the cargo without being detected. From Kealt it proceeded to its next stop, Ardala, and eventually would have followed its normal route all the way to where father is waiting.

"Unfortunately the ship's captain was injured when a conduit exploded just after reaching Ardala. The *Zazor* has been sitting on the tarmac ever since, supposedly waiting for a new captain. Once we found one we trusted, i.e. you, the problem was, how could we get you aboard without raising suspicions? You know that Polis, Ivege, and I are the only Ardalans witting of our little conspiracy. We hired an unwitting Ardalan, who has cleared customs and has since boarded the ship. When we're ready, we'll beam him off and you on."

"Won't he go to the authorities?"

"Doubtful. I'm going to ask Abby to return him to his colony. We'll pay him three times what he was going to get for piloting the *Zazor*. If that isn't enough to keep his secret, I'm sure his fear of revealing his role in our little conspiracy would be. Aden, are you sure you want to do this? Neither the ship nor this mission is safe."

"I have to. You know the stakes."

"I do," she admitted unhappily. "Ardala doesn't want a war and won't start one; but we won't back down from one, either. Brawn acts as if we're weak, but I think the capabilities of our forces will surprise him. Neither side would win this war!"

"We?" he asked. "When did you become 'we?'"

"My children and my husband are of this world. This is my home now! Its fate is mine." When he didn't answer, she said, "This is how this is going to work: When I give the signal, Abby is going to use her transporter to send you to the *Zazor* and the Ardalan to her ship. Hopefully Ardalan security won't be able to detect her transport beam.

"Once you're en route, your vidscreen will malfunction, which will prevent interested ships from getting a good look at you in the event you're stopped; but you'll be able to see them. The ship you'll be piloting is old, and, as I mentioned, used primarily to transport toxic waste. I doubt anyone will want to board it. Even smugglers would never use such a dangerous ship.

"The qrell are a neutral species, respected by both sides. It isn't unusual for waste recyclers like this one to go back and forth across Ardalan and Kealt space. Both sides are delighted to have someone else carry out the toxic trash. Your route will eventually take you to the Frone Colony, near the edge of Ardalan space. From there you'll break off your planned route and make your way to where my parents are waiting."

She reached into the satchel he was holding and pulled out a data crystal. "See this?" she asked, holding it up. "Once you get to Frone, follow the coordinates on this data crystal. They will lead you to a short-range beacon that will guide you to father's location. Whatever happens, this crystal mustn't fall into unwitting hands! It's almost dinner time here. Cleanup, and I'll prepare us something to eat. The transport will occur later this evening."

"If she'll do what you ask of her."

"Why wouldn't she?"

"Because I'm an idiot."

Later, over a simple dinner, Celesta cried while remembering Edris, the biological father she shared with Aden; Sarin, her mother-in-law; and her good friend Sia. "Who do you think committed these crimes?" she asked, wiping away tears.

Aden put down his fork and wiped his mouth with a napkin. "I don't know," he replied pensively. "I'm sure whomever it was will eventually reveal themselves."

"They never recovered Sarin's body. We couldn't even bury her!"

"I know. It was a plasma coil overload. When one of those explodes…"

"The Ku Assa believes she was murdered."

"Most likely. The chances of an accident like that are exceedingly slim. The fact that it only affected her quarters is even more suspicious."

"Do you trust Abby?"

"With my life."

"I never liked her, Aden. She's an opportunist. Whenever Sia was out of the picture, she jumped in as fast as she could. I think she'd do anything to be with you."

Aden smiled. "Some people would call that loyalty...or love."

"Is *that* what you'd call it? I'd call it obsession, fanaticism, or maybe, just plain old lust!"

"It doesn't matter," he replied wanly.

"Why?"

After Aden explained the circumstances of their last goodbye, she said, "I almost feel sorry for her—almost. Now, you have a half hour before you leave." When Aden again expressed doubt that she'd be there for him one more time, she replied, "You forget, brother, she's spent time on Ardala. Against my will, I've gotten to know her. While I don't appreciate her buzzard-like interest in you, she is...predictable. I doubt she'd ever let you down, no matter how badly you treated her."

She was right: At the appointed time, Aden switched places with the ship's hired pilot.

Later that day, after Abby had concluded her business with King Ivege and returned to the ambassador's residence, Celesta paid her a visit.

When Abby admitted her, she declined her offer to sit.

"How is your guest?" she asked.

"He's fine," answered Abby. "He's confined to his quarters for now, but seems to accept the deal he's been offered. I get the impression that to him this is just business—he'd rather make three times the money doing nothing than captain a waste recycler. Who wouldn't?"

"I am…I'm grateful to you for your assistance in this matter," said Celesta. "Aden trusts you, so, against my better judgment, I must as well. I also want you to know that I don't like you, and I don't appreciate your interest in my brother, or the way you use your body to influence him."

"I have no influence over Aden, Celesta!" retorted Abby angrily. "None whatever; I'm no more to him than an extended one-night stand, if even that. Still, I'd give my life for him, and may before this over."

"Did you kill Sia?" asked Celesta bluntly.

"What? No!"

"Who did?"

"I don't know! I do know this: Aden needs us both. So you can go on blaming me for whatever it is you think I've done, or we can work together and help him!"

Celesta glared at her without responding, then turned abruptly and left.

Celesta was correct about one thing: Aden's ship, the *Zazor*, wasn't much. It was old, slow, dirty, and balky. In order to limit the exposure of crewmembers to toxic waste, it was largely automated and required little input once its course was set. His journey out of the solar system was uneventful, partly because, as Celesta noted, even smugglers avoided using ships like the *Zazor*. He was rarely challenged, and when he was it was merely perfunctory.

The few times military patrols took note of the her, they never expressed an interest in boarding her, and only asked the most cursory questions before sending her on her way. Once outside the solar system Aden breathed a sigh of relief. He quickly entered hyperspace, a much faster and safer means of travel, since neither Kealt nor Ardala could track unbeaconed ships outside of regular space.

He followed his flight plan as written, periodically stopping to pick up waste products from a number of small colonies. As the voyage stretched into its second week, he found it harder and harder to relieve the crushing boredom. As his thoughts invariably drifted to Sia and his never-to-be-born son, his emotions vacillated from sadness, to anger, and back to sadness in the space of seconds. He also thought of his father, who grew wiser in his mind by the day.

He frequently went over the facts of the attacks in an effort to divine clues to the perpetrators. Nothing made sense. Another force was at work in Laima, one that was malignant, manipulating, and intelligent. He remembered Trent's warning about OSEC. The more he thought about it, the more he wondered if they were the ones pulling the strings.

The problem was, whomever was behind the attacks must have had an in-depth knowledge of how Kealt worked. They would have had to have known that the podium was lined with carbanite, which blocked routine scans. In addition, OSEC couldn't have known that, of the several typically used for such events, it was the one Edris preferred because it was a little taller, and that it would be the best place to put a bomb intended to wipe out the Kealt Government. Lastly, they would have had to have known where the podium was kept in order to beam the bomb into it. Even if they had been tapping into all of Kealt's communications and databases, it was unlikely that OSEC, on their own, could have gained such specific knowledge of the inner workings of Kealt society so quickly.

Try as he might, he also couldn't keep his mind off Abby. When Sia was alive, her intense light blinded him to Abby's own brilliance. Even in death it continued to shine brightly. However, while it would never be extinguished, it was gradually dimming, enough so that Abby's light was beginning to shine through. He tried to turn away from it, but his attraction to her was undeniable. In retrospect she was correct: He took from her when it was convenient for him, but gave little in return.

Of course, Abby herself had contributed to his attitude toward her. When he first met her, she was an EA spy pretending to be a dopy refugee from the Zon War named Drusa Prine. He took an immediate liking to her, but her affected demeanor, by design, made it impossible for him to take her seriously.

The more he thought about it, the more he wondered if Sia was correct: Perhaps being Drusa allowed Abby to express herself in ways she couldn't when she wasn't acting. He was sorry he hadn't been more considerate of her when he'd had the opportunity—another regret for him to add to a growing heap now just short of a mountain.

With just a week to go before reaching Gris, he was finally beginning to let himself relax. He ate a light meal, ensured all systems were operating properly, and turned in for the night. He was in the middle of a rare good dream when the ship's proximity alarm nearly knocked him out of bed.

He leapt to his feet and rushed to the bridge without bothering to get dressed. Less than a thousand meters away and closing fast was a huge ship of an unfamiliar configuration. He pulled the *Zazor* hard to starboard, but the larger ship matched his maneuver. With less than five hundred meters between them, he brought his ship to a full stop.

When he hailed the much larger vessel, it ignored him and locked a tractor beam onto his hull. He set his engines to full reverse, but to no avail—the other vessel drew his ship into it effortlessly. Realizing the futility of his situation, Aden turned off his engines, lowered his landing pylons, and waited.

The *Zazor* came to rest in a huge hanger, surrounded by many other ships whose configurations also were unfamiliar to him. He pulled the data crystal containing the coordinates of his final destination out of the computer, put it on the floor, and vaporized it with a plasma weapon.

After he secured the pistol, he threw on some clothes and made his way down to the cargo hold. He lowered the loading ramp and walked down to the deck, where he was met by a large contingent of heavily armed soldiers, who had their weapons trained on him. A woman pushed her way through them and put her hands on her hips.

"Hmmm," she said, "we were led to believe the pilot of this ship was a man named Gus

Harper. I have no idea what he looks like, but you look a lot like High Prince Aden Cade."

"Major."

"I should shoot you now for betraying Kealt!"

"You and Brawn are the ones guilty of that."

"Major," said an armed man named Stanford, "I'd be happy to loosen him up for you. He looks like someone who needs to be taught a lesson!"

"Negative!" insisted the officer in charge, whose name was Henry. "Our orders are to bring him back in one piece. Brawn and Gross will decide what to do with him."

"I wouldn't be so eager to pick a fight, Stanford," added Aija. "Especially one you might not win."

"Are you kidding me?" replied Stanford. "He's big, but he's a fricking prince! What does he know about fighting?"

"All right," answered Aija, over Henry's objections. "Have it your way. Max, take his weapon."

The one called Max did as ordered, and the rest of the men formed a loose ring around the two combatants. Stanford removed his shirt, revealing an impressively muscled chest. He wasn't quite as tall as Aden, but he was even thicker. When the two men began to circle each other warily, waiting for the other to engage first, Aija became impatient.

"You wanted him, go get him!" she insisted. "We're getting bored watching you two dance!"

When Stanford lunged at Aden, he easily sidestepped him and slapped his head. Stanford regrouped, and responded with a series of punches that Aden slipped with ease. Now thoroughly frustrated, Stanford bellowed and charged. Aden didn't move, but unleashed a straight right hand that stopped him in his tracks.

"You five!" exclaimed Aija, pointing to a group of men. "Get in there and see if you can do any better!"

"Major!" protested Henry. "These men are spec ops trained! They'll kill him!"

"Get in there!" she demanded, over his objections.

The men fought furiously, punishing Aden with repeated blows. However, despite their best efforts, they failed to subdue him and one by one they left the ring with various injuries.

When the bloody and bruised Aden was again alone in the circle, Aija stepped inside it. "OK!" she said. "Now it's time to show you how it's done!"

"Major!" warned Aden, "I will hurt you if you insist on doing this."

"Thanks for the warning!" she retorted, as she spun and threw a kick that just missed his head.

Aden quickly recovered and the two battled each other furiously while the others watched. Just when it seemed neither would falter, Aden took advantage of an ill-timed kick and countered with a punch to Aija's ribs that left her gasping and spitting blood. She hunched over, held her bruised ribs and struggled to speak.

"You...bastard...you broke...my ribs! I...can't...breath!"

"Finish her!" demanded a man named Roberts, when Aden hesitated. "She's been nothing but a pain in the ass!"

When Aden let down his guard and went over to assist her, she straightened suddenly, punched him in the groin and knocked him out with a kick to the head.

Aija nodded to the remaining men. "Bind him before he comes to. Then secure his ship and find out where he was going. Search it for anything of intelligence value. You three, clean him up and bring him to my quarters in an hour."

As she was walking away, Roberts said, "You weren't really hurt, were you? You tricked him!"

She walked over to him and said, "I bit my lip and used it to my advantage. Every man has a weakness. His is compassion." She pointed to a spot behind Roberts. "See that?" When he turned to look in the direction she was pointing, she shattered his jaw with one blow. As he laid on the ground moaning and spitting teeth, she said, "Yours is stupidity!"

As she ordered, Aden later found himself in Aija's quarters, heavily bound and sitting in a chair facing her and Henry.

"Nice of you to join us, high prince," said Aija sarcastically. "What brings you to this portion of the galaxy?"

"I needed a job."

"I'm sure that's true, but I doubt that's why you're here. Your documentation says one of your vessel's stops was Ardala. Considering our current 'warm' relations with them, you're a spy either for them or for someone else. Now, do you have a better answer?"

When Aden remained mute, Aija nodded toward one of the guards watching the door. He opened it, and two men came in hauling a large crate between them. After they left, she threw open the lid, revealing an impressive cache of military grade xanide crystals.

"We found these tucked away in your ship. Quite an impressive haul. You know it's illegal for a civilian to have this much xanide without a license. With Seti's moratorium on mining, how did you get your hands on so much mil-grade xanide and who is it for?"

When Aden didn't answer, she said, "Ardala needs this almost as badly as we do, yet you left there with it, so it wasn't for them. OSEC tipped us off to your clumsy smuggling operation, so it wasn't them. You weren't heading anywhere near Kealt, so it wasn't the resistance. It certainly wasn't for the provisional government.

"That leaves the greedy, avaricious, and grasping EA. Add to that the fact that your ship left Ardala the same day you and your EA girlfriend arrived and, well, two plus two equals four in every galaxy. Fortunately, little Miss Watanabe is scheduled to return to Kealt soon. When she does, we'll have a welcoming committee for her. With the right persuasion, she might be willing to shed some light on your new 'job.'"

"Abby knows nothing about this," he insisted. "Besides, she's a diplomat. Do you really want to antagonize the EA?"

"We're not afraid of them," Aija retorted. "Anyway, we're not going to torture her, we're going to torture you. If she's as close to you as we believe, she might be more than willing to give up what she knows."

"I told you, she doesn't know anything! She was never anything more to me than an easy means of physical gratification."

"As much as I like the sound of that, she must know something—she agreed to smuggle you to Ardala, after all."

Changing the subject, Aden asked, "Who are your new friends, Aija?"

"The future of our solar system, high prince. If you survive long enough, you better get used to it."

"How did you find me…oh, it was OSEC that performed the second scan on Ardala!"

"Yes," admitted Henry. "We wanted to confirm you were onboard. We had to wait until you reached Ardala, because we were afraid the EA officer would detect our scan. We know Ardala scans all incoming ships, so we took a chance she would think they did it. Apparently it worked. After that, we monitored her ship for transporter activity, which eventually led us to the ship you were on when we captured you.

"Without beaconing your ship, we couldn't follow you in hyperspace. However, it was easy to obtain a copy of your flight plan, since on Ardala they're available to the public. We were waiting for you, cloaked of course, each time you jumped into regular space. We wanted to see where you'd lead us and whom you'd meet, but we were running out of time. According to your flight plan, we caught you at your last jump before you were supposed to head back to qrell space. We doubted that was going to happen, and we were afraid we'd lose you if we let you reenter hyperspace.

"We hoped we'd be able to determine your ultimate destination from your ship's computer, but you obviously kept it out of the database. I assume the fresh burn mark on the deck of your ship occurred when you blasted the data crystal containing it. Now the major and her friends are going to have to torture it out of you."

Aija asked to be left alone with him. When the door shut behind the last man, she went up to Aden and caressed his cheek.

"You are such a handsome man!" she cooed. "I have no interest in seeing you ruined. We merely need some information. We'll find out what we need to know whether you tell us or not. Why not make this less painful for all of us?"

When he didn't answer, she undid her blouse and bared her smallish, but well-formed breasts. She leaned over him until she was so close, he could have kissed them. "Wouldn't this be preferable to what's in store for you?" she teased, while caressing his hair. "Tell me what I want to know and you can have me any way you want, and I mean any way! In fact, I prefer it 'any way!'"

Aden couldn't help but stare at her tense, inviting nipples, and inhale her nearly intoxicating fragrance. Against his will, he felt a fire igniting in his loins. However, realizing she was just taunting him, he cleared his head with some effort. "I'd make love to you," he replied, "except the stench from your maggot-infested soul makes an erection impossible!"

Aija stood up and slapped him. "Have it your way!" she hissed. "When I get through with you, you won't be fit for a bolba tree!" She spit on him for good measure and stomped out of the room.

Despite their vast distance from Kealt, they made orbit just two days later. To Aden's surprise, they didn't further abuse him during the brief voyage. He assumed that was because Aija and Brawn wanted to interrogate him on Kealt, where their leverage was…

Chapter X

When Abby returned to Kealt she hoped Aden would find his way to her, despite the acrimonious nature of their last parting. When he didn't, she swallowed her pride and went to his quarters. His servants informed her that they hadn't heard from him, and that he planned to be away for some time. Not sure if that was a good sign or not, she went about her duties as though nothing had happened and waited for her replacement, Jeff Dandridge, who was an old friend.

On the day he was to arrive, she went to the spaceport to meet him. When he stepped off the EA transport, she waved to him and he came over to her.

"Abby Watanabe, as I live and breathe!" he exclaimed, dropping his bag and embracing her heartily. "We all thought you'd been swallowed up by the jungle of that fascinating world you discovered!"

"Well, it's nice to see you too, Jeff!" she replied, gasping for breath. "I hope your trip was quick and uneventful."

"Yes to both. Abby, I'm sorry about John. I know he meant a lot to you."

"He did," she agreed. "He saved my life, literally. How are Miranda and the kids?"

"They are fabulous! Mindy can't wait to see her Godmother again! They'll be joining me after school lets out."

"My goodness, she must be so big by now. Unfortunately, I'll be long gone by then. Come on, our car is waiting over there. I'll take you to your new quarters; afterwards, if you're up to it, how about dinner on me?"

"Can't imagine anything I'd rather do!" he agreed.

Later that evening, Abby took him to the Public Inn. As the waiter seated them, she said, "Not very fancy, but I really like this place."

"I can see why," he said. "Very cozy and unpretentious. I think it suits us well!"

"It suits me, anyway," replied Abby. "I'm not particularly popular with current regime. I try to stay off the beaten path."

"So I heard. Tough times on Kealt. I'm looking forward to meeting…High Prince is it? Aden Cade. He seems like an amazing fellow."

A waiter interrupted them, and at Abby's request he scurried off to find them a bottle of Kag wine. When he was gone, she said, "I…I haven't seen him for a while. He's left the planet and might not be back."

"Is he in trouble?"

"I don't know…maybe…I hope not. You know we were close at one time."

"I read about his exploits on Seti. I understand he discovered the taal?"

"Rediscovered is more like it. The taal and the people of this system once knew each other well, until the taal became skittish and retreated into their jungle lair centuries ago. If it weren't for Aden, I suspect they never would have revealed themselves again, war or no war. I gather they were quite comfortable in their anonymity."

"As I said, I would very much like to meet him. It's not often you come across a living legend."

"I know," agreed Abby with a grin. "I've never met anyone like him."

"If I didn't know better, I'd say you're still smitten with him."

"What? No!" she replied emphatically. When Dandridge looked at her skeptically, she added, "OK, I like him—everyone who knows him does—but I don't think he or his family ever got over my deception prior to first contact."

"Ah, the Drusa Prine affair! Surely they don't still hold that against you?"

Before Abby could answer, the waiter returned with their wine. After dispensing it with the proper ceremony, he left with their food order. When he was gone, she said, "I'm afraid they do, especially Celesta, his homicidal Ku Assa sister."

"An impressive woman in her own right," he answered, before taking a sip of wine. "Abby, this is quite good!"

"I like it."

"Shame about his wife and unborn child. Have they ever gotten to the bottom of that mess?"

"No," replied Abby, "they haven't, although they don't lack for suspects, including the EA."

"Surely you don't think we had anything to do with this?"

"Of course not."

"Well, for his sake, I hope the perpetrators are caught." When Abby didn't reply, he said, "I have your orders. You'll be returning to Earth whenever you're ready. I don't know what they have in store for you, but I've been told it's big."

"Unfortunately, after my adventures in this galaxy, I'm afraid everything is going to seem a little smaller!"

Dandridge leaned back in his seat and rested his hands in his lap. "So, are you looking forward to going home?" he asked. "I don't think you've been back since…"

"Can we not talk about that?" she responded tensely.

"I'm sorry Abby; but you can't keep pretending it didn't happen."

"Why not?"

"Abby..."

"I'm sorry Jeff. I don't mean to be short with you, but I'm really not ready for this."

Eventually they moved on to happier subjects, and when dinner was over, Dandridge leaned back and said, "I've eaten at the finest tables in the Milky Way, but I can't remember enjoying a meal more than this one! Thank you very much."

"I'm glad you liked it. There is something about this place. I've enjoyed a lot of good memories here." She rested her arms on the table and leaned forward. "I'm sorry I haven't been very good company. I have a lot on my mind. To tell you the truth, I'm worried about Aden, and Kealt itself for that matter. Things are not going well here."

"I know how much you like this solar system, Abby. Would you like to stay? I could arrange it if you want."

"Thanks Jeff, I appreciate it; but I've overstayed my welcome here. I need to leave."

The next day she was packing her sparse belongings when a servant told her a pair of stern-looking soldiers were waiting for her at the entrance to the residence. When she opened the door to greet them, one said, "I'm sorry to intrude ma'am, but General Brawn has requested an audience with you immediately."

"Oh, what's so urgent?"

"We weren't told."

"I see. Do you mind if I dress properly?"

"Of course, we'll wait out here."

Abby went back inside and took her time. She remembered how Celesta had chastised her about her appearance. Although her admonishment was mean-spirited, she realized she had a point. After brushing her hair, she applied some makeup and a small dab of perfume a previous guest had left behind.

When she stepped outside to join the soldiers, they gawked at her speechlessly until she reminded them, they had somewhere to go. A short while later an aide brought her into General Brawn's office. Aija also was there, and stared at her in a way that made her uncomfortable.

"Good morning general, I understand you wanted to see me?"

"Yes," he said affably, sitting down on the front of his desk. "How are you?"

"Fine. I assume you wanted to ask me something more substantive?"

"Very good, all business! I appreciate that. How close are you to Aden Cade?"

"Not close at all. In fact, at the moment, I'd say we're not on speaking terms."

"Yet you violated Kealt's prohibition on citizens traveling to Ardala."

"I'm not a Kealt citizen," noted Abby. "The EA's treaties with Kealt and Ardala permit me to move freely between both worlds."

"Cade is. And we have proof that you took him there."

When Abby started to protest, Brawn held up his hand.

"Captain, before you add lying to your resume, we can prove it." He pushed the intercom on his desk and asked his secretary to send in a waiting guest.

"OSEC!" exclaimed Abby, when Gross entered the room. "You're working with them? You have no idea what you're dealing with!"

"My goodness, if it isn't the lovely Abby Watanabe!" replied Gross condescendingly. "Unlike the EA, we're here to help Kealt."

"Mr. Gross's men scanned your ship when you reached Ardala," said Brawn, "and to our surprise, Cade was onboard. Later, you teleported him to the very quarters of the high prince and princess."

"Am I under arrest?" she asked testily.

"Of course not!" Brawn assured her. "You're a diplomat, for now, and have immunity from our legal system. You can leave any time. In fact, we would prefer you did."

"Very good," she replied, and turned to leave.

"Before you do, I thought we should tell you that we have the high prince in custody. He hasn't told us anything yet, but my men can be very persuasive."

Abby stopped in her tracks. "Is he…hurt?"

"Oh, he's fine...for now. Let me show you." He pushed a button on his desk, and an image of Aden appeared on the vidscreen on the wall across from it. He was secured to a chair, slumped over, with his hands strapped to a table in front of him. "Would you like to talk to him?" he asked in a solicitous manner. "I'm sure he'd enjoy your company."

"Please," she replied.

"Aija, would you mind? I have some further business with Mr. Gross."

"Of course not," she answered brightly. "We're holding him downstairs in an interrogation cell."

At Aija's request, Abby followed her out. When they got to Aden's cell, Aija ordered the guards to open it and they both stepped inside. "Wake up sleepy head!" she said cheerfully. "You have a visitor!" When he didn't move, Aija instructed one of her men to throw cold water on him. As he jerked up, Abby saw that his face was a mass of welts.

"Aden!" she exclaimed. "What have they done to you!"

"Major," he croaked, "I told you she doesn't know anything. I swear, if you hurt her, I will personally peel the skin off you *and* Brawn!"

"While that sounds like fun—for you anyway—in your present position I'm afraid that's not likely. At any rate, I've already told you I have no intention of hurting her. Guard!"

At her command, another soldier stepped into the cell and handed her a mallet and some slivers of wood. "Aden," she said airily, "who were you taking that xanide to?" When he didn't reply, she stepped up to the table, positioned a sliver of wood under a fingernail, and drove it home with the mallet.

His screams brought tears to Abby's eyes. "Stop it, you monster!" she exclaimed.

Aija positioned a second sliver under another fingernail. "Either of you can stop this at any time."

"I don't know anything!" Abby insisted. "Aden, tell her what she wants to know!"

When he remained mute, Aija drove home the second sliver and laughed manically when he screamed so loud the guards stepped back in alarm. "I can do this all day!" she said, as she positioned the third sliver. "And another thing: We've finally had a chance to go over the books.

It seems a huge amount of resources have been going to the military."

Aden, who by now was barely consciousness, rasped, "Why should that surprise you? Two thirds of our fleet was destroyed or damaged during the war with the zon!"

"That's not the part that bothers us. What bothers us is that, for all the money Kealt has earmarked for the military, all we've gotten from it is a handful of half-finished Dipsa class warships and barely enough xanide to keep the rest of our fleet minimally operational. Where did all that money go?"

"How would I know? I'm not in the government anymore."

"You were. You mean King Edris never told you, his son, the former overlord of the Kealt War Machine, what he was spending all that money on? That's hard to believe high prince. If I didn't know better, I'd say that you, your father, and certain members of the Council of Commons were stealing from the till." Before he could answer, she drove home the next sliver, eliciting the expected scream. Then she took yet another sliver and placed it under one of his rapidly diminishing intact fingernails. "Well, how about it?"

"We're not thieves you twisted, evil bitch! My father was a secretive man. He never even told me about Celesta until Glyn forced him to!"

"Ah yes, Glyn, your mysteriously unaccounted for sister. Where is she, Aden? And your brother in law, for that matter." When he refused to answer, she drew back the mallet.

"Please, leave him alone!" Abby pleaded, grabbing her arm and stopping her in mid-strike. "He'll never tell you anything, can't you see that? I'll do anything you want, just, please, leave him alone!"

"*Anything*?" repeated Aija, moving her eyes suggestively up and down Abby's body. "*Anything* covers a lot of ground, sweetie!" When she remained mute, Aija leered at her. "Guards, get him out of here and clean him up. I'm going to stay here and talk to the ambassador for a bit…and we're going to need some privacy!"

The guards smirked at each other as they untied the now unconscious Aden and dragged him out of the room. When they were alone, Aija pulled the door shut. She put a hand to her mouth, then walked over to Abby and circled her slowly, pausing to sniff the back of her neck.

"You are delicious!" she said brightly.

She put her hands gently on her shoulders and turned her around to face her. "Let's see how badly you want to save your beloved Aden!"

Fighting the urge to cry, Abby stood quietly as Aija slowly pulled down the zipper on her uniform before pushing it off her shoulders. Then she reached behind her back, unhooked her bra, and freed her straining breasts.

With Abby now naked from the waist up, Aija put one hand around her waist, roughly grabbed a bare breast with the other, and leaned in as though to kiss the smaller woman. She blew on Abby's lips gently, and put her mouth on hers. When she slipped her tongue between her teeth, Abby realized it was pushing a small object before it. She accepted it, then, in warning, bit down gently but firmly on Aija's lingering tongue. Aija released her and laughed.

"Unfortunately, today I don't have enough time to enjoy your quite remarkable and tasty body properly," she said. "Put your clothes back on, captain, we'll have to finish this later. Don't worry, we will—I'm sure you'll like me as much as I like you!"

After Abby had finished dressing and fled, Aija summoned one of her soldiers.

"Sergeant, how is Cade?" she asked.

"He's pretty banged up, but he'll live."

"Good; if he's still with us in the morning, I want him castrated. Then I want him tied naked to his beloved goliathan tree for everyone to see."

"Sir, he's not a dog."

"Did I ask for your opinion, sergeant?"

"No sir."

"It's a big tree. There's plenty of room for you as well. So unless you want to meet his fate, don't question my orders again!"

Chapter XI

When Abby reached her quarters, she took the data crystal Aija had slipped into her mouth and plugged it into her computer. If she was reading it correctly, Aija had given her the frequency to a type of subcutaneous transponder routinely injected into prisoners, as well as the code for lowering the force field around Aden's cell.

Later that night, without telling Dandridge, she transported herself from her quarters to her ship. Then she cloaked it and lifted off. When she reached orbit, she located the transponder signal, lowered the shield around Aden's cell, and beamed him aboard.

He was unconscious, clearly having suffered additional torture. She dragged him onto an antigravity stretcher and took him to the infirmary, where she tended to his injuries. Using a hand scanner, she quickly found and removed his transponder. To her surprise, she found a second one. *That* was why Aija had helped her: She was going to use the second transponder to track them to whomever Aden was working with! What a conniving, vicious bitch, she thought grimly.

She continued her scan, which reflected that, while his injuries were painful, he had suffered no permanent damage. When he eventually came to, she was still cleaning his wounds.

"Where am I?" he asked groggily.

"Onboard my ship," she replied, wiping his face with a fresh towel. "We're in orbit around Kealt."

Aden suddenly grabbed his crotch and squeezed it determinedly.

"What on Earth are you doing?" asked Abby, trying not to laugh.

"I was told Brawn's pet monster was going to castrate me."

When Abby ensured him that he was still intact, he asked her how he had found his way onto her ship.

"Aija helped me get you out," she answered.

"What?"

"It's a long story."

"OK. Won't they find us?"

"No. EA cloaking technology is far more sophisticated than yours—even OSEC can't penetrate it."

"Where are we going?"

Abby smiled gently. "I was waiting for you tell me!"

"I need to talk to Celesta."

When he tried to stand up, only Abby kept him from falling.

"Do you make it a habit of going against doctor's orders?" she asked. "Give yourself a little time."

Later that evening, Aden found her sitting in the galley nursing a drink. When she saw him, she leapt up and said, "Aden, you shouldn't be up yet!"

"I'm fine. Do you mind if I join you?"

"Of course not."

"I don't suppose you have any more of that fine French wine?"

In reply, she walked behind the bar and looked underneath. She pulled out a bottle and put it down on the stone surface. "I'm afraid not, but I have some Kag wine. To be honest, I like it just as much."

When Aden nodded, she filled two glasses, handed him one, and they walked over to the couch. When they were settled, he lifted his glass in a toast. "Here's to you. My life wouldn't be the same without you. In fact, it wouldn't 'be' at all!"

"Well," she replied, tapping his glass with hers, "a lot of people can say the same thing about you. And you have the bruises to prove it!"

Aden tried to smile, but to Abby it looked more like a grimace.

"So," he said, "I have time for a long story. How did you get me out?"

She tried with only partial success to keep her emotions in check as she told him. When she finished, all he could say was, "Well, it's a good thing you were able to find that second transponder!"

"It wasn't hard, it was practically screaming at me. I thought Kealt's technology was more advanced than that."

"I can assure you, it is. I have to assume whomever implanted it didn't know what they were doing."

"Just lucky, I guess."

"Abby, you should have just walked away. I could have handled it."

"A simple thank you would be nice," she answered curtly. "At least it didn't go as far as I thought it would! A kiss is one thing, but I...I don't know if I could have handled the rest of it."

"I don't know what to say. I can't ever repay you for what you did."

Abby smiled wanly. "You were right, Aden."

"About what?"

She got up, went to the bar, and brought the wine bottle back to the small table in front of them. After she refilled their glasses, she said, "Not telling me what you were up to. I see now why you didn't—I would have told them everything, done anything, to get them to stop hurting you."

"Abby, we're missing something."

"That's obvious, but what?"

"You heard Aija—according to her, the fleet is in tatters and there is a xanide shortage. It wasn't that long ago I was in charge of Kealt's military. When I left, we had an adequate stockpile of xanide, and the restoration of the fleet was proceeding on schedule. We were redirecting significant resources—including xanide—to another project, but neither my father, the council, nor I would do anything to compromise the ability of Kealt to defend itself.

"Even if there was a legitimate xanide shortage, there were more than enough mil-grade crystals in Gris's 'birthday present' to power several dozen Dipsa class ships. So where did all that xanide go? Why isn't the fleet in better shape? Brawn is up to something, and it can't be good."

Abby poured herself more wine. "Maybe he and Major Vilas are the ones who are stealing?"

"I doubt it. Brawn doesn't care about money. He's bent on destroying Ardala, whom he blames for killing his wife and other assorted sins. Vilas seems more intent on torturing people. Which brings up another point: Brawn is a member of the Sarfas clan, one of the oldest and most powerful clans on Kealt. They also are one of the most chauvinistic clans, even more so than the Mars. It's almost inconceivable that he would allow a member of the Sokk clan, like Aija, into his inner circle. As I said, they are up to something, and even the Ku Assa is in the dark, at least so far."

"Aren't they all knowing?" she asked, sarcastically.

"Since the military got its hands on zon scanning technology, they can't hide behind their personal cloaking technology anymore. They have to do their spying the old-fashioned way. It's much more cumbersome and time consuming."

Later that evening, Aden got through to Celesta, who was ecstatic that he was safe, if bruised from his ordeal.

"What, no hologram?" she asked, playfully. "Aden! We cannot have a war!"

"All hope isn't lost," he replied.

"I still have extensive contacts on Kealt. They told me OSEC had captured your ship. They also told me what you went through. I was wrong about Abby. She's a real hero. So, we lost the xanide. Is that it? Is this over?"

Aden smiled grimly. "Not yet. I happen to know where a very large supply of it can be found."

Grasping his meaning, Celesta said, "You can't go there! It's locked down except for the handful of minors the taal allowed to stay to maintain critical infrastructure. I know Brawn has sent several ships and none came back. They are serious about staying neutral."

"I'm hoping Bang will make an exception. If she doesn't, I've beaten them before."

"That was different. They claimed they let you do it, remember? Besides, when was the last time you even heard from her? You said Bang was old. There's no guarantee she's even still alive!" When he didn't answer, she said, "Polis has been dying to talk to you!"

"Hello old man!" Polis exclaimed, as Celesta stepped aside. "Can't stay out of trouble, can you? What I don't understand is how you always come out alive!"

"Polis, I'm sorry about Sia and your mother."

"And I about your many losses. Monsters are loose in Laima, Aden."

"Yes, but there is more going on here than meets the eye."

"Most certainly, but every day Brawn is becoming more and more belligerent. We'd be fools to want war after what we've been through, but we'll defend ourselves!"

"I know, my brother. On the bright side, we're still technically at peace. We still have time. Gris is waiting patiently, and I believe I can replace the missing xanide."

"Yes, I heard—from Seti. I think you place too much trust in the taal. They're not a trustworthy bunch."

"Perhaps not. Take care of yourself, my sister, and my nephew! I'll be back soon!"

"I pray you are."

When he ended the transmission, Abby set course for Seti. When he saw what she was doing, he stopped her. "Abby," he said, "you've gone out on a limb for me repeatedly. I owe you my life several times over. You're right; our relationship has pretty much been a one-way street."

"What are you saying?"

"I need to go this alone. If you help me any further, you risk dragging the EA into this, and no one wants that. You also could die; as it is, I can barely get through each day having one woman's memory on my mind. I prefer to think of you happy and safe, following a path of your choosing."

"What if this is the path I've chosen?"

"It can't be, not this time. I need to do this myself."

"How will you get there?"

"The taal allow one supply ship from Kealt and Ardala to land every few months. An Ardalan supply ship is en route now and will arrive within the week. If you beam me aboard before it gets there, no one will be the wiser."

"If the Ardalans find you, they might flush you out an airlock."

"Is that wishful thinking?"

"That's not funny."

"I'll be OK, I always am."

"Aden," she replied, "all things die eventually. You will too. There's no need to tempt fate. You're already so deeply in its debt, I question how much credit remains in your account. Let me come with you!"

He embraced her tightly and stroked her hair. "My love for Sia is overwhelming," he said. "I may never get over her. You can't imagine what it's like to lose a love like that. I'll not rest until her killers face justice. My quest may indeed consume me, but I refuse to let it take you as well."

Abby angrily broke his embrace and slapped him so hard his head snapped back. "You bastard!" she exclaimed. "You self-important, self-centered, arrogant son of a bitch! Don't you dare assume you know me! You've never even tried! After all this time, I'm still just 'easy little Drusa' to you! You know nothing about me...NOTHING!"

Aden rubbed his cheek. "Abby I...I..."

"Shut up!" she bellowed. "What the hell was I thinking? I actually felt sorry for you. I should have saved my pity for me! I'll take you to your precious supply ship, but you better pray I don't just beam you into space or onto their bridge!" Now crying freely, she stepped up and pulled back her hand as if to strike him again. Instead, she turned abruptly and stomped off.

She barely spoke to Aden the rest of the trip. When they reached the supply ship, it was still four days from Seti. Abby cloaked the *Hyperion* and drew within beaming range. When he was ready for transport, she handed him a shoulder bag.

"I'm beaming you to what looks like an isolated storage room. It's small, but it has life support. The bag I gave you contains enough food and water for several days. I'm sorry for my behavior the other day. Not to be overly dramatic, but once more, I doubt we'll see each other again. After I transport you, I'm going to the nearest EA base to turn myself in for taking this ship."

When he opened his mouth to reply, she held up her hand.

"Please, enough has been said already. Good luck Aden Cade."

When he vanished, she wiped a tear from her eye and headed back to the bridge. She plotted a course to the nearest EA base, about three weeks distant. She was about to open a hyperspace window when an anomalous reading caught her eye. A small time-dilation appeared to be following the Ardalan supply ship. A look of concern crossed her face as she recalibrated her sensors. They confirmed what she suspected: It was a cloaked OSEC ship…

Chapter XII

General Brawn asked Aija to meet him in the royal gardens under the goliathan tree. As she drew near, she remembered her previous conversation with Aden. She wondered if he recalled it as fondly as she did. When she reached Brawn, he said, "Quite a magnificent tree, isn't it? Wood from such a large specimen is very valuable. I've been thinking of cutting it down, making a desk from it, and selling the rest to help fund the military."

"Where I come from," she replied, "people carry slivers of goliathan trees for good luck; but they must come from trees that died of natural causes. We believe that anyone who harms a live tree would be cursed."

"What a quaint custom! I'll keep it in mind." He pointed to a bench and after they both sat down, said with a smirk, "That was quite a show you put on in Cade's cell! Why did you stop?"

"She's attractive, but not my type," she replied, returning his smirk. "I was just trying to see how far she'd go for him. I think the stupid bitch would have cut her own head off if I'd asked her. Personally, I don't get it. My plan worked though; they took the bait. Unfortunately, they found the transponders and disabled them. Apparently we underestimated EA tech."

"Yes," Brawn agreed. "In retrospect, it would have been better if we'd just killed him and been done with it. We won't make that mistake again! On another topic, it's also too bad the xanide you commandeered was substandard."

"What? That's impossible! I scanned it myself! It was mil-grade!"

"Well then," he replied gruffly, "get your scanner recalibrated, because what we have is barely suitable for farm equipment. No matter though, we may have another opportunity."

"Oh?"

"I'm sure the indomitable high prince hasn't abandoned whomever or whatever it was that needed his xanide in the first place. I have no doubt he'll try again."

"Where can he get that much xanide…Seti, of course! Even he wouldn't dare take such a risk!"

"The Cades are fools, but their courage is without question. He's going there, one way or another. Our OSEC friends are already there waiting for him. Their instruments can't pinpoint a ship using an EA cloak, but when he sets foot on the planet, he'll be vulnerable. They're also following an Ardalan supply ship heading for Seti in the event he managed to hitch a ride with them. He, and possibly Watanabe, will both be in custody before you know it. Hopefully they'll have secured another bounty of xanide for us. This time, they won't get away."

"Watanabe is a diplomat."

"Not anymore. We revoked her diplomatic status for helping Cade escape. She also absconded with one of the EA's ships, and they would like to get their hands on her as well."

"Won't the taal try to interfere? We don't know the range of their abilities."

"OSEC believes they can block their telepathic influence," he reminded her.

"You know we'll never break Cade," noted Aija, "and I've come to believe Watanabe really doesn't know anything. If she did, she would have given it up in his cell that day. I think the idiot loves him. The irony is, he probably doesn't trust her any more than we do."

"Correct on all points, I'm sure; however, you'll undoubtedly give him your best effort. When he finally dies from your tender care, it won't be as a martyr, but as a traitor and common smuggler. That should end any remaining nostalgia for his father's misguided and corrupt rule.

"As for Watanabe, you can have whatever fun with her you like, just don't injure her too badly. I share your reservations about OSEC, and would prefer not to provoke the EA unnecessarily. They'll accept that we arrested her for breaking the law, especially since she lacks diplomatic immunity, but I wouldn't want to push them too far."

"General, you are too kind to me."

"Yes," he replied with a chuckle. "Now tell me, how goes the battle here?"

Aija grimaced. "As you're aware, Pador Province is home to several major military installations. The rebels there are proving to be a formidable foe. They're demanding a return to civilian government, and are threatening to bring the fight here if you don't move in that direction. If our Dipsa class ships aren't available soon, they may be able to—they command thousands of our best-trained and equipped troops. Harma Province, on the other hand is poor and ill equipped for war. Its collapse is imminent. If General Drall ever gets around to ordering the final assault, we'll be done with it."

"Excellent!" exclaimed Brawn. "And when he does, we will obliterate it as a message to other provinces that may have similar ideas."

"Sir, there are many Sokks there!"

"I know," replied Brawn with an insincere frown. "They are most-loyal citizens. They will understand this is necessary in our war against the Ardalans."

"We're at war?"

"Earlier today I ordered several ships to Moon Base Ozals. We've learned the Ardalans recently deployed two ships there. I believe they're intending to stage significant forces there, which will give them an important strategic advantage."

Moon Base Ozals circled Goran, the fifth plant in the System. Goran was uninhabitable, but a rich source of metal ores, minerals, and other non-xanide related raw materials crucial to the economies of Ardala and Kealt. Since it lacked the cultural and political significance of Seti, both worlds had long shared it peacefully. Due to the large amount of mining-related traffic, the planet also featured several high orbit space docks, built to accommodate the needs of all space travelers.

"Sir," replied Aija, "I saw the intelligence on that. Those ships are civilian vessels, there for repairs, which is allowed by treaty. There is no indication they have any hostile intent."

"Their very existence signifies hostile intent!" he growled. "I have demanded that Ardala remove them immediately, and they have refused. I've ordered several ships to proceed to Ozals. We will remove them by force, if necessary."

"Are we ready to challenge them so directly? In its present state, it's questionable if our fleet can defend Kealt. Offensive operations against an adversary as formidable as Ardala are out of the question!"

Brawn smiled cryptically. "You underestimate Kealt ingenuity, major. We have a surprise up our sleeve, and a big one. But first, we have to convince the good citizenry that drastic measures are called for."

"I'm afraid I don't understand."

"You will, soon." Brawn leaned back with his arms outstretched, resting on the top of the bench, and took a deep, exaggerated breath. "I love the way this place smells. I see why Edris enjoyed sitting here so much. I think it's time I moved my administration to the palace. The people of Kealt need to get used to the idea that we're in charge now, and that neither the Cades nor their short-lived democracy will be back."

"Yes sir."

"I want this tree taken down."

"Yes sir."

"Dismissed."

Later that day, as Aija prepared for bed in her modest quarters, she picked up a portrait of Ludis off her dresser. He was immaculately groomed, handsome, and resplendently dressed in his best uniform. She gently touched the glass covering the picture before placing it back on her dresser. Then she pulled open the top drawer, reached in and felt above it. She yanked something down, and when she withdrew her hand it was holding another picture. She gazed at it briefly, kissed it, and held it to her breast before returning it to its hiding place.

Chapter XIII

"I don't know boss," said Arvid Denk, chief of logistics for Seti mining operations, "but unless we can get some guys out here to take care of this place, I don't think there'll be much left of it in another few weeks."

"You're right," replied Borg Hassan, who was Arvid's boss as well as the chief of Seti mining operations. "The jungle is moving in fast. We come out here every couple of weeks and each time we come back, there's more of it. It's the same at every mine across Seti. Hell, we can barely keep the roads open. We really do need to keep some guys out here, but with only a couple of dozen hands, we have to pick our priorities. This is one of our older and less productive mines. Maybe we should just let it go."

The men, old friends who had spent over twenty years wresting precious xanide from an unyielding world, stood looking over what had once been the most productive mine on Seti. Now the cacophony of huge earthmoving machines, explosions, and bustling men was stilled, and only the sounds of the encroaching jungle filled the air. The mine itself was quickly disappearing beneath a riot of jungle foliage, and soon little sign of mans' handiwork would remain.

"I guess we could reclaim it later," answered Arvid.

"We could," agreed Borg, "but I don't know if it'll be worth the effort."

"My first assignment on Seti was as a grunt working this mine," said Arvid. "I'd hate to see her go."

"Me too," replied Borg. "You know I started here as well. The taal agreed to let us keep a skeleton force to maintain our infrastructure until everything blows over, but their idea of an adequate caretaker crew is far different from ours. Realistically we'd need a couple of hundred men to even begin to preserve our assets."

"Funny," said Arvid, "I can remember when a couple of hundred men was all we had, and it was plenty."

"Yeah, well, that was before the taal granted us greater access to the planet and Kuste became a small city. Boy, didn't that happen overnight? Anyway, the bigwigs insist that we maintain Kuste as our first priority. They'd rather not sacrifice their own convenience, if and when this stalemate with Ardala ends. Right now, the mines are just an afterthought."

Arvid started to reply, but was interrupted by a series of loud cries emanating from the jungle, and uncomfortably close. The men nervously slid their hands down over the triggers of the weapons they wore slung around their necks.

"Come on Arvid," said Borg uneasily, as he swiveled his head around, looking out toward the jungle. "It's getting late. People have been gone from this place for too long. I'm afraid the local fauna no longer feel the need to keep their distance. We better get out of here while we can still drive home in the light!"

"You don't have to tell me twice!" agreed Arvid emphatically. As the two men walked to their nearby hover car he added, "Next time we come out here—if there is a next time—we need to bring more guys. This place is getting too creepy for me."

Thankfully, the drive back to Kuste was uneventful. However, when Borg pulled the car into the large warehouse that housed the motor pool, a group of agitated men immediately surrounded them.

"Something's happened!" said Borg, as he parked the car and shut it off.

When they stepped out, Einar Leok, the senior Ardalan on Seti, exclaimed, "Where have you two been? We've been trying to reach you. Kealt destroyed two Ardalan freighters docked for repairs at Moon Base Ozals. Ardala retaliated against a military base on Kealt's moon. Before they left, they dropped a xanide bomb on Klavan Province!"

"What?" answered Borg and Arvid in unison.

"It's true," confirmed Cale Scaar, a Kealt. "Fortunately the bomb went off in a wasteland. Had it landed in a more populated area…"

Realizing the two were armed, another Ardalan named Fric Sirmuls said, "Are you going to shoot us?"

"Come on Fric, you know we just came back from making the rounds at the mines," replied Borg angrily. "It's not safe to go out there unarmed anymore!" He lifted the weapon off his shoulder, ensured the safety was on, and tossed it to the startled Ardalan. "There aren't many of us here, and that jungle is coming closer every day. I don't know what's going on back home. I do know that, if we don't work together, we're all in trouble."

"I'm sorry," said Fric, who took Arvid's weapon as well. "These are strange times."

They were still talking when the communications officer burst into the room excitedly, shouting that the supply ship *Vaden* had established orbit and would land within the hour.

"About time!" exclaimed Arvid. "They're late and we're running low on just about everything."

"Well Einar," asked Borg, "wanna come?"

"Why not?" he responded. "I'll drive."

"Thanks. You're coming too, Arvid. We'll need another ten men as well. Have them meet us there in another vehicle. Einar, take those weapons back from Fric, we might need them. I've seen some strange things out there this time of day."

Einar went over to Fric and retrieved the weapons, while Arvid secured one for himself. Einar pointed to a huge wheeled truck and said, "Should we take Big Bessie?"

"Might as well," agreed Borg. "Better to take everything in one load. Less exposure to those damn vampris birds. They can carry a man off, and have. The worst part is you never see them."

Vampris birds were not really birds, but large, flying carnivores big enough to pick a man up off his feet. They were feared man-killers whose skin coloring changed to match their environment. They were generally active at dusk, when their natural camouflage was most effective, but they could appear any time they were hungry.

157

Before long Einar pulled the massive vehicle up alongside the supply ship, which had landed shortly before they arrived. Before getting out, Borg took a controller from his shirt pocket and pushed a button, instantly flooding the rapidly darkening tarmac with light. He said, "I don't know if the light makes us safer, or just an easier target."

"Yeah," agreed Einar. "I hate it when the ships come at night; just too many ways to die around here."

The three stepped out of the cab together, holding their weapons alertly, and walked over to the large cargo ramp that was slowly lowering, revealing a cavernous maw. When it hit the ground five armed men walked down it, escorting another man with bound wrists.

When they reached the tarmac one of them said, "I'm Captain Harold Williams. We caught this stowaway two days ago when our biosensors picked up an extra man in one of our storage rooms. I understand he's wanted on Kealt. Considering the state of our current relations, we won't be going there anytime soon. Other than hitch a free ride, he hasn't done anything to us." He walked up to him, pulled a knife out his pocket, and freed his hands. "So, over to you."

"Hello high prince," replied Borg. "Never thought I'd see you like this!"

"There's a first for everything, dear friend! It is good to see you, and you Arvid, even under these circumstances."

Just then a horrendous screeching sound filled the air. Two men who had walked around to the back of the truck seemed to be flying away of their own accord. Aden bolted over to Borg and yanked his weapon from him. He pointed it in the direction of the men, pulled off two quick shots, and they fell to the ground. The rest of the party ran over to them, and, after insuring they weren't seriously injured, headed back to the supply ship. Einar backed Big Bessie up onto the ramp so that they could load the supplies from the safety of the ship.

When they were finished, they drove back to the main warehouse and, with the help of the ship's crew, quickly offloaded the supplies. Afterwards Captain Williams and several senior crewmen accepted Borg's offer to spend the night in Kuste's one functioning hotel. After cleaning up, the men met in the hotel bar, where the settlement's fulltime cook and two junior logistics officers served dinner.

Aden, Borg, Arvid, Captain Williams, and his first officer, Commander Allen Sax, sat together at their own table. Captain Williams had lent his own steward to the meal, and he ensured that everyone's glass remained full.

"Ahhh, Ardalan Ale!" exclaimed Aden, before downing the better portion of his glass. "I can't imagine anything better!"

"Nice job on the tarmac, high prince," said Williams. "If you hadn't shot those things, those men would probably be in some unholy nest right now, being torn into a thousand pieces by some equally unholy brood."

"I don't know if I hit them or not," replied Aden. "There wasn't any blood on the tarmac. Anyway, those things are as much God's creations as we are. They are deadly to be sure, but beautiful in their own way."

"If you say so. I'm just glad we got our men back."

"Hopefully those two, at least, will look for food elsewhere from now on."

"Now that we brought you here," replied Williams, "are you finally going to tell us what's so important that you risked being thrown out an airlock to get here?"

"I need xanide."

Borg nearly choked on his beer. "Xanide?" he repeated. "You're not going to get it here! We've shut down every mine. Key equipment is in storage. It would take weeks and a few hundred men to bring the best-preserved mines back on line."

"I never told anyone this," Aden replied, "but when Sia and I were marooned in the jungle, we stumbled across a cave that had so much xanide you could pull it off the walls with nothing more than a pick. I'll need to borrow one of your shielded cargo ships. With it I'll be able to get close enough to the cave that I can get what I need and get out before I draw too much attention from members of the 'unholy brood,' as the captain here so colorfully put it."

"That's crazy Aden…uh… high prince," replied Borg. "And even if you succeeded, how would you get it out of here?"

He nodded toward Williams. "Perhaps the good captain could offer me a ride, if I slid some xanide his way."

"What, me?" sputtered Williams, in mid-sip. "I'd have to be crazy to help you! For all I know, that xanide is headed back to Kealt where your military will use it to power more of those super ships you used to attack the zon."

"Kealt desperately needs xanide, but do you really think they'd employ such a cockeyed scheme to get some?" asked Aden.

"It would be a really good one, if it worked, but I see your point," responded Williams. "So why do you need it? You don't strike me as a common smuggler."

"Captain, Kealt is trying to start a war. If they succeed, only the EA and OSEC will win. I have a means to stop this war, but I need xanide and I need a ship. Will you help me?"

"You're serious, aren't you?"

"Yes."

"War is bad for business. I also have three sons in the Ardalan Military. If I agree to help you, how much risk will my crew be in?"

"I won't sugarcoat it; we all could die."

"Cheery thought, that. And will this journey take us through Kealt space?"

"At times."

"I see. I like challenges. Very well, high prince. I'll consider your request, but only if my crew agrees. Some xanide would go a long way…"

"I understand; so, Borg, how about that ship?"

"Under one condition: You take me with you."

"I can't do that old friend—too dangerous."

Borg laughed. "You're talking to a guy who's spent the last twenty plus years on the most dangerous habitable planet in the universe. I think I can handle it. Besides, you're going to need help hauling all that xanide!"

"You have a point," he replied. Then he finished his ale and slammed the glass down on the table. "Well captain, I eagerly await your decision. In the meantime, I'm going to turn in. Borg and I need to get an early start."

Early the next morning Aden met Borg at the spaceport. Like every other manmade manifestation on Seti, the jungle was devouring it rapidly. It reminded him of the end of the world.

"So, Borg, is this the best you have left?" asked Aden, banging on the aged and pockmarked hull of a ship that sported the name *Endro* in running, barely legible letters.

"No it's not, but in the event we don't make it back, I'd rather not waste one of our better transports. Anyway, it's in better shape than it looks—can't judge a book by its cover and all that!"

"I hope that's the case," replied Aden dubiously. "I assume you've already loaded everything we need?"

"Except this," he answered, reaching into the back of the truck he and Aden had ridden to the spaceport. He pulled out a worn-looking sword that was secured in an equally worn shoulder sheath. "Here, I know you never feel at home around here without one of these."

Aden took the weapon, pulled it out of its sheath, and turned it over in his hand as he studied it. He tested the edge, which was dull, and noted its corroded and scarred surface.

"So Borg, what have you been using this for? Prying open crates and chopping wood?"

Borg snorted in reply. "Yes, as a matter of fact! Until recently, we had no need of such an archaic implement."

"There are better choices at my family's lodge."

"Sure—if we could reach it safely. The road there was iffy on its best days. We could take a hover car, but I'm sure the lodge has suffered the same fate as everything else around here."

"No time for it anyway," replied Aden. "Let's go."

"To where?"

"To the place the taal brought Sia and I down."

"That area is soaked in xanide radiation. This ship is heavily shielded, but even so, we'll only have about a 24-hour window. Will that be sufficient?"

"It should be. We encountered the cave less than half a day from the wreck."

An hour later Borg announced they were beginning their descent. As the *Endro* approached the small clearing that contained the remains of the ship that had once stranded Aden and Sia, he frowned at the gauges in front of him.

"Something wrong?" asked Aden.

"The radiation is even more intense than I expected. Our window is going to be less than

24 hours—18 hours at best. After that the ship's reserves will be too depleted to get us home."

"Well," replied Aden cheerily, "we'll have to work fast!"

Borg brought the *Endro* down just fifty meters from the wrecked ship. The men quickly filled their backpacks with tools and supplies and checked their projectile weapons. Aden pulled out a map and a compass and laid them on the deck. He found a marker, circled their present location, and drew a short line to where he recalled stumbling upon the xanide.

"Here," he said, tapping the marker on the map. "This is where we need to go. It's just about four kilometers from here. As I recall, this leg of our journey was relatively easy."

When they stepped out into the clearing, it was smaller than Aden remembered it, but looked very much like it did when the taal brought him here to see Sia one last time. Borg pointed past their old ship and said, "You do know there's a bolba tree less than a hundred meters from here?"

Of course he did. It was there when he and Sia crashed. It had grabbed him with its slimy, detachable tentacles and attempted to drag him into its now slumbering mouth. Despite its current dormant state, its tentacles waived back and forth from the tree's branches in a sort of macabre dance. The base of the tree was obscured by piles of bones that marked the final resting place of various creatures, large and small, that had wandered too close at the wrong time.

"Yes," replied Aden with a sardonic chuckle. "I know it well—it was almost the end of me. Don't worry, it's dormant during the day, unless it's disturbed. We should be back long before it stirs again." He walked over to his old ship and briefly thought about going inside, before deciding it would take too long to uncover the foliage-encrusted hatch. Besides that, he wasn't ready to face the emotions it would evoke.

"What keeps a clearing like this open?" asked Borg. "The jungle swallows everything up so fast."

"I'll tell you when we get back. I'm pretty sure you'd prefer that."

With that, they headed off into the jungle following the heading on Aden's map. The path he and Sia had taken out of the clearing was no longer evident. It had probably been nothing more than the trail left behind by a taal or some other massive creature capable of forcing its way through the thick underbrush. The going was tougher than Aden anticipated, and after three hours they had only progressed a couple kilometers.

Just when he was beginning to despair they would reach the cave with sufficient time to return safely, they broke through the thick brush onto a fresh trail that headed in the right direction. Fortuitously, it took them all the way to where Aden remembered seeing the cave, except that it wasn't there.

"It should be here!" he insisted, more to himself than to Borg.

"We could be right on top of it, or kilometers away," replied Borg. "The jungle changes every day."

"It's got to be around here! We're running out of time!"

Suddenly he felt a calmness descend over him, along with the conviction that the cave was just over the rise to his right. "Come on!" he exhorted his old friend. "It's just over there!"

Borg followed Aden, who was now running up the rise. When he got to the other side, the maw of a large cave greeted them. "That's it!" he exclaimed, pointing emphatically.

He was about to head toward it when Borg grabbed his arm. "Aden, we can't just walk in. Who knows what could be living in there! And during the day, something large probably is."

"All right," he replied, "what do you suggest?"

"I packed a couple of stun grenades. They won't set off the xanide, but should stir up anything living in there. Let me toss them inside and see who's home."

Succumbing to his logic, Aden agreed. Borg pulled off his pack, found the grenades, and hung them from his vest by their pins. Then he walked up to the cave slowly and angled off to one side. When he was in position he nodded to Aden, who removed his own pack, readied his weapon, and sought protection behind a large tree. Borg let go of his weapon, grabbed the grenades and yanked down. He tossed them into the cave and waited.

The subsequent explosion sent a huge cloud of dust billowing from the cave. When nothing else came out, Aden stepped toward it until a gesture from Borg stopped him. From deep inside they heard a rustling sound that grew in intensity. Seconds later a rush of dozens of dog-sized, rodent-looking creatures with large fangs and slavering jaws issued from the cave, disoriented and angry, snapping at everything in their way. They took no notice of Aden and Borg as they ran past them and quickly disappeared into the jungle.

When Borg stepped toward the cave after the last one bolted by, it was Aden's turn to urge caution. However, before he could gain his attention, a huge version of the vicious creatures that had just scurried off emerged from the cave, directly in front of him. Fully seven meters at the shoulder, it was larger even than a taal, and very angry.

When it spotted Borg and moved toward him, he opened fire on it, which only enraged it. It swung a clawed paw at him, catching him in the chest and driving him into a tree. Stunned, he laid helplessly while it advanced on him with ill intent.

Aden attempted to fire at it, but his weapon malfunctioned. Like everything else on Seti, it suffered from a lack of maintenance. He yanked out the old sword and charged the creature from behind. He began hacking at the back of one of its hind legs, but the dull blade had little impact on it. When it continued advancing on Borg, he threw it down and picked up Borg's weapon, which still worked. He began firing at the behemoth and, finally feeling the impact of the high-energy projectiles, it turned and followed the smaller creatures into the jungle.

When he was sure the immediate danger had passed, Aden went up to Borg to assess his injuries. As it turned out he was only stunned, and more embarrassed than hurt. After a while he stood up and dusted himself off.

"Thanks, high prince," he said, once he fully regained his senses. "I've seen the little ones before. What the hell was that thing?"

"Their mother. They were just babies."

"Great; and I thought I'd seen everything around here. I assume it's safe to go in now?"

"Let's find out," replied Aden, picking up the nearly useless sword and shoving it into its sheath. Then he found his weapon and quickly fixed the source of the malfunction. Satisfied he could defend himself if any other beasts lurked inside, he returned to his backpack and pulled out an electric torch, as did Borg. Together they made their way into the cave.

Once inside, their lights revealed the largest concentration of xanide crystals Borg had ever seen. He whistled softly and said, "Boy, you weren't kidding." He shined his light down the deep tunnel. "There's nothing but mil-grade crystals in here! I've never seen this much high quality xanide in one place before. In fact, I'll bet this cave contains more xanide than we've shipped out of here in twenty years!"

"Maybe," replied Aden, "but it's not ours. Come on, let's get what we need and get out of here!" They emptied everything out of their backpacks and quickly refilled them and two duffle bags with high quality crystals. When they were full, Aden yanked the drawstring on his backpack. "That's enough," he said, "lets head back to the ship."

Fortunately raw xanide crystals were relatively light, and their backpacks weighed less than they did when they left the *Endro*.

They left everything else behind except for the sword and their projectile weapons, and headed back to the ship.

Despite making better time than they could have hoped for, when they reached the *Endro* its reserves hovered near the redline. Borg was able to initiate the engines, but the ship labored mightily to gain enough altitude to escape the thick canopy. In order to conserve power, he flew at tree top level, and maintained just enough speed to keep them airborne. When they reached the spaceport, the *Endro* exhausted the last of its reserves just as it touched down. Borg and Aden carried their haul to the truck and returned to the hotel. Aden summoned Captain Williams and, when he arrived, put enough raw xanide on the table to pay his men's salaries for two years.

"Wow!" exclaimed the stunned captain. "You were serious."

"Well, do we have a deal?"

"I spoke to my crew, and I have to say, they had significant reservations. Some because you're a Kealt, and some because of the risk involved. Still, they're merchants after all, and when they see the profit in it, I suspect they'll come around. As far as I can tell, helping you isn't technically against any of our laws, so you have that going for you. That said, if any of this xanide makes its way back to Kealt, our necks will be in a noose."

Aden held out his hands and displayed his misshapen fingernails. "You see these?" he asked. "I got these at the hands of Kealt's military junta. I have other equally painful wounds under my clothing. I can assure you, it's not going there."

With the added incentive of a personal fortune in xanide, Williams' balky crew came around quickly. The *Vaden* lifted off the next day, with Aden aboard. They had barely left orbit when an explosion rocked the ship.

"Battle stations!" bellowed Williams. "Get those shields up and find out where that came from!"

"Sir!" exclaimed Sax, "The energy signature is unfamiliar, but I believe it came from a cloaked ship!"

Williams glared at Aden. "Only Kealt's ships can fire while cloaked!"

"No, EA and OSEC's ships can as well!" Aden assured him, as another blast rocked the ship.

"We're a civilian ship, we can't defend ourselves against this!" exclaimed Williams. He turned toward a younger officer. "Tell them we surrender!"

When their hidden foe met their offer with another volley that sent the *Vaden's* weapons officer flying from his post, Aden took his place. He quickly plotted the other ship's relative position, and when it fired again, he immediately fired back. From the resulting explosion it was evident he'd inflicted damage on the phantom aggressor. The next enemy volley took out the *Vaden's* shields.

"Sir!" advised Sax, "they scanned us and now they're attempting to board us!"

"The xanide!" exclaimed Aden.

"They better hurry then, our engines are about to go critical!" exclaimed Sax.

"Abandon ship!" bellowed Williams. "Ensign, beam everyone back down to the planet."

"We're too far, sir. Transporters are off line anyway."

Aden, who had continued to fire with some effect, stood up from his adopted post and bellowed, "I'll be damned if I'm going to let them have the xanide! Where are your weapons?"

After Williams told him they were in a locker on the other side of the ship, he pulled out the old sword he'd brought with him from Seti and promptly left the bridge.

No more blasts shook the *Vaden*, as OSEC had succeeded in disabling it and was focused on capturing the xanide its scans had revealed. It was located in the most heavily shielded hold on the ship, which preventing them from beaming it off. OSEC's transporters were good, but not as good as those on a frontline EA ship.

When Aden reached the hold, four OSEC commandos were leaving it with the xanide. He had the advantage of surprise, and used his sword to bludgeon two of them into unconsciousness.

The remaining commandos dropped their cargo and drew their particle weapons. Although they fired wildly, a blue beam struck Aden in the shoulder, propelling him into a bulkhead. The commandos advanced on the wounded high prince and aimed their weapons at his head. Just as they squeezed their triggers, an explosion knocked them off their feet. The ship was coming apart.

Not knowing what to else to do, Aden grabbed the xanide—which was still in the packs he and Borg had used to carry it out of the jungle—and ran toward the bridge. Seconds later a massive explosion shook the ship. Aden looked back and saw a fireball coming up the corridor. Before he could blink, he was standing on the bridge of the *Hyperion*.

"Abby, what in God's name…?"

"No time Aden!" she replied tensely. He looked at her vidscreen and saw three huge warships decloaking that were similar to the one that had captured the *Zazor*. She fired her main weapons and one of the three ships exploded. When the remaining two ships fired missiles that seemed far too small to be a threat, Abby backed away from them as fast she could, opened a hyperspace window, and jumped. She studied her instruments intently, and finally breathed a sigh of relief. She turned and said, "Welcome aboard King Aden." Seeing his wounds, she exclaimed, "You're hurt! We need to get you to sick bay!"

"What about the others?"

"They're safe as well. I didn't know if you trusted them or not, so I beamed them directly to the cargo hold and locked them in."

"Not that I'm not immensely grateful, but what are you doing here?"

"Saving your butt again!" she replied emphatically. "After I beamed you onboard the Ardalan freighter, I detected cloaked OSEC ships following it. I followed them, figuring you might need help. Aden, they sent a false distress call using an Ardalan emergency frequency. They claimed you were under attack by a Kealt warship."

"Good strategy if you're intent on ratcheting up tensions between us. Why didn't you take on the remaining ships? They were obviously no match for this one."

"We've learned that OSEC has a bio weapon stolen from the zon. It's deadly to the selkie. Those missiles we dodged were carrying it."

"Deadly? You mean it can kill one of these things?"

"Easily, and it has. Xanide would help a selkie fight it off, but would only delay the inevitable."

"I'm sure there's a…a…vaccine or something!"

"Maybe, but if there is, we haven't found it."

Aden shivered at the thought of something so dangerous it could fell a selkie. "Come on," he said, "let's free those men."

Chapter XIV

bby insisted that before anything else, Aden report to sickbay. While his shoulder was burned and bruised, the weapon had been set to stun. With the ship's advanced medical facilities, he would heal quickly. After she satisfied herself that his injuries weren't life threatening, she freed Williams and his men and assigned them quarters. Then she showed them where the galley was, and invited Williams, Sax, and Aden to her stateroom.

Once they were comfortable, she offered them some coffee. Then she proceeded to explain, with Aden's assistance, the events that led to their current predicament.

"Well, what happens now?" asked Williams, when she was finished.

"If Abby is willing," replied Aden, "we'll take you home. Then I'll return to Kealt, where I'll try and find yet another ship to complete my mission."

"Aden, if this is so important to you, I'll take you where you want to go," replied Abby.

When all parties agreed to her offer, she returned Williams and his men to Ardala. As they were about to beam down, he walked over to Aden and dropped his share of the xanide at his feet. He said, "This is for my boys. There are monsters out there that would destroy all of us. I know you're a good man, a trustworthy man. I'm convinced that if anyone can save us, you can. I mean, you've done it before.

"I haven't told you this, but I was an officer in the Ardalan Defense Force when the zon attacked us. My ship was badly damaged. One of your ships sacrificed itself to save us. You don't forget something like that. Put this to good use, Your Highness."

One by one, his men did the same. After they were gone, Abby smiled condescendingly.

"Well done king, I think you could charm the stripes off a hungry tiger."

"A what? And if you're going to help me, could we dispense with the sarcasm?"

"What sarcasm?"

"Stop calling me 'king.' That was my father's title."

"Well it's yours now. After we left Kealt, your Council of Elders held an emergency session. Against Brawn's warning they crowned you king in absentia. They were beaten and jailed for their efforts, and two of them are dead.

"Your friend Abeg declared the Council of Commons dissolved, and transferred all political authority back to the monarchy. He also was jailed, and the group of them are now at the mercy of your vicious lesbian major. You are now the legitimate political authority on Kealt. Aden, a lot of people are counting on you. I don't envy you."

"How do you know this?"

"My friend Jeff contacted me while I was on my way to Seti."

"I thought you were an outlaw?"

"That was until you became king. Now I've been ordered to aid you in any way I can."

"I see," he replied dryly. "Crowning me king took a lot of courage from a typically weak and feckless bunch. Things must be even more desperate then I realized."

"Well, congratulations. Where to now?"

"I'll need to talk to Gris first."

"Here," she replied, pointing to the captain's chair, "have a seat. You can contact anyone you want across two galaxies." When he stayed where he was, she said, "Don't worry, I'll leave. I can assure you I won't monitor or record your conversation."

"Abby, I…"

"Do what you have to do," she responded curtly.

Before he could protest further, she was gone. Now alone, he walked up to the captain's chair. Not knowing what to expect, he lowered himself onto it slowly. After he sat down, he realized she hadn't told him how he was supposed to operate the equipment. He was still trying to figure it out when he felt another consciousness intruding onto his own.

"Hello Your Highness, how can I help you?" It was the ship, communicating with him telepathically.

"I...I...need to talk to my friend." He said it aloud, but knew it was unnecessary based on previous telepathic conversations he'd had with the taal. Still, he found it easier to present his thoughts when he could hear himself speaking them.

"I know," she replied. "Would you like me to try and reach him now?"

Aden realized that at that moment she knew everything he did. "Yes," he said, "that would be fine." Seconds later Gris appeared on the vidscreen with his wife, Aden's older sister Glyn, standing next to him.

"Aden," asked Gris, "how are you communicating with us? We're receiving no signal, although our communications console is active."

"I'm aboard an EA ship. I have to confess, I don't understand the technology. You look good my brother. My beautiful sister must be taking good care of you."

"The best, as usual," he replied, feigning sarcasm. When Glyn glared at him unappreciatively, he ignored her and said, "A lot has happened since we last spoke. You, my friend, have nine lives. Hopefully you're calling to tell me you're on the way with the…the…"

"This is Abby's ship, my brother. She's been tasked by the EA to support me. She knows about the xanide."

Gris frowned. "Does she know what it's for?"

"Not yet."

"Are you planning on bringing her here?"

"Gris, if there's anything I'm sure of, it's that I can trust her. She's more than proven herself."

"I know," answered Gris. He looked down and appeared to be operating a keyboard. When he was satisfied, he looked up and said, "I just sent you a set of coordinates for the badlands. These are different from the previous set Celesta gave you. Once you arrive safely, I'll forward additional coordinates to a series of beacons that will lead you to us."

When Aden reviewed them, he said, "Not a very friendly region of space."

Gris laughed. "No, but a lot better than the 'badlands' we're hiding behind! We'll see you in a few days, if that EA rust bucket you're riding in can manage it." When Aden answered affirmatively, he added, "Oh, and congratulations Your Highness, you have large shoes to fill."

"I love you Aden," interrupted Glynn. "I am so sorry about Sia. We all loved her. Please, take care of yourself. We will prevail."

"We will. I love you too. See you soon."

When the transmission ended, the selkie said, "Sia was a wonderful woman."

Feeling awkward talking to a ship, Aden replied, "And how would you know?"

"I see her in your mind and in Abby's; other's as well. Abby respected her greatly."

"Well…thanks. I'll be turning you back over to her now…"

Before he could get out of the chair the selkie said, "Please be considerate to her. She has lost much. She is also very fond of you. She feels what you feel. Her heart is and has always been in your hands. That is a heavy burden. Be worthy of it."

"You're a ship, how can you know such things?"

"We are a sentient race, Your Highness, even more so than the Earthers know. We have many secrets, and we know many things."

"Why would you tell me this? You barely know me."

The selkie ignored his question. "One more thing, Your Highness: Good friends of yours are in trouble on Kealt. You must help them soon, before it's too late."

"I have many good friends in trouble on Kealt. Can you narrow it down?" he asked.

"The resistance in what you call Pador Province is protecting them. They are under great stress and cannot hold out much longer. You must return to Kealt when you've accomplished your mission here."

"Anything else you'd like to tell me, while you're feeling expansive?" When she ignored his attempt at humor, he said, "Abby told me you're mean to her."

"I was angry with her. I wrongly blamed her for not saving John Trent. Of course, there was nothing she could have done. I forgave her some time ago."

"OK. Can we reach Gris in the time allotted?"

"Easily."

"Thank you."

"You're welcome."

Still feeling awkward and not knowing what else to say, Aden got up and tracked Abby down in her stateroom.

"How did it go?" she asked, with a knowing smile, when he stepped inside.

"Uh, well…"

"Yes?"

"To be honest, it was a little weird."

"Yeah, you get used to it after a while."
When he just stood there staring at her, she
giggled. "What are you doing?"

"I'm sorry, it's just that…the selkie…she
said some things about you…"

"What kind of...things?" she asked
nervously.

"Nothing very specific. Just enough to know
you're right: I've never bothered to get to know
you. If you'd let me, I'd really like to try."

"Oh, I see," she replied, looking relieved. "I
know I threw that in your face when I was angry
with you; but the truth is, there's really not much
to me. You'd find me rather boring."

"Oh, I seriously doubt that." When she
didn't respond, he said, "I know something
terrible has happened to you. I'd like to be there
for you, like you've been for me."

"Aden, that is so sweet!" she replied, in a
way that sounded less than sincere. She went up
to him and stroked his scarred cheek gently.
"I'm fine, but thanks for the thought. Now, it's
late and I need to get to bed. See you in the
morning!"

As they drew closer to Gris's coordinates,
Aden went down to the hold where he had left
the xanide, and took a portion of the crystals
back to his quarters. There were more than

enough for Gris, and a separate stash might come in handy one day, he thought.

Abby remained cool and distant. No surprise, he thought, considering his perpetually callous and thoughtless behavior toward her. At the end of the second day, they were eating a strained meal together when an alarm went off. Abby jumped from her seat and headed quickly to the bridge. Aden followed and watched over her shoulder as she stared intently at a panel in front of her.

"It's a distress call from an OSEC ship called the *Boston*. That's one of their newest and most capable ships. She's under attack, but they don't say from whom. She's less than a light year from here. At top speed we can be there in half an hour."

"This is a huge galaxy. How is it that one of their best ships is virtually right on top of us?"

"Good question. Perhaps they've been following us, somehow."

When they reached the *Boston*, it was burning and on the verge of exploding. Abby scanned it for life signs, but found none. She scanned the area for survivors who may have abandoned ship, but again found nothing.

"Any sign of who did this?" asked Aden, while Abby continued to study the wreckage.

"No," she replied, "it seems the only thing that survived is their black box. I'm not sure what condition it's in, but I'm beaming it onboard now. Hopefully it will at least tell us who attacked them."

Later that evening, she invited Aden to her stateroom. The scarred and dented black box was sitting on a table in front of her.

"Well," he said, "any luck?"

"I'm about to find out. It seems to be functioning. I've downloaded the data and I'm ready to review it."

"Let's get started!"

Unfortunately, it turned out that most of the data was corrupted. All that was salvageable were the last three hours before the *Boston's* destruction. Aden and Abby watched as the ship's crew went about their tasks, hoping to glean clues as to why they were so close to the *Hyperion.*

They gathered that OSEC had gained the coordinates of Gris's base, and the *Boston* was on its way to join a fleet of ships that was intent on destroying it. They were oblivious to their proximity to the *Hyperion,* but had been monitoring Celesta's transmissions, which eventually led them to Gris.

Near the end of the data stream, a series of explosions rocked the ship. The captain ordered his men to raise shields and launch fighters. The stream ended before the *Boston* identified their attackers.

"Did the EA do this?" asked Aden.

"I doubt it. We don't have a lot of ships in this galaxy, and we're not in the habit of destroying other ships, even if they belong to OSEC. If it were us, I'd be able to pick them up on my sensors."

"Kealt has allied themselves with OSEC, it couldn't have been them," answered Aden. "Ardala could have done this, but we're far from any of their colonies or shipping lanes. Who does that leave?"

"I don't know," replied Abby, "but I suggest we proceed to your brother-in-law's base with greater urgency. We don't know where the rest of OSEC's fleet is, and it could be closer than we are."

When they arrived at the rendezvous point without encountering any hostile ships, they breathed a sigh of relief. As promised, Gris provided the frequencies and encryption codes for the beacons.

As they followed them in, Abby said, "This is some neighborhood Aden. Radiation, black holes, some of the densest asteroid fields I've ever seen, time dilations, and any number of other deadly stellar phenomena. Even with our sensors, we could literally be on top of a thousand ships and never know they were here. With the proper coordinates we could reach Gris without these beacons, but it would take much longer."

As it was, using the trail left by the beacons, less than half a day later the *Hyperion* suddenly and without warning broke through the badlands and found itself on the edge of a solar system.

"According to the coordinates provided by the last beacon," noted Abby, "the base is on the third planet."

When they reached it, they established orbit. Abby gasped when the planet's horizon gave way to a massive shipyard.

"Aden," she said, "they're building dozens of your super ships here! Enough to give even the EA pause!"

"Yes," he agreed with a smile. "But currently they float above the planet as nothing more than huge chucks of metal."

"The xanide."

"Right. They have some, but it's not all mil-grade and only enough to power the yards. Now the ships are nearly finished, but there isn't sufficient xanide to bring them on line."

Abby signaled Gris, and she and Aden beamed down to his base of operations on the planet's surface. When they materialized inside his office, Glyn immediately embraced him.

"Aden, my brother," she sniffed, "I despaired of ever seeing you again!"

When the embrace ended, he said, "I'm sure you both remember Abby?"

"It would be hard to forget her!" answered Gris playfully. "Although I don't believe we ever actually met 'Abby.' She was Drusa at the time our paths first crossed. Still beautiful, but I doubt nearly as interesting as the real thing!"

Seeing how Gris was ogling her, the regal-looking but perpetually stern Glyn glared at him and said, "Can you ever behave yourself? She not only represents a foreign government, she's our guest! Abby, you'll have to forgive my husband. He is as crude as any man I have ever met!"

Before Abby could answer, Aden pointed to the crate of crystals that had beamed down with them. He said, "My brother, you must get this to your fleet immediately. We have learned that a fleet of OSEC warships is looking for your base. We believe they aren't far behind us."

"That is troublesome," he replied. "We're lightly defended. Two or three of their larger warships would be more than sufficient to destroy all of our work. However, I doubt their entire fleet could handle three dozen fully armed and operational Dipsa class ships."

He called in one of his men and said, "Colonel Thrick, please insure this xanide is distributed and integrated into our fleet as soon as possible, and that we begin space trials as soon as the ships are ready. Time is of the essence!"

After the colonel summoned additional men and left with the crystals, Gris said, "Well, let's hope you reached us in time. While we're waiting for our imminent destruction, would you like something to eat?"

"Gris Haberat!" chastised Glyn. "How can you think of your stomach at a time like this?"

"If I'm going to die, I'd rather not die hungry."

"There is a certain logic to that," agreed Aden.

Later, over a rich dinner, Abby said, "Gris, those ships you produced out of thin air—I guess that was where all of Kealt's missing resources were going?"

"Yes," he replied. "Almost immediately after the zon were defeated, Edris, Aden, and the Council of Commons set the wheels in motion to revitalize our forces. However, we knew that building such a massive, powerful fleet in the open would unnerve regular Ardalans, despite our good intentions. We also were concerned that the EA would attempt to sabotage the effort, and perhaps even steal our technology. So, we worked out a deal with the qrell."

"What's in it for them?" asked Aden.

"If they gave us unfettered access to one of their more isolated shipyards, we in turn would protect them from the zon and any other hostile species they might encounter. The qrell are a tough, entrepreneurial race, but they're not fighters. They were an easy target for the zon, even if they preferred us to them."

"I see," answered Aden, sounding almost disappointed.

Gris took note of his demeanor and snorted derisively. "There was something else…"

"Yes?" replied Aden expectantly.

"I understand in your younger days you spent a year here as Kealt's representative?"

"I did."

"And you were close to the queen?"

"For a time."

"We had to work around that, it seems she hates the idea of your very existence."

"Oh," noted Aden.

"How did you build so many ships so quickly?" asked Abby, seeking to fill the uncomfortable silence that followed Aden's terse reply.

"The qrell are master shipbuilders," answered Gris. "Much of the process is automated. And the badlands contain an abundance of raw materials—minus xanide, of course—which can be processed quickly in factories that were already here when we took over the facility. At any rate, we're not completely finished. While the motherships are ready to enter service, we've only completed a fraction of their fighters and tactical spacecraft."

"You trust the qrell that much?" asked Abby skeptically.

Gris smiled grimly. "Normally, no," he said. "But, the zon decimated them. We have vowed to protect them—it's in their best interests to help us. I've always found self-preservation to be a powerful motivator."

"Nonetheless it's an amazing feat, protecting such a vast 'conspiracy,'" answered Abby. "Especially considering the resources the project consumed and the number of people involved. Congratulations on pulling it off. I assume Celesta knew about it, and Polis as well?"

"Yes," replied Gris. "We're actually building a significant number of these ships for Ardala. They're well aware of our operation. In fact, many of our workforce are Ardalans. We couldn't have built these ships without their help."

"How come your ships will soon be fully operational and Brawn's aren't?" wondered Abby.

"It was only with the help of one of your own engineers that we were able to overcome our technical problems," answered Aden, after putting down his ale. "He did it out of desperation, when it looked like his own ship was about to join the fate of our other three prototypes.

"When Brawn took over, the original technical lead of the Dipsa project, Chief Engineer Alex Stick, a very bright man, realized how dangerous even six of these ships would be in his hands, so he essentially disabled them. Fortunately for him, it was very easy for everyone to believe the EA was the culprit. Of course, Gris had the fix all along."

"Abby," said Gris, "even with the xanide, it may be days before our ships are ready. Can OSEC find its way through this briar patch as well as your ship did?"

"Not quite," she replied, "but with the exact coordinates they will eventually find their way here."

"Well the good news is: I doubt they have the exact coordinates or even know what we're up to. Almost everyone who knows this base's coordinates is here. Even if they were listening in to our coms, which is probably how they found out about us, we never broadcast them, and Celesta and Polis don't even have them. The qrell know, of course, but they're a tight-lipped, secretive bunch. Someone could trace the signal back to the beacon that lies on the edge of the badlands, which is probably what OSEC did, but that would be the closest they could get. After that, they'd be left with trial and error. That could take them months."

"Either way," replied Aden, "we can't stay until your fleet is ready—I must return to Laima. Even if OSEC found its way here before you're ready, I doubt the *Hyperion* would be able to protect you from so many ships."

"Aden," asked Abby, "what will you do when the fleet is ready—use it to attack Brawn?"

"Undoubtedly it will play a key role when it's ready, but until then, I must help the resistance win on its own."

The next day, they departed. As they approached the edge of the badlands, Abby noted a series of distress calls. It was OSEC, and their fleet was under attack. Abby cloaked the *Hyperion* and entered the coordinates of the broadcast. When they reached them a half hour later, they found thirty wrecked ships, including four frontline motherships, and no survivors.

They stayed long enough to try to determine the cause of the carnage. As they surveyed the debris field for evidence of what caused the fleet's demise, Abby said, "These were powerful ships. This ended quickly. Like the *Boston*, it may have happened so quickly they never knew whom it was that attacked them—I can't even detect a black box. It's as though someone deliberately destroyed them. Gris's ships better be ready soon."

Stunned at the scope of the destruction, Aden merely nodded in agreement. After advising Gris of what they found, they set course for Laima.

Chapter XV

Ardala's use of a xanide bomb on civilians had enraged Kealts across the planet. Even though it failed to hit its intended target and exploded with little effect in a largely uninhabited region, calls for revenge grew louder by the day. Brawn quickly took advantage of the situation and launched an attack on an Ardalan military outpost; however, Ardala's superior forces easily repelled Kealt's largely rag-tag fleet, sending what was left of it scurrying back to Kealt in humiliation.

Ardala responded to the attack by destroying a Kealt garrison in Rilan. The attack wounded Aija, a fact that further endeared her to Brawn and increased her resolve.

Brawn resisted committing his Dipsa class ships to the fight, even though Kealt desperately needed them. Despite their promises, OSEC had failed to fix the lingering problems with Kealt's most formidable warships, and then there was the ongoing xanide shortage that OSEC also had failed to alleviate. Without those ships, Kealt was an easy target for Ardala, which, except for the one xanide bomb, had exercised restraint in retaliating for attacks on its territory.

Kealt's defeats, combined with Brawn's manipulation of the media, had also galvanized much of the population against the few pockets of organized resistance to his rule that remained. The most significant of these was focused in the Pador Province, where many xanide mines once operated. Why some of the resistance—that led by Colonel Frune Jasper—had chosen the mines to make their stand was a mystery. While their location near the mines discouraged Brawn from using xanide munitions against them, the terrain around these particular mines was mostly barren and flat, and difficult to defend.

Although the resistance possessed state of the art air defense systems that had successfully kept Brawn's superior air forces at bay, they were rapidly depleting their stocks of missiles and other munitions, as well as power supplies, fuel, and food and water. They were fighting a war of attrition they couldn't win. It was time for the rebels to move to more defensible positions, but Colonel Jasper was adamant they stay where they were.

His men supported him without question, but with each passing day he could feel their resolve crumbling. If they didn't receive help soon, the resistance would not survive much longer.

This day was a good one, though, thought Jasper, as he stood at the entrance of an old mine his troops had further excavated to serve as his headquarters. He watched with pleasure as his second in command, Major Jaak Kalle, returned from a successful mission. They had ambushed a large government firebase and captured an impressive booty of weapons, food, and other supplies. As the vehicles made their way into the large cavern, Kalle got out of the lead vehicle and went over to Jasper.

"Nice work, major!" Jasper exclaimed, grasping his hand strongly. "I'm afraid to ask what this treasure trove cost us."

"Two soldiers with minor wounds. We also lost a couple of vehicles."

"It looks like you more than made up for it! What did you do with the government troops? I hope you didn't kill them all?"

"No, we let them go. We figured we'd get more value out of them if we let them return to Brawn without their boots and try to explain how 250 men took down a fortified military installation of 5000."

"Your plan worked brilliantly."

"Well, I had some inside help."

"Yes, the Ku Assa. Good work nonetheless. Take care of your men, major. I'll have someone else inventory your catch."

Kalle snapped to attention, saluted sharply, and exclaimed, "Yes sir!"

As he walked away, Jasper knew their joy would be short lived. Brawn would seek to extract a high price for the humiliation his troops had received. Until recently, for reasons unknown to Jasper, General Bendiks' forces had been concentrated around a number of nearly played out and difficult to defend xanide mines. However, after weeks of pleading, Brawn finally heeded Bendiks' request for a significant influx of men and materials. The resulting offensive was putting a severe strain on the rebels' own finite resources.

Before reinforcements arrived, the government had been reluctant to use their heavy artillery because they knew the rebels possessed weapons that could locate the source of the barrage and destroy it. However, Bendiks had guessed correctly that Jasper was running low on these munitions and was no longer capable of responding effectively to every attack.

To make matters worse, without the ability to suppress Bendiks' artillery, Jasper's air defense batteries were coming under sustained fire. As a result, more and more aircraft were getting through and dropping their ordinance.

As Jasper and his men hunkered down deep underground, the walls shook and dust filled the air. He knew they couldn't stay any longer. He reluctantly summoned his chief lieutenants to formulate a plan for moving to positions that were more defensible.

"So that's it, gentleman," he said, after providing his grim assessment of their situation. He took a pointer, stood by the large map hanging from the wall, and tapped it in two places. "We need to consolidate our forces here and here. We have adequate supplies at these bases, which are shielded, easier to defend, and were actually built for military purposes.

"Major Kalle, the next time there is a lull in this cursed barrage, and hopefully before our air defense batteries are obliterated, I want you to manage our retreat. It will be risky, but I believe we still have sufficient assets to keep Brawn's forces at bay until you reach these bases."

"You're staying, sir?"

"Yes, with a handful of men. We'll cover your retreat."

"What about our…guests?" asked a young lieutenant. "Are they coming with us?"

"One is, lieutenant. That one you must protect all costs, if there is to be any hope of peace once we have overcome Brawn and his henchmen."

At the conclusion of the briefing the men began to file out of the room except for Major Kalle.

"Sir, it's not safe for you to stay. Without your leadership, I'm afraid things might not go well."

Jasper put his hands on Kalle's shoulders. "Jaak, to be honest, they're not going that well anyway. I'm playing for time. We have an ace in the hole, but it's not ready yet. It will be soon. Have a little faith."

"Yes sir!" answered Kalle, smartly.

Jasper smiled humorlessly. "Regardless, you know that the ambassador is not well and must stay here. We're dug in pretty deep; we'll be able to hold out for a while. Keep our other guest safe at all costs. I'll rejoin you when I can."

"As you wish," replied Kalle. "Of course, the men would appreciate knowing *whom* it is they are protecting with their lives."

"I know, and I trust them; but you and I both know Brawn has spies here. If he knew who it was, he would tear these mines apart even if he consumed Rilan in the process."

Kalle chuckled mirthlessly. "He would at that!" he replied. "And the Ku Assa?"

"What about them?"

"Will they be assisting us? I mean, that's what they do."

The Ku Assa, Kealt's most elite soldiers, were the personal protectors and servants of the royalty, and owed their allegiance directly to them. They maintained their own command structure, and their identities, as well as their numbers and capabilities, were hidden from all but the king and the leader of the Council of Commons. They occupied all walks of life and toiled as ordinary Kealts until their services were required. Their stealthy and occasionally deadly manners made them greatly feared, even on Kealt, but on other worlds, such as Ardala, they were the stuff of nightmares. High Princess Celesta Mar, adopted daughter of Gris and Glyn Haberat, and full sister of Aden Cade, was herself revealed to be a Ku Assa soldier during the Zon War.

"I wish I knew, major," replied Jasper, "but even I don't know who they are. Their communications to me have been sporadic and anonymous."

"You—and they—really believe Aden Cade will come through?"

"I've known him for some time. He's an amazing man. Now that he's king, no matter how reluctantly, I'm sure he's working on a plan right now. And knowing him, it's a big one!"

"Perhaps," replied Kalle, "but if he doesn't

do something soon, he won't have much of a kingdom left."

"Agreed; now major, you need to get the rest of the men and equipment out of here!"

Over the next two days, Major Kalle and his men organized preparations for their strategic retreat. It involved moving thousands of soldiers and civilians and tons of equipment dozens of kilometers over open land. They would move at night, but with the technology available to Brawn's forces, that would be a negligible advantage. Once they reached the rest of the resistance, they would be able to defend themselves far more effectively and for a longer time.

The downside was that once they were a sufficient distance from the mines, Brawn would no longer be constrained from bringing his most effective weapons to bear, including tactical xanide munitions. Even though the rebels had advanced defensive capabilities, including some of Kealt's most modern and deadly aircraft, if just one such weapon got through, it would be sufficient to obliterate a base. The one thing they had in their favor was that Brawn's ships had to decloak to fire their weapons, which made them vulnerable.

The night before Kalle was to move out with the bulk of Jasper's forces, he made his way to where the ambassador was staying. "Hello Jaak," she said, when he entered her quarters.

"You know why I'm here. How is she?"

"Her heart is heavy and her spirit is torn, but she is strong. She will do what must be done, as will you."

Early the next day Kalle announced that he was ready to move out. Jasper gave the order and the evacuation commenced. When the last of his army straggled out by the middle of the next day, Jasper redeployed his few remaining forces around the handful of choke points Bendiks' men would have to navigate past to get to the ambassador.

She was very weak. Jasper estimated he had less than a week to get her to safety. In desperation, he ordered one of his men to take a cloaked ship to Rilan. There he was to contact the EA ambassador and request that he help them get a message to Aden. It was a long shot, but the last cards he had to play…

On the other side of the galaxy, with the

xanide safely in Gris's hands, Abby reluctantly agreed to return Aden to Kealt. Their relationship remained strained. She attempted to avoid him, but, while the *Hyperion* was a good-sized ship, it wasn't large enough for her to ignore him indefinitely.

On the third day, she came into the galley while he was eating. When she saw him, she turned abruptly and walked out. Aden jumped up and ran after her. When he called after her, she only walked faster. He broke into a jog and caught up to her just as she was about to enter her quarters.

When he grabbed her by the arm, she turned and with a disgusted look hissed, "Will you leave me alone!" Then she forcefully broke free from his grasp, entered her quarters, and secured the door behind her.

Not knowing what to do, he made his way to the bridge and sat in the captain's chair. "Hello, Your Highness!" the selkie greeted him brightly. "Can I be of assistance?"

"You know why I'm here!"

"I'm afraid I can't help you."

"Why not?"

"If I got involved it would become a

threesome, and I find those distasteful."

Not sure if she was serious or not, he replied, "I can assure you, if you help me, we will not be a 'threesome!'"

"Well then, in that case, I have a suggestion."

"Yes?"

"She has strong feelings toward you, but she is no longer willing to serve as a mere receptacle for you bodily fluids."

"A receptacle for…that's ridiculous!" he replied. "I've always cared for her, even if I don't always show it properly. Regardless, that is a statement, not a suggestion!"

"Her reticence isn't just about your lack of attention. She is afraid."

"Of what?"

"That is for her to share."

"And your suggestion?"

"She wants you to keep trying, Your Highness, so keep trying!"

"I have been, but she won't even look at me anymore!"

"Try harder!"

"OK, watch this!" he exclaimed, as he stood up from the chair and strode purposely toward

Abby's quarters. He paused briefly in front of her door, then banged on it insistently with his fist and shouted, "I've had enough of this! Open the damn door!"

When she didn't open it, he banged harder and repeated his demand. He was about to do it a third time when the door slid open. He went inside, and when he didn't see her in the living area, he stomped back to her bedroom. She was sitting on her bed, fresh from the shower, wearing just a bathrobe and drying her hair with a towel.

"OK," she said, as she continued to towel off her hair. "You're in. What do you want?"

Aden was taken aback by her state of undress and her sweet, clean scent. When he recovered his senses he replied, "When we part in a day or two, we may never see each other again. After all we've been through, our current relationship seems…inadequate."

"Well," she answered brusquely, "if you think you can get me to spread my legs for you one more time just by forcing your way into my quarters and reminiscing about times that I recall less fondly than you, you're not as smart as people think you are."

While she was working on her hair, the belt on her robe was loosening, exposing an exceptional amount of cleavage and her thickly covered crotch. She knew he was staring at her, but did nothing to cover herself up.

Aden realized she was baiting him from the slight smile playing on her lips, but there was nothing he could do to calm his unwanted, but now nearly bursting erection.

"Abby," he replied, "I have to admit, right now it's difficult to think of anything else. You are so beautiful…"

She clucked at him dismissively.

"…but you are so much more than that. I've been a fool. I can't undo the things I've done. Can we at least be courteous towards each other?"

Her face softened for a moment, but it passed quickly. "Sure," she answered. "Now, please leave so I can go to bed."

The next day she met him for breakfast and actually conversed with him. Politely at first, but before long they were speaking to each other more comfortably than they had in a long time. As Kealt drew near, it saddened Aden to think that soon she would be out his life for good, especially since he still knew next to nothing about her.

Remembering what the selkie had said, he went to her quarters their last night together. When she opened the door, he was disappointed she was fully dressed. He asked if he could come in, but she refused, saying she was tired and needed a good night's sleep.

He went to bed himself and dreamed about an old woman, sick and starving, and living in a dark, damp place. She wasn't a prisoner, but she was far from home and despaired of ever seeing it again. She called to him by name and implored him to help her.

When he arose the next day, Abby summoned him to the bridge and told him Dandridge had relayed a message to him from someone named Colonel Jasper. The resistance was failing, and without his leadership, would soon collapse altogether.

When she was finished, Aden asked if such communications weren't interfering in the internal affairs of other worlds, something the EA was loath to do. She advised that as the King of Kealt and its senior legitimate representative, they were merely responding to a request for aid, something they were bound to provide under the treaty they had signed just before attack. When they reached Kealt and Aden asked her to beam him down to Jasper's encampment, she balked.

"Aden," she said, from her captain's chair, "it's too dangerous for you down there! I'm not going to give that sick, sexually confused bitch another chance to rip your skin off…or abuse me!"

He stood in front of her and caressed her shoulders gently. "I know; time for me to let you go. I'm going to need one more favor from you. Wait in orbit until you hear from me. I may need you to take a friend home. When that's done, I want you leave this solar system. Go home. Have a life!"

"That's not what I meant. I'm not going to leave you. You wouldn't last ten minutes if I weren't watching over you!"

Aden appreciated her attempt at humor. "Sadly," he replied with a chuckle, "that is probably true. Still, I care too much for you to put you at risk again. This is my battle. It's time I took it on."

Abby stood up. "Your battles are my battles," she insisted. "They always have been."

She eventually gave in and beamed him down to Jasper, who was waiting for him at the entrance to an old mining tunnel.

"So," Jaspar greeted him enthusiastically when he materialized, "you *are* still alive! And you got my message."

"Surely you never doubted it?"

Jasper snickered. "I haven't been sure of many things lately, high prince...I mean, king. These are hard times."

"I understand you're protecting a friend of mine."

"How would you know that? That wasn't in the message I sent. Did she tell you?"

"I'm not sure. How is she?"

"Not well. She needs to go home."

"I think I can manage that. Can I see her?"

"Of course," Jasper replied. "She's waiting for you down there." He was pointing down the tunnel. "Follow me."

When Jasper turned and headed into it, Aden followed him. The tunnel was dimly lit by widely spaced light globes, and it was cool and damp. One hundred meters in, Jasper paused in front of a large side shaft and gestured down it. "She's in there."

"Could you give me a minute alone with her?"

"Go on. I'll wait here."

She was on her feet when he entered the chamber, considerably thinner than the last time he saw her, and her eyes weren't as bright. Her fondness for him remained unmistakable. He went up to her and said, "Time for you to go home, mother."

Chapter XVI

"Past time, my son," replied Bang, the head of the Taal Prime Council. As with the selkie, she presented her thoughts in his mind, not through his ears. "I should have left months ago. However, when our beloved Sia died, along with most of your government, I no longer had a way home. I would not reveal myself to the one you call Brawn—I don't believe he would have let me go willingly, and I wasn't strong enough to influence him to change his mind."

"How long have you been on Kealt?"

"Not long before your father gave up the reins to your Council of Commons, he, they, and the Ardalan Government negotiated a treaty with us that required each world to provide diplomatic representation to the other. We agreed, but being naturally introverted, we insisted that only the top levels of your respective governments be aware of our presence. This was for our protection as well as yours—we had no interest in being put on display, and the humans were concerned that the general populace would be unnerved by having such powerful telepaths in their midst, especially after what happened the last time we lived together."

She was referring to taals' telepathic manipulation of Ardala and Kealt that had encouraged the centuries-long conflict between them. Only when the war between the zon and the EA threatened to consume the entire Laima System did the taal step out of the shadows in a successful attempt to unite its inhabitants against a threat they couldn't handle on their own. Many on both planets still harbored resentment toward them for their role in the bloodshed.

"You were here before my friends and family were murdered!" exclaimed Aden. "Why didn't you stop it?"

"If you entered a room with thousands of people all speaking loudly," replied the taal, "would you know what people in arm's length of you were saying unless you focused your attention on them?"

"Well...no."

"Imagine millions of voices shouting at each other over vast distances. That is how it is with us. Without being aware of such a plot, we did not know to listen for it. I assure you, if we had..."

Trying not to sound hurt, Aden asked, "Why didn't you reveal yourself to me?"

"I'm sorry; but under the terms of the treaty, only a handful of senior government officials were privy to our presence. By then you had left the government, which prevented me from contacting you as long as I was on Kealt."

"That changed when I became king."

"Yes, but by then I was so weak, I could only reach you when you were sleeping."

"Did Celesta know you were here?"

"We do not often reveal our names to non-taal. She was aware only that Kealt had a taal representative, not whom it was. Even if she knew it was I, under the terms of the treaty she couldn't have told you as long as you were out of the government. We would have known if she had."

"Thank you for letting me see Sia and my child before their deaths."

"I didn't do it alone; I required the

assistance of other taals. One isn't strong enough to bring three human souls together in that manner."

"Nonetheless, I am forever in your debt. How do you survive here?"

"Even a depleted xanide mine contains enough residual radiation to sustain us for a time; even so, we must eventually to return to Seti to nourish ourselves properly."

"Do you know who killed Sia and the others?"

"The ones you call OSEC."

"Did Brawn having anything to do with the generational ship memorial bombing?" asked Aden.

"No, although with OSEC's urging and support, he was involved with what happened later to Sarin. Your friend Colonel Jasper will provide you those details."

Aden grinned sardonically. "It seemed too obvious to be true. They had to have inside help—someone who knew his way around the upper tiers of Kealt society."

"Yes."

"Who?"

When she told him, Aden erupted. "Tell me

where that weep hog is!" he bellowed, "so that I might drag him by his feet to the bolba tree that almost finished me!"

"Beyond my reach, and yours, for now," answered Bang. "Be patient my son, he will eventually come to you, I am sure of it."

"What is Brawn up to?" he asked. "What is he doing with all of Kealt's missing resources?"

"He and OSEC are building a weapon that will destroy Ardala. It is almost finished."

"A weapon that could destroy Ardala…the xanide! That's what he's been doing with it! He's building a mega bomb!"

"Yes. He will attempt to provoke Ardala into attacking Kealt in force. That will leave Ardala lightly defended, and increase the odds of his 'mega bomb,' as you aptly describe it, getting through. He is also responsible for dropping the xanide bomb on Kealt in order to increase the tension between your worlds. However, I intervened and ensured that the officer who programmed it set incorrect coordinates and armed it for a low yield."

"That evil son of a bitch! Where is this bomb?"

"Seti."

"What?"

"That is part of *our* plan. OSEC, which is actually building the bomb, believes they have technology that blocks our ability to manipulate them. They do not, but we are using that fallacy to our advantage. We encouraged them, subconsciously of course, to build the bomb on Seti, where we can ensure it will not work as intended."

"A bit of a risky gambit, isn't it?" said Aden. "What if their technology does work?" When she didn't answer, he said, "So far Ardala has resisted his provocations. What is he planning this time that will force them to act?"

"A cloaked ship is on its way there now. I was not strong enough to stop it. It carries a tactical xanide bomb and is programmed to drop it on Dilax."

"The palace! Celesta and her family are there! It must be stopped!" When Bang didn't answer he said, "Wait a minute, if there is a taal on Ardala, couldn't he stop it?"

"No, our ambassador to Ardala left shortly after the attack on your government. Regardless, the ship is automated."

"Do you know the flight path?"

"Yes."

"How long?"

"Twelve hours."

"Not enough time for Abby to take you home and reach it before it's too late."

"I will wait. Your sister is precious."

"So are you!" he retorted. "I don't have to read minds to know you need to go home now. There must be another way! And I think I know what it is…"

After Bang finished providing the details of OSEC and Brawn's plan, Aden contacted Abby, who, as requested, was still onboard her ship in orbit around Kealt. Without telling her whom it was she was helping, Aden asked her to beam Bang directly to the *Hyperion's* cargo hold, where she would be provided further instructions. He also told her about the cloaked ship and his plan for stopping it. Then he attached an extraction beacon to the huge creature's mane and when Abby was ready, said goodbye.

Chapter XVII

W hen Aden signaled that he was ready to transport his mystery guest to the *Hyperion*, Abby locked on to the extraction beacon and beamed her to the cargo hold as he had requested. Then she made her way back to the hold to see whom it was she was helping. When the doors opened and she stepped inside, the sight of the huge taal stunned her.

"I...I...hello!" she greeted her awkwardly, not knowing what else to say. "I assume I'm taking you to Seti. If that's the case, it will be a short trip. In the meantime, is there I anything I can do to make you more...comfortable?"

Bang swayed unsteadily, her strength ebbing rapidly. "No," she replied weakly to Abby's inquiry. "Thank you for taking me home. You have been very good to Aden. Thank you for that as well."

"You're Bang!"

"Yes."

"Aden speaks highly of you. Not to be rude, but what were you doing on Kealt?"

Bang explained the taals' treaties with Kealt and Ardala, and how she came to be trapped in a dank, dark cave.

"You're the reason the xanide bomb fell harmlessly, and why the resistance has survived this long, aren't you?"

"I played a role in those matters," she admitted, "but so have many brave humans, some of whom would surprise you. Now that Aden has returned, I suspect the resistance will gain momentum on its own."

"So, even the taal believe he has magical powers," said Abby, with more than a touch of sarcasm.

Sensing her irritation, Bang replied, "He is all too human. His heart aches, as yours does. It's time you trusted him enough to tell him the truth. He will not disappoint you. But that is not what you fear, is it?"

Surprised by the turn of the conversation and unable to deceive a creature that could read her mind, Abby declined to answer her.

"If you're afraid I'll reveal your secrets, it's true I can't help but hear them, the way they scream at me, but I'm under no obligation to share them. That is up to you to decide at a time and place of your choosing. Abby, I weep with you."

Abby felt the taal's sadness wash over her. "Bang," she said, reeling from her intense emotions, "I'm enjoying our conversation, but I need to go to the bridge and set course for Seti. Please let me know if there's anything else you need."

When Bang didn't answer, she fled to the emotional safety of the bridge. She sat in her chair, plotted the course, then leaned back and closed her eyes tightly.

"Bang is right."

Abby nearly jumped out of the chair at the selkie's observation.

"What?"

"You should trust Aden, he's such a nice man. You've each carried your burdens alone for too long. You need each other. He is ready to let go. You must do the same."

"Not you too! I really wish telepathic creatures would at least grant me the *illusion* of privacy! Why do you all make it a point to torment me?"

"Not fair Abby Watanabe!"

"It is from where I'm sitting."

"Consider us your…conscience!"

"Just get us to Seti as fast as possible!"

As Abby promised, using hyperspace the trip was a short one. After she established orbit, she went to the cargo hold to see Bang off. Before beaming her to the planet, she asked her if she was going to be OK.

"I will recover quickly," she assured her. "We are resilient creatures."

"Forgive me for being blunt," said Abby, "but we don't have much time and I may never have a chance to ask you this again. While I regret it to this day, I once fooled Aden into thinking I was someone I wasn't. I understand he considers your relationship with him to be like mother and son. Are you fooling him too?"

"You think he is naïve and easily manipulated. Yet as a boy, he once captured a taal, tricking her, as you would say, at her own game. A game we have played far longer and better than most humans can imagine."

"That is an evasive answer, Bang, if I've ever heard one."

"I could say anything to you and make you

believe it, if I wanted to. Humans in Laima have an expression: 'What a person does, a person is.' That applies to taals, as well. It also applies to you. You ask the right questions Abby Watanabe. Keep asking them."

"As good an answer as I could have hoped for, I suppose," she replied. She walked up to the taal until she was so close the massive creature had to bow her head to see her. "I promise you, if you ever hurt him, you will answer to me!"

Bang continued to look down on the almost diminutive Abby, whom she could have swallowed in one bite had she so desired. "For a human, Aden picks his friends well. He is blessed to have you at his side."

"Thank you for the advice," answered Abby. "I might even take it." When Bang didn't reply, she initiated transport. Once her sensors confirmed Bang was safely on Seti, she set course for Kealt.

Chapter XVIII

When Bang was gone, Aden left the cavern. He found Jasper where he left him, and said, "I must talk to Polis Selarney."

"The Ardalan High Prince?" he replied. "Why?"

Aden told him about Brawn's planned attack on Ardala, and his need to warn Polis in time to stop it. While the resistance lacked the ability to communicate with Ardala, Aden was sure Abby's friend Dandridge would assist him. After using one of Jasper's cloaked aircraft to take him and his men to their new headquarters, he flew to Rilan and beamed himself into Dandridge's quarters. When he materialized, he found himself trapped in a force field. Dandridge entered the room, went to a panel on the wall, and freed him.

"Well, Your Highness," he said good naturedly, "I've been looking forward to meeting you, but never thought you would come as a common thief."

After Aden assured himself the field was down, he stepped toward him and held out his hand. Dandridge shook it firmly and said, "You are indeed, quite literally, larger than life. Welcome to the sovereign territory of Earth. Abby told me you were coming. What can I do for you?"

"I am sorry to intrude ambassador, but it seems you have the only efficient means of interplanetary communication General Brawn can't jam. I must speak with Ardala's high prince."

"Ah, Polis! Of course, it will be my pleasure; and please, call me Jeff."

Dandridge led him into the room where Abby had previously allowed him to communicate with Celesta. When Polis's hologram established itself, Aden relayed the information he'd received from Bang.

When he finished, Polis said, "At the risk of sounding like a common bureaucrat, now that you're a king you really should be having this conversation with my father."

"You're right," agreed Aden, "but at this

point I barely know him. You and I have known each other a long time. I will leave it to you to convince him of our plan."

"Very well." answered Polis. "What *is* our plan?"

"Anything large enough to destroy a planet would contain so much active mil-grade xanide it would be difficult to cloak for very long and probably slow and automated. Even if it's capable of hyperspace travel, it will eventually have to transit regular space, at which time it will be vulnerable. It will require a significant escort to protect it."

"That all makes sense," replied Polis, as his hologram sat down in a chair. "And our play?"

"You will find and destroy Brawn's latest provocation before it drops its payload. Become outraged and commit the bulk of your fleet to a devastating counterattack. I believe that with most of your forces committed to the campaign against Kealt, Brawn will take the opportunity to deploy his planet-killer."

"I won't leave Ardala undefended."

"I've already contacted Gris. His fleet is ready and it's on its way. I've placed him under your command. When Brawn's mega bomb reaches Ardala, he'll be waiting in the shadows. If your remaining forces aren't sufficient to eliminate the threat, he'll be ready."

"So, do you know where the bomb is?"

"Yes."

"Why don't you just destroy it before they deploy it?"

"We need to force OSEC and Brawn out into the open. Otherwise, they'll continue to manipulate both of us. They're very good at it. I believe if we wait until the bomb reaches Ardala before destroying it, we'll have a better chance of exposing their little conspiracy, since I don't believe the bomb can get there without OSEC's overt involvement. If we destroy it on the ground, they can deny having anything to do with it and perhaps even blame Ardala for building it, leaving them free to try again."

"We're playing with fire."

"Oh, it's worse than that! If our plan works, I doubt OSEC will stand idly by, even if it means confronting the EA. I also fear for the taal, who will be unprotected unless I can convince Abby and the EA to help them."

Polis laughed ironically. "Well then, into the fire with us, old friend. This will be worth many ales between us if by God's Providence we come out of this alive!"

After Aden ended the transmission, Dandridge quickly agreed to support his plan. Aden then contacted Abby.

"Hello captain," he greeted her. "I assume by now you've reached Seti and dropped off your guest?"

"Yes; next time you want me to transport a massive, legendary creature, you think you could at least warn me? Regardless, she's safely away; Aden, she wasn't well. I don't know if I got her home in time."

"We'll have to worry about that later. Are you still in orbit above Seti?"

"I am, but I was preparing to leave."

"I'm afraid that if things don't go OSEC's way, they'll be looking for revenge. Since our fleets won't savage each other as they planned, Kealt and Ardala will be too heavily protected for them to confront. That leaves Seti. We have no ships to spare, meaning the *Hyperion* is the only thing resembling a warship in position to protect the taal. Fortunately, your friend Jeff has also agreed to redeploy whatever resources the EA has available to Seti."

"That can't be more than a handful of frontline ships," noted Abby. "They'll be far superior to the *Hyperion*, but there won't be enough of them to hold out very long against the forces OSEC can bring to bear, especially if they deploy their bio weapon."

"I know," agreed Aden. "I didn't tell you this, but I withheld a substantial number of xanide crystals in anticipation of this situation. You'll find them in the quarters you provided me."

"All right, we'll do what we can. What are you going to do now?"

"I don't know. Just wish me luck!"

With that Aden signed off, thanked Dandridge for his support, and returned to his ship. Later that evening he sat down to dinner with Colonel Jasper.

"So, Frune, now that you've helped me, how can I help you?" he asked, as the food made its way around the table.

"Brawn is tearing Kealt asunder," he responded. "I command the only meaningful resistance. Before long, we also will be forced to capitulate."

"What can I do?"

Jasper took a long pull on his ale, then put his glass down and wiped his mouth. "Brawn is a demagogue who has taken advantage of Kealt's grievous injury. We need someone to remind us of who we are and lead us past our fears. Only you can do that."

"How?"

"Not everyone who fights for Brawn believes in him. General Drall and others have never fully supported his rule, but they believe he is Kealt's best chance of preventing Ardala from winning a military confrontation. Drall is poised to destroy what's left of Harma Province. You must stop him, and convince him there's another way!"

"Frune," Aden answered, "Ardala doesn't want a war! OSEC is plotting to destroy both our worlds and take over this solar system. That fool Brawn has played right into their hands."

"You're probably right on all counts. Most clans have little stomach for our civil war. Members of Brawn's clan are driving this, with help from the misguided Sokk. Nonetheless, he's pushed both worlds to the edge. If we're to have a chance, you must take charge of the resistance, starting with Drall."

"How will I get to him?"

"Using one of our aircraft, of course," replied Jasper, stating the obvious. "However, once you're on the ground, I'm afraid you'll have to rely on your quite superior wits for the rest." When Aden didn't reply he added, "Before you go, I must show you something…"

It was early next morning when he reached General Drall's encampment. Without prior warning, he landed his ship near his headquarters, walked up to a shocked soldier, and asked to be taken to him.

"Your…Your Highness!" stuttered the soldier. "We're under orders to arrest you on sight!"

"Well then arrest me, soldier," he replied, holding out his wrists.

"Sir, that will not be necessary!"

Aden's presence quickly caused a stir among the other men as the young soldier led him to Drall's quarters, located in a large, portable shelter. He left him standing outside and went in to report his capture to the general. He stomped out seconds later, and seeing no restraints, bellowed, "This man is supposed to be under arrest!" Noting the sword slung over his back he added, "And he's armed!"

"I am, general." replied Aden. "Under arrest, that is. Your man did as he was ordered to do. He arrested me and brought me here. I am at your mercy."

Drall stared at Aden, until his impassive face gave way to peals of laughter. "Please Your Highness," he gasped between guffaws, "would you join me in my humble abode. Many of us thought you were dead. I'm most intrigued by what could possibly bring the storied King of Kealt to my humble doorstep!"

Once inside, Drall pointed him to a sofa and poured them both some brandy. He took a seat on a sofa opposite him and put the bottle down on the table between them. "I'm sorry about your family Aden. I've known your father since he was my first commanding officer. His loss was…devastating."

Aden thought he saw the old man's lip quiver.

"General," he replied, skipping any pleasantries, "you can't slaughter these people. Over the centuries these clans have given Kealt enough blood to fill an ocean, often in return for nothing more than bread crusts."

Drall again stared at Aden. Finally, he said, "You not only look like your father, you sound like him. You will be a good king."

"Will you stop this, then?"

"You have his courage as well." He threw down his brandy and refilled his glass. "Weeks ago, I was supposed to have given the order to destroy what's left of this place, but I can't bring myself to do it. My late wife was born here. Some of her relatives still live here, if I haven't killed them already. Major Vilas, Brawn's psychopathic little shrew, is on her way here personally to relieve me. The man who will replace me will not hesitate to finish this. There's not much more I can do."

"We can stand together and join the resistance. Brawn draws most of his support from divisions dominated by members of his clan. The rest he has scared in line by whipping up fears that Ardala is waiting to pounce on us. You know that's not true."

"Perhaps, but I'm sworn to defend the government of Kealt."

"Haven't you heard? I'm the government of Kealt."

Drall laughed. "You are, aren't you?" He stood up and finished his second brandy. "I'll talk to my men tomorrow. Will you stand by me?"

"Of course."

Drall ordered his men to put Aden up in suitable quarters. Word of his presence spread through the encampment at light speed. By the time Drall summoned his officers the following morning, a crowd had gathered around his quarters hoping to catch a glimpse of their king. With Aden next to him, Drall had little difficulty convincing his men to take up arms against Brawn. That settled, they prepared for the arrival of Aija and General Albert Brass, Drall's replacement…

Against her wishes, and on Brawn's orders, Aija agreed to escort General Brass to his new headquarters. In the event Drall had it in his head to resist his reassignment, Brawn was confident she would have no trouble bringing the aging general back in line. Also, against her will, General Brass insisted on flying across Pador Province, even though no cloaked ships were available, because he was unwilling to take the extra time to use slower, but safer, near-ground transportation.

When they reached the edge of Pador Province without incident, she finally began to relax. Almost immediately a missile hit the ship. The pilot struggled to regain control with little success. When he gave in to the inevitable, he shouted, "Brace yourself, we're going down!"

Aija recognized the severity of the damage inflicted by the missile, and for a moment was sure they wouldn't survive. However, the pilot was a skillful officer who fought to bring the ship down in a controlled, if violent fashion.

Seconds later, they plowed into a field and slid along the ship's belly before coming to an abrupt rest at the edge of a small lake. Aija, who was briefly unconscious, awoke to find the pilot dead and Brass badly injured. While she also was bloody, bruised, and dazed she didn't believe her wounds were serious.

Realizing the rebels would be upon them shortly, she unbuckled herself and secured a weapon. When she went back to check on Brass, he too was dead. She tried the com system, but it had been damaged in the crash. With nothing left to do, she opened the hatch and stepped outside.

To the west she saw a small town, and to the south she could see two vehicles speeding toward her. Realizing her situation was hopeless, she dropped her weapon and waited for them to reach her. When they got there, fifteen soldiers spilled out onto the field, followed by their commanding officer, Major Kalle.

Kalle was startled when he realized who she was. When he got over his shock, he said, "Major Aija Vilas, I hereby arrest you on grounds of supporting General Brawn's illegal coup. Other charges may be forthcoming."

"You're making a mistake, major! Brawn will be looking for me. If you let me go now, I promise we'll go easy on you when this insurrection is over!"

"Haven't you heard?" replied Kalle. "King Aden has returned. Drall's forces have already switched sides, Bendiks' have as well, and we've had overtures from other generals. I'm afraid it's you and the rest of Brawn's loyalists who will require mercy, and soon."

"Aden Cade? I thought that coward had fled the planet! I'm sorry I didn't kill him when I had the chance!"

When one of Kalle's men moved to strike her with the butt of his weapon, he stopped him. "We're not like them!" he insisted. "We will treat her with dignity!" Turning his attention back to Aija he said, "Sounds like another charge! Maybe you'll be able to tell him yourself."

Wrists bound tightly, Aija rode sullenly, refusing to answer Kalle's questions. When they arrived at Jasper's headquarters, he placed her in the brig. Before long, Jasper himself came to see her with a medic by his side.

"Hello major," he said. "You look like you've been injured. If you'll permit her, Captain Nardo will check you out. If you need treatment, you'll get it."

"I'm fine!" she replied gruffly. "I'd prefer she keep her dirty hands to herself."

"As you wish. I'd like to ask you a few questions."

"You don't really think I'll answer them!"

"You will if you ever want to see the other side of those bars again. If you cooperate with us, I'm prepared to offer you some form of amnesty once this is over."

Aija spit on him in reply.

"Have it your way," he said calmly. He ordered two men to keep watch over her, and left with Captain Nardo.

With nothing else to do, Aija laid down on a cot and went to sleep. Early in the morning, someone woke her by tugging on her arm. It was a guard, but not one of those who had been watching her earlier.

"Major, wake up!" he insisted.

Thinking he was trying to assault her, she reacted instinctively and struck him in the head. While he was still reeling from the blow, she bolted up from the bed and took his weapon from him. She put it against his head and told the other guard to drop his own weapon and slide it into the cage.

While the guard complied, he said, "We're going to get you out of here."

"I believe I'm doing that on my own!"

"No, you don't understand, we're loyal to General Brawn. We're on a mission to kidnap someone important Colonel Jasper is hiding here on the base. When we learned you'd been captured, we moved up our timetable. The rest of our team should be here shortly. We need to go now!"

"Who is it?"

"You'll see, we have a vehicle and it'll be here shortly."

Her curiosity outweighing her caution, she agreed to follow them. As promised, a military transport arrived minutes later. A soldier threw open a hatch, and above the sound of explosions and gunfire crackling throughout the base, exclaimed, "Get in, we don't have much time!"

The three climbed into the car as commanded. After grabbing a set of body armor and a weapon, Aija took up a seat in the back next to the prisoner, whose features were concealed beneath a hood. Once they were underway and certain they weren't being followed, she said, "OK, I give up. Who is this?"

"You won't believe it!" replied one of the men, with an ear-to-ear grin. He reached across the aisle, threw off the hood, and shined a light on the prisoner's face.

Aija gasped. After the soldier leaned back in his seat and she recovered from her shock, she leaned over and whispered something to the prisoner only she could hear. When she finished, Queen Sarin suppressed her own surprise.

Chapter XIX

Armed with Aden's intelligence, Ardala easily found and destroyed Brawn's robot ship. It displayed the expected outrage, and prepared for the massive retaliation Brawn had been counting on. Later, as Ardala's huge fleet advanced on Kealt, Howard Gross came to Brawn's office to assure him everything was happening as they planned. He had in tow a hooded visitor.

When the door closed, Brawn asked, "Why all the drama Gross? Who's our cloaked guest?"

At Gross's request, Tock Horat, former chief aide to King Edris Cade, threw back his hood and said, "Hello general, it's ga ga good to be back."

"What is this traitor doing here!" exclaimed Brawn.

"Ya ya you've only heard one side of the story!" stuttered Tock. "The Cades' side. I was trying to protect Kealt. Had the EA not intervened and destroyed the zon, I wa wa would be a hero."

"Go easy on him general," requested Gross. "Without his keen knowledge of Kealt's inner workings, we wouldn't be on the verge of eliminating Ardala."

"Again, why is he here?"

"He's earned a front row seat to our grand conspiracy," answered Gross. "He wants to come home."

Brawn shook his head distastefully. "I'll tolerate him for your sake, Gross. I just hope your weapon is ready." Then the uncharacteristically nervous general began to pace in front of his desk. "Our ships still aren't fully functional, despite your promises," he whined. "And once Ardala is destroyed, what's to stop their 'grand armada' from doing the same to Kealt?"

"It's been ready for weeks," Gross replied impatiently. "It's on its way to Ardala now. When your ships rendezvous with it, we'll turn over the weapon to you and you will escort it the rest of the way. Using hyperspace, this can all happen very quickly."

"Hyperspace travel within a solar system is a tricky thing, Gross. Most of our civilian vessels aren't capable of it—reliably, anyway. Is it safe, or even possible, for a ship carrying that much energized xanide to travel that way?"

"It is, but the weapon itself has limited propulsion," answered Gross. "We'll have to tow it with ships designed for that purpose." As though suddenly bored by the discussion, he walked over and helped himself to a stiff pour of Brawn's whiskey. He took a sip and held the glass aloft. "I generally prefer scotch, but this is very good. I'll have to bring some back with me when this is over…oh yes, you were asking about the weapon. Now that you've succeeded in luring their fleet here, your fancy new warships, fully charged with the xanide we managed to spare from the weapon, should be more than sufficient to ensure it reaches Ardala, even in their current state."

"And their fleet?"

"OSEC will honor its treaty with Kealt to defend it from all aggressors. Our ships are more than capable of dealing with them."

"Aren't you concerned the EA will intervene?"

"We've been over this, general!" Gross replied impatiently. "They have, by our estimate, no more than three or four front line organic-hulled warships in this sector that are available on short notice. We have committed a far more sizeable number of ships. In addition, they are aware of our weapon. I doubt they'll want to get involved in this."

"The EA's conventional ships are quite capable. You said so yourself. Your bio weapon will not deter them."

"General, please," answered Gross from the chair he'd just filled. "All this handwringing is unbecoming! We have a plan and it's a good one—no time to get cold feet now! The Ardalans will be here within a day. You should be ensuring your preparations are complete."

In response, Brawn pulled up his vidscreen. "Ah, Colonel Darvin! Is the fleet ready? The Ardalans will arrive shortly. I want our Dipsa class ships away before they get here."

"Too late sir, they're here now!"

"What! Well then, they'll have to fight their way out!"

"Yes sir, they'll deploy immediately."

Onboard the *Kreg*, Admiral Polis watched with pride as his fleet assembled above Kealt. When Kealt initially failed to mount a response, or even acknowledge their presence, First Officer Ari Olonious asked for orders.

"For now we wait, Ari," replied Polis. "They're up to something; I'd like to know what it is before we act rashly."

"We have all their major military installations locked in," advised Ari. "We can hit them at will."

"I know commander."

"Here we go!" exclaimed Ari. "Six warships have just left the surface. They're coming right at us!"

"Stop them commander!"

The *Kreg* opened fire as Kealt's warships approached. Four of the ships raised shields in an attempt to protect the other two, which were deploying their main weapons. The ships focused their fire on the *Kreg*, which stood between them and open space. Explosions rocked the Ardalan flagship as it attempted to block their escape.

Return fire from the *Kreg* destroyed one of the unshielded ships, but the other five got by and immediately jumped into hyperspace. As the *Kreg* returned fire, a high-energy relay exploded and threw Polis from his chair. Ari rushed to the fallen admiral and found him unconscious, but alive.

"What are our orders, sir?" asked a young ensign.

"Open fire! Target their major military installations and spaceports!"

As volleys from the Ardalan fleet began to rock the palace, Brawn lowered the shields protecting it long enough to allow the stolen transport carrying Sarin and Aija to enter.

When they made their way to the throne room minutes later, Gross said, "All right, it's my turn to ask: Who is this, and why is she here?"

"Ah," Brawn replied, "you're not that new to this solar system are you Gross? This is Her Royal Highness Sarin Selarney, the queen of Ardala."

"Queen…I thought you'd killed her!"

"I did as well. Perhaps later she'll tell us how she escaped."

"So why is she here?"

Brawn smiled smugly. "In the event your forces are not as superior to Ardala's fleet as you profess, she's an insurance policy. Ardala won't attack us if she orders them to stop."

"You don't really think I'll help you, do you?" replied Sarin haughtily.

"You are of Kealt. I doubt you'll standby and do nothing while your subjects blast it to hell."

Sarin held out her bound hands. "Is this really necessary?"

Brawn nodded to Aija, who produced a knife and cut the cords binding her wrists. Then he turned his attention to Aija herself. "Major, you've been injured. Are you all right? What are you doing here?"

"Our airship was shot down," she replied. "Brass was killed and I was captured. Your men freed me as they escaped with the queen. I learned on the way that Drall and Bendiks have joined Colonel Jasper's forces. That's five divisions in the past week. Soon there will be more of them than us!"

"Patience major!" replied Brawn. "Soon Ardala will be destroyed and we'll be heroes. That will be the end of this little rebellion, and those that betrayed us will hang!"

"With due respect, sir, how will we manage that?"

"In due time. For now, I need you to recall every division that's still loyal to us and have them redeployed around Rilan. This will all be over very shortly…"

Chapter XX

When Aden returned to Jasper's base after convincing Drall to switch sides, a young officer presented himself and exclaimed, "Sir! Colonel Jasper requests an immediate audience with you!"

"What is it? Has something happened?"

"We were attacked last night. Our guest was taken!"

In short order he was standing before Jasper, who provided him the details of Sarin's abduction, and Aija's capture and subsequent escape. Jasper explained that, shortly after he locked Aija in the brig, teams of commandos infiltrated the base with the help of Brawn's spies and began attacking force field generators and other critical base infrastructure. While the commandoes intentionally drew his attention away from Sarin, a small team kidnapped her and freed Aija.

Aden asked if Aija's capture and the attack that followed were related.

"I don't know," Jasper replied, "but it seems too convenient to be a coincidence."

"Indeed, that woman is a demon and a clever one. Either way, we must go after them! If something happens to Sarin, nothing will save us from Polis's wrath."

"I agree," replied Jasper. "Fortunately Brawn isn't the only one with spies. The Ku Assa have a number of good ones as well, and they tell me, anonymously of course, that they've taken her to the palace, most likely to the throne room. Brawn plans to use her to prevent Ardala from attacking in the event OSEC doesn't. The problem is, the palace is too fortified for a frontal assault, and even if it weren't, such an approach could injure the queen."

"There are a series of tunnels beneath the palace built by previous kings, primarily to offer an avenue of escape from encroaching enemies," noted Aden. "As a youth, I studied them extensively. I doubt Brawn and his men know they exist. Even if they do, there are tunnels I'm sure I alone know about. I could lead a small team into the palace, and, with any luck, we could find our way to Sarin."

"The palace is shielded. How will you get around that?"

"The shield is intended to protect the palace from airborne attacks, it doesn't extend below ground. The tunnels extend outside the shield in places. We will use one of them."

"Very well Your Highness," responded Jasper, "but other than you and Kalle, I'm not sure whom I can trust for such a mission."

"I can't think of a better team!" said Aden with grin. "What are we waiting for?"

Using a cloaked ship that was much faster than the vehicle transporting Sarin, the three quickly reached the outskirts of the palace. Aden put them down in an isolated section of the vast gardens that surrounded it.

After checking their weapons, he produced a hand scanner and surveyed the area. Satisfied he'd found a route that would lead them to a tunnel without being observed, they set out. Jasper shivered when they stopped in the middle of a small, overgrown graveyard holding the remains of long forgotten royals and their retainers.

After ensuring they were unobserved, Aden walked over to a grave covered with a large stone slab. He reached under it and felt around until a satisfied grunt signaled he'd found what he was looking for. Manipulating a mechanism Jasper and Kalle couldn't see, the slab rose slightly. With some effort, Aden swung it away from the grave, revealing a narrow staircase.

Jasper and Kalle turned on their electric torches and followed him down the steps. When Jasper's foot crunched a bone fragment, he shivered again. "You never mentioned these tunnels also serve as an ossuary!"

"Sorry Frune, it slipped my mind!"

"From the looks of it," said Kalle, "they've been used in this manner for some time! Why are the bones scattered about like they are? I would assume even down here the dead would be disposed of with a little more formality."

"Oh, I can assure you they were!" replied Aden. "But when the tunnels started to fill up a few centuries ago, a former king introduced mor francachs to free up some space."

Jasper gasped. "Mor francachs, you say? Those things can bring down a man!"

"And have!" agreed Aden. "But they much prefer dried bones. I doubt they'll make their presence known while we're down here."

"If you say so," replied Jasper. "I pray when I finally breath my last, my remains will be handled with a little more dignity!"

"Don't worry old friend, I'll be sure to oversee your interment myself!" answered Aden cheerfully.

"Yes, that makes me feel better!" retorted Jasper. "The way we're going, you won't live any longer than I--uh, Your Highness!" he quickly added.

Before Aden could reply, the ground shook and dust fell from the ceiling.

"What the hell was that!" exclaimed Kalle.

When multiple explosions followed in quick succession, Aden said, "Something has gone wrong. The Ardalans must be firing on us!"

"Are you sure it's them?" asked Jasper.

"Pretty sure. Their fleet would have reached Kealt by now. I doubt OSEC would be brazen enough to take them on directly. The EA only has a handful of ships in Poseidon and isn't looking for a fight, so I doubt it's them. Besides those three, yours are the only forces capable of such an onslaught. Obviously it's not them."

"Why? They're supposed to be protecting us!"

"No idea!" Aden replied. "Maybe they're defending themselves. But if Brawn has Sarin, and she's alive, she can stop it. If something's happened to her..." He didn't need to finish.

As the ground continued to shake from the Ardalan bombardment, Aden led them through a labyrinth of underground tunnels, which were still full of bones despite the alleged presence of mor francachs. He took so many twists and turns Jasper and Kalle were sure he was lost. Eventually he paused at the bottom of a short, but steep staircase.

"Up there is a door that opens into a little-used anteroom to the throne room," he said quietly. "We should be able to enter it unobserved. When we get to the top of the steps, turn off your torches."

He started up the stairs with Jasper and Kalle following closely. When they reached the small landing in front of a rough-hewn door, they extinguished their lights. Aden turned the knob and pushed the door in cautiously, concerned it would open noisily after years of disuse. His concerns were unfounded, it opened smoothly; but even if it hadn't, it would have been hard to hear anything above the sound of the intensifying bombardment.

The three cautiously stepped into the empty anteroom through a bookcase that served to conceal the door. Hearing voices coming from the throne room, they edged toward it. Aden was pleased to see Jasper's intelligence was correct: Brawn and Sarin were in the throne room, along with Gross, Aija, and to Aden's surprise, Tock Horat. All but Horat and Sarin were armed.

While volleys from the Ardalan fleet shook the room, Brawn and Gross were arguing. Brawn wanted Sarin to contact her fleet and order it to stand down, but Gross was insisting they save her for insurance and wait for OSEC's fleet. When Aija raised her weapon to force the issue, Gross stepped behind Sarin for cover and shot her.

Without waiting for the others, Kalle rushed into the room and gathered the fallen woman. Their hand forced, Aden and Jasper followed quickly, pointing their weapons at Brawn and

Gross. They forced Brawn to drop his weapon, but Gross grabbed Sarin and pointed his at her head.

"Your Highness," said Kalle, ignoring Gross, "we need to get her to a med unit quickly!"

"We will," Aden replied, "as soon as we deal with these criminals."

"Very touching," said Gross, wrapping an arm around Sarin's waist while continuing to point his weapon at her with the other. "I suppose even rabid dogs should be put down humanely. Now don't do anything stupid or the queen gets it!"

When Kalle stood up and advanced on him threateningly, Gross pulled Sarin closer.

"Easy, big boy. Right now, this pretty lady is all that stands between us and a bunch of pissed off Ardalans. Polis has already lost his mother once. If it happens again, I doubt even the king here will be able to stop him from wrecking this place."

"I know you won't hurt her because she's also all that stands between you and me, you coward!" exclaimed Aden. "I know you killed Sia and my son!"

"Ardala did that!" answered Brawn angrily.

"No!" Aden corrected him. "Do you really think King Ivege would blow up his own pregnant daughter? Gross and his friends did it, with considerable assistance from Tock. You're a hateful, angry fool who played right into their hands.

"Tock knew you'd believe without question that Ardala placed the bomb in the podium, and that it would be easy to convince you to retaliate by going after Sarin and commit other provocative acts, hoping you would ignite a war that would end with the destruction of both worlds. You're also responsible for the xanide bomb that fell on Harma, aren't you? You blamed that on Ardala hoping to drive a wedge between us. Thankfully the taal got wind of it and saw that it fell harmlessly."

"Why would OSEC attack Kealt?" asked Brawn scornfully, ignoring Aden's accusation.

"They wanted Ardala out of the way, but they didn't want to take them on directly for fear of dragging in the EA. While they had a weapon that was effective against the EA's organic ships, they were less confident they could prevail over their conventional forces, which, I'm told, are also quite formidable.

"Even if that weren't the case, it would only be a matter of time before the EA found a vaccine for their ships. So why provoke them if it wasn't necessary? Now, if the EA thought *Kealt* destroyed Ardala, they would consider it a local war and wouldn't get involved. Problem solved.

"By killing my father and most of the Council of Commons, OSEC knew, based on Tock's knowledge, you would likely take charge and wouldn't need much of an excuse to go after Ardala. However, you lacked the resources. So OSEC, which believed it had the technology to keep the taal at bay, set up a base on Seti to build a weapon sufficient to do the job.

"Even though they also believed they had access to all the xanide they needed, they claimed they needed more and tricked you into scavenging every spare crystal you could find. You disabled much of Kealt's defensive capability in the process, making it an easy target for Ardala.

"When OSEC was ready to implement their plan, they had you attempt to attack Ardala with a tactical xanide bomb, believing that would goad them into committing the bulk of their ships to a massive counterattack. With their fleet on its way to Kealt, they would have no way to defend against OSEC's mega bomb, especially since they'd convinced you to send all of your Dipsa class warships to protect it. Conveniently, that meant Kealt would be unprotected when Ardala showed up."

"That's not true," insisted Brawn. "OSEC has sworn to protect us!"

"That's where you've been a particular fool! OSEC has no intention of protecting Kealt! In fact, they were anticipating Ardala would smash it. When they were finished, Ardala would still possess a formidable fleet, but no practical means of maintaining it, and their population would be reduced to a few thousands.

"Without a planet they could return to, and having insufficient numbers to rule a devastated Kealt, they would ultimately have to leave Laima and resettle on one of their distant colonies, leaving OSEC in charge. With the obliteration of Ardala and the destruction of Kealt, nothing would stand between their conquest of Seti and access to a virtually unlimited supply of xanide with which to trade and power their next generation warships.

"On what was left of Kealt they also would have access to a large supply of skilled and manual labor to work the mines. Of course, the EA might object to OSEC taking Seti directly, but they'd manage that through their Kealt proxy. Kealt might not have much of a military left, but Seti has none, and with OSEC's supposed telepath-blocking technology, the taal would have no way to stop it.

"OSEC would have all the xanide they could ever want, without firing a shot. Of course, they couldn't be 100% sure the EA wouldn't get involved anyway, but from a strictly business perspective, it would be well worth the risk.

"Unfortunately, the taal were one step ahead of them the entire time, and so were we. Based on their information, we have a fleet of fully operational Dipsa class warships waiting for OSEC when their weapon reaches Ardala. And Ardala's ships are here to protect Kealt, not attack it.

"So now the game is up. OSEC is exposed, Kealt and Ardala will not be destroyed, and, as king of Kealt and a close ally of the taal, I will do what I can to ensure the EA has access to the xanide it needs to protect its ships from your bio weapon. Things aren't looking very good for OSEC right now. If I were you, I'd get out of the Laima System as quickly as possible."

"From the way your 'good friends' the Ardalans are pummeling this place, I'd say something has gone terribly wrong with your own plan!" snorted Gross. "That aside, we knew you were up to something in those badlands, but assumed you were experimenting with weapons prototypes or other new military technologies. We had no idea you were building an entire fricking fleet of your most advanced warships! Now that was quite a feat, keeping it from us and Brawn!"

When Aden made a subtle move toward him, Gross tightened his grip on Sarin and warned him to stay where he was.

"Very good, your kingliness!" Gross continued. "You got it almost all right. That is, except for the part about us leaving Laima. We're not done here yet! No Sir Ree Bob, not by a long shot!"

"You!" exclaimed Brawn, staring down Gross. "You did this! I'm nobody's fool!" As he reached for his weapon, Gross blasted him.

"I'll give you credit Cade," replied Gross with a forced cheerfulness, "you are certainly as impressive as your reputation. We should have killed you when we had the chance. If it weren't for you and the damn taal, my plan would have succeeded and then some! They will soon pay dearly for their role in this. You'll have to wait, I'm afraid."

"What now, Gross?" asked Aden. "You'll never get out of this room."

"Oh, I most certainly will!" He assured him.

He released Sarin, but kept the gun on her while he used his free hand to pull an extraction beacon out of a jacket pocket. He stuck it to her shoulder, then reached into another pocket and pulled out a small device. He held it up and said, "When I push this button, the lovely queen and I will be transported to my ship, which, fortunately, is cloaked and has so far survived Ardala's fusillade."

"Leave Sarin!" demanded Aden. "If you do, I promise we won't pursue you."

"Normally older women aren't my thing," replied Gross brightly, "but you have to admit, she is exquisite! Kind of a 'Taste of Sia,' wouldn't you say? I think we'll enjoy each other's company, at least for a while. Besides that, she's my insurance policy in the unlikely event you find me before I'm safely back in the Milky Way."

"You better take up his offer, Gross," warned Sarin. "Between Aden, my son, and the taal they will find you, and my presence will not save you."

"Ga Ga Gross," stuttered Tock, who had been cowering quietly behind him, "wha wha what about me? They have many grievances against me. If you leave me here, I'll perish!"

"You're right my dear friend, that would be cruel!" agreed Gross. Then he casually pointed his weapon at him and burned a hole in his shallow, unprotected chest. "There, now they'll never get their hands on your traitorous, emaciated body. Well, they will, but it will be dead!"

"This was your plan all along, wasn't it?" said Aden. "Tock and Brawn were the only Kealts with firsthand knowledge of your little conspiracy. I doubt even Major Vilas knew what was going on. You intended to kill them both from the beginning. You needed someone to blame for Brawn's death to keep OSEC's hands clean, and Tock, being a wanted traitor, is as believable as anyone. Unfortunately for you, we stumbled onto your little scheme."

"Well, I think it's pretty obvious to all of us that my plan was less than perfect!" Gross replied sarcastically. He lifted up his device. "It's been fun folks."

Just as he initiated transport, Sarin ripped the beacon off her shoulder and threw it onto Brawn's body. Gross's face had time to register shock before he and Brawn were transported away.

"Aden," exclaimed Kalle, "we need to get Aija medical attention now! Her armor took much of the damage, but the weapon that did this was set to kill."

In response, Aden strode over to the com panel and summoned a medical team.

"I must contact Polis and stop this attack!" insisted Sarin, as another volley rocked the palace.

Aden waved her over to the com panel and hailed the Ardalan flagship.

Onboard the *Kreg*, an ensign said, "Sir, we have an incoming transmission from Kealt—it claims to be from Queen Sarin! She is demanding that we stop the bombardment!"

"Cease all weapons fire, now!" ordered Ari.

"Sir, it can't be, she's dead!"

"I'm aware of that ensign. I would prefer not to kill her again. Put her on screen."

The ensign complied, and Sarin herself appeared. "Hello Ari. It's good to see you are well. Where is Polis?"

"He's been injured, Your Highness. We're assessing his condition now, but I believe he'll be fine. We thought you were dead!"

"I know, I'll explain later. Right now, King Aden must speak with you."

Sarin stepped aside and Aden took her place on the *Kreg's* vidscreen.

"Ari old friend, I hope you are well. On behalf Kealt, I apologize for any damage your fleet has incurred as a result of our actions. The previous, illegal regime has been deposed, and the legitimate government is back in control.

"We knew that Brawn, with assistance from OSEC, was going to attempt to destroy Ardala with a massive xanide weapon. Polis and I were playing into his plan in order to force his hand and expose them. Those ships that escaped are supposed to ensure the bomb reaches Ardala."

"Your Highness, with all due respect, most of our forces are here. What kind of plan is that?"

"We have a surprise for them."

"Let me talk to the queen."

Aden stepped aside for Sarin.

"Is this acceptable, Your Highness?"

"Do what he says. He will not let anything happen to Ardala."

When the transmission ended, Aden turned back to Aija. The medics hadn't arrived yet, but Kalle had found a first aid kit and was helping her out of her armor. While he was working on her, Aden noted the way Kalle stroked her hair and handled her tenderly.

"I don't understand why you're so concerned about her, major. She would have eaten us both in an instant."

"She's my wife," he responded.

"Your wife!" exclaimed Aden and Jasper in unison.

"Aden," said Sarin, "she's also Ku Assa."

"Ku…she tore off my finger nails! She threatened to castrate me!"

"I knew you could take it!" Croaked Aija, who had revived enough to sit up on the couch Kalle had laid her on.

"So please explain why you tortured me, abused Abby, and allowed Brawn to commit his various atrocities?"

"Brawn wanted you dead and so did Gross. I couldn't think of any other way to keep you alive, except to pretend I enjoyed torturing you. It was my idea to implant the second transponder and allow you to escape, supposedly to track you. I made sure your friend Abby couldn't miss it.

"I'm sorry I accosted her, but that was all part of my act, which in retrospect was certainly effective.

"When Brawn rounded up the Council of Elders, two died of heart attacks during the arrest. He wanted the rest killed as well, but I convinced him they were cowards who would do whatever we wanted after a little torture. He agreed, but I made sure we never got around to it…the same with Abeg Mar. I'm also responsible for ordering General Bendiks to redeploy his men in defensive positions around those old xanide mines, buying time for Colonel Jasper."

"How did Brawn learn Colonel Jasper was protecting Sarin?" asked Aden.

"From spies he managed to infiltrate into Jasper's camp when the taal was too weak to detect them consistently. When he was ready, he sent in a spec ops team to abduct her. By then the taal had left, and could no longer protect her.

"Coincidentally, and fortuitously as it turned out, Jasper's men shot down my ship as I was on my way to Drall's camp, where I was to relieve him of his command. They captured me and brought me to Jasper's headquarters for questioning. There I learned from Brawn's spies he was protecting a VIP, whom they were going to kidnap that morning.

"They freed me at the same time, and that's when I learned whom it was Jasper had been protecting. They had orders to bring her to the throne room, which is well protected and has the broadcast equipment Brawn needed to show her to the rest of the world. He figured the Ardalans wouldn't fire on us if they knew she was alive and a prisoner here. He believed her presence would also assure the people of Kealt they would be safe from an Ardalan bombardment."

"It was you who advised us where they had taken her, wasn't it?" asked Jasper.

"Yes."

When Aija coughed weakly and appeared to be on the verge of passing out, Kalle told her to rest, but she insisted on continuing:

"I placed a beacon on Brawn, a much better one than I placed in you, Your Highness. We should be able to find him even if he's in hyperspace; or, at least what's left of him."

"Mother," asked Aden, while Aija paused, "how did you know she was Ku Assa?"

"Something she said on the way here—a line from an old Ku Assa ballad: 'The sky will crumble, the ground will swallow the ocean, the sun will fade, and Seti will give up its secrets before harm will to come to those we serve.'"

"Aija," asked Aden, turning his attention back to the wounded woman, "how did you get so close to Brawn in the first place?"

Grimacing from the pain, she replied, "When King Edris still ran the government, he assigned me to Brawn. He didn't trust him and wanted me to keep an eye on him. He knew I was Ku Assa, and that Brawn had killed my half-brother Ludis for refusing to fire on unarmed Ardalans protecting a celestial claim.

"At first Brawn kept me at arm's length. I was a lowly Sokk, after all. However, his clan was too small to win a civil war—he needed our support. After a while he thought he could use me to his advantage, and allowed me into his inner circle.

"The only reason I didn't kill him long ago was because we suspected OSEC's plan wasn't complete when they destroyed our government, and that they needed Brawn. If I dispatched him before knowing what they were up to, OSEC would merely find someone else to do their bidding. There were certainly plenty of willing subjects among his clan."

"So the taal never told you OSEC was building a bomb on Seti?" asked Aden.

"I never spoke to the taal and Brawn never mentioned it to me."

"Didn't he know you were married to Jasper's second in command?" asked Sarin.

"No. We're from different clans that don't get along. Our parents would not have approved of our marriage, so we did it in secret to prevent interference. We intended to tell them after it was a fait accompli, but before we could, OSEC attacked our government and we thought it best to keep our secret a secret. I never took Jaak's name, something I will rectify immediately."

She was at the end of her strength when the medics arrived. With Kalle's help they loaded her onto a gurney, and then zipped up Tock's body. After they left, Sarin came up to Aden and hugged him. When she released him, she said, "You've come through again, for all of us! Sia would be so proud of you!"

"I've had a lot of help."

"Yes, including Abby Watanabe. My daughter was quite annoyed with her at one time. However, near the end of her life she spoke highly of her. Celesta does as well, if grudgingly. Of course, Bang helped too. How is she, by the way?"

"I don't know," replied Aden. "Abby got her safely to Seti. After that…"

"And Abby?"

"Abby?" repeated Aden.

"Be true to your heart, Aden; let something good come of all this evil." When he didn't reply, she asked, "Well, what now?"

Aden gazed at his mother-in-law. Tall, lithe, blond and fair skinned, with pale blue eyes and full lips, she looked so much like Sia he had occasionally confused the two at a distance or when the light was right.

"You, my beautiful and beloved mother, are well missed by your devoted son and husband, daughter in law and grandchildren. I must get you back to them immediately. Then I will contact Gris, and with luck, confirm he has destroyed OSEC's weapon. After that, I will organize a search for Gross and ensure he gets the justice he deserves, as well as Brawn, if he's still alive. Then I will order elections to give our government back to the people. Once that is done, I am going back to Seti. I have unfinished business there."

"Grand*children*?"

"Yes, while you've been trapped here, Celesta has given birth to a beautiful, orange haired girl. They are all eager to see you."

Word of Aden's presence and Brawn's demise spread quickly throughout the palace. His few remaining supporters quickly swore their allegiance to their new king, effectively marking the end of Brawn's reign of terror.

Chapter XXI

As promised, OSEC delivered the bomb to Brawn's men. It was on an automated ship over four kilometers long. Slow moving in normal space, and with no defensive capabilities, it would be vulnerable until it was deployed. The five Kealt warships that had escaped the Ardalan blockade, along with two OSEC ships, set course for Ardala with the weapon.

Almost immediately Ardala's remaining forces engaged them, but they were no match for even partially enabled Dipsa class ships, and they continued on to the planet unimpeded. As they passed Ardala's moon, they began to deploy the weapon; before they could initiate it, three dozen cloaked warships emerged from the darkness.

Gris Haberat, commander of thirty-six fully operational, second generation Dipsa class warships, hailed the enemy ships and demanded their unconditional surrender. To his horror, the weapon cloaked.

"Sir," exclaimed his second in command, "the enemy is retreating!"

"I don't care about them, find that weapon!"

"We can't sir. They're using an EA-style cloak."

"Damn it! That's impossible! Plot its likely course and put us in its way!"

When the weapon reappeared over Dilax, it was too far from Gris's fleet to be intercepted in time to stop it. He watched helplessly as it powered up and exploded. Expecting the annihilation of his own ships since they were so close to a planet-crushing explosion, he was stunned when his overloaded sensors came back on line and both his fleet and Ardala were intact.

"Science officer!" he bellowed. "What the hell just happened?"

"Sir, apparently there was only enough xanide onboard the weapon to destroy it and emit an EMP sufficient to blind us."

"Sir," called his communications officer, "your daughter, uh, High Princess Celesta, is hailing us."

"Put her on."

"Father!" she exclaimed, unable to hold back her tears, "your plan worked! You saved us!"

"Sweetheart, I didn't save you and this wasn't my plan. Someone else sabotaged the weapon."

"Who?"

"Well, if even the Ku Assa don't know, only one suspect presents themselves."

"The taal," replied Celesta. "Have you heard from Aden?"

"No dear, not since he ordered me to protect Ardala. I don't expect to until this is over. Have you heard from your own fleet?"

"Yes," she replied with a frown. "When the ships that were sent to protect OSEC's weapon escaped Kealt, they fired on the *Kreg*. I've been told Polis was injured, although I've been assured not seriously."

By the end of the day, Gris and Celesta learned the resistance had routed Brawn's remaining forces, and restored Aden to the throne. They also learned that Polis was fine, having only suffered a mild concussion. Unsure of OSEC's next move, the respective fleets agreed to stay where they were in order to prevent OSEC from catching them out of position as they transitioned back to their respective home worlds.

Back on Kealt, waiting for the Ardalans to ensure it was safe to beam Sarin up to the *Kreg*, Aden was still reeling from the reappearance of his mother-in-law.

"You are a beautiful sight mother," he said. "I see Sia's eyes in yours. How did you survive the explosion and how did you end up here?"

"Your friend Bang became aware of Brawn's plot to kill me in retaliation for the assassination of your government by, he believed, Ardalans. She warned me and ensured that everyone was looking the other way as I left the ship before it departed. The Ku Assa then led me to Colonel Jasper, who, I understand, is a friend of yours. He took me in, along with Bang, and watched over us. So my son, what now?"

"This isn't over yet. I don't believe OSEC has played their final hand."

Just then Jasper, who had gone to ensure the palace was secure after the last of Brawn's loyalists surrendered, burst into the room.

"We just received a distress call from Abby—a huge OSEC fleet is heading for Seti! Three EA warships have joined her, but they still haven't found a countermeasure for OSEC's bio weapon. Once they get there, they won't be able to hold out for very long from the sounds of it."

"They can't touch Kealt or Ardala, so they're going to take revenge on the taal!" replied Aden. "I feared as much!"

"Aden," said Sarin, "our ships are at your disposal!"

"Thank you, mother, but right now they are all that protects Kealt."

"Then Gris's ships."

"They're protecting Ardala."

"We have to help Abby!" insisted Sarin.

"I know. I didn't give Gris all the xanide. When I heard about the bio weapon, I stashed some on Abby's ship. She told me it would help their ships fight off the infection. Colonel, can you get me to the Kazt shipyard? We need to get to Seti."

"Kazt?" replied Jasper. "We don't keep space-worthy ships there; and most of what's left of our fleet had their xanide cores stripped by Brawn. There's nothing left that can take you to Seti in time."

"The *Garm*."

The *Garm* was the aged former flagship of Kealt's space fleet. It had been severely damaged when, on Aden's orders, Gris rammed it into the bridge of a zon mothership. It destroyed the mothership, but suffered significant structural damage. While it was able to limp home, Kealt engineers deemed it not worth repairing, since the first of the Dipsa class ships were coming on line.

"Are you kidding?" answered Jasper. "They're turning that old relic into a space museum. It was too old and damaged to bring back into service."

"Technically the *Garm* was never out of service, merely moved to our reserve fleet," noted Aden. "Admittedly my information is dated, but she was still considered combat ready the last time I checked. Against our engineers' recommendations, my father insisted she be brought back to spec as much as possible. She's space worthy again, and even has a xanide core—albeit one near the end of its service life. Hopefully Brawn overlooked it as he raked in most of Kealt's xanide for the mega bomb. The ship even has a crew assigned to it; I merely require a first officer."

Jasper saluted. "Aye aye, sir! First Officer Frune Jasper at your service!"

Aden clapped him on the shoulder. "Well old friend, we don't have time to waste!"

After beaming Sarin up to the *Kreg,* Aden contacted Abby and told her he would join her soon. She advised him that the EA ships had integrated the xanide he'd left behind. However, while there was more than enough for the *Hyperion* and the other EA ships, they both knew it would only buy them time, not defeat the virus that soon would be eating at the ships' hulls.

Jasper placed Kalle in charge of the forces guarding the palace, and commandeered a hover car to take him and Aden to the *Garm.* When they came aboard, the ship's captain immediately turned the *Garm* over to them.

Aden had not been aboard his old ship since it limped home following its last engagement with the zon. He was impressed with the effort that had gone into restoring her. He asked for a proper uniform, which was quickly provided. In fact, it was his old uniform, which was being kept on display onboard the ship. When they lifted off, Jasper was astonished that most of its systems were working properly, albeit minimally, except for the weapons systems, which were off line.

Upon reaching Seti, Aden asked Abby to beam over the surplus xanide, which Chief Engineer Stick used to refresh the *Garm's* nearly exhausted core. With the ship now at full power, Stick and his team worked feverishly to bring the weapons on line. Just as he was about to perform a test, one hundred and fifty frontline OSEC warships and Kealt's five rogue Dipsa class ships jumped into normal space. OSEC immediately launched their bio weapon but, as expected, the xanide slowed the virus's ability to degrade the hulls of the EA ships.

"Stick!" exclaimed Aden, "I hope our weapons are on line!"

"Sir," he replied, "they're functional, although without testing them I can't say to what degree or for how long!"

"We're about to find out! Colonel, open fire, all batteries!"

"Aye sir!" replied Jasper emphatically.

Multiple plasma beams lanced out from the *Garm*, inflicting significant damage on several ships. However, the EA's weapons were far more effective, destroying multiple motherships with their initial volleys.

As the battle raged the five ships were holding their own, but the selkie soon began to weaken despite the xanide's added boost. Before long, their shields were on the verge of collapse and their weapons were losing their effectiveness. With their demise imminent Aden offered to beam Abby and the crews of the other EA ships to the *Garm*, but they refused to abandon the selkie, which in a matter of seconds would be too weak to fight. Just when it seemed hopeless, Abby hailed him.

"Aden, did you send this?"

"Send what?"

"It's the genetic structure of an antivirus that attacks whatever it is that's eating our hulls. The selkie are synthesizing it now—our systems are coming back on line!"

"That's great!" he exclaimed, as multiple fusion cannons rocked the *Garm*. "But they just sent in another hundred and fifty ships. They're targeting the surface, but we can't tell what they're aiming at."

"They're firing on the taal! They have the same sensors we have and can find them anywhere on the planet. They've already killed dozens of them!"

The *Garm* and the EA ships continued to battle OSEC, but their superior numbers made it impossible for them to protect Seti. As they began to buckle under the strain, hyperspace windows opened all around them. Dozens of additional ships poured through, but they weren't OSEC's—they were zon!

"I can't believe this!" exclaimed Abby, "OSEC is allied with the zon! We can't take them both on!"

"We won't have to—look at your vidscreen," replied Aden.

The zon had placed their ships between OSEC and Seti and were firing on them; but while the addition of the zons' firepower slowed OSEC's onslaught, it merely delayed the inevitable. As more OSEC ships joined the fray, it wasn't long before the zons' fleet also was on the verge of collapse.

"Aden!" exclaimed, Jasper. "More hyperspace windows are opening!"

"Tell me that's good news!" he demanded.

"It's Commander Gris. I'll put him on the vidscreen."

"Gris," bellowed Aden, "you're supposed to be taking orders from Polis!"

"I am sir," he replied. "He ordered me to report to Seti with fifteen ships. From the looks of it, you can use the help." As OSEC weapons fire rocked his ship, he added, "It is good to see the old lady back in action."

"Target only the OSEC ships, Gris. Leave the zon alone."

"What?" exclaimed Gris. "Did I hear you right?"

"No time to explain, just do it!"

"My pleasure!" answered Gris, as OSEC ships continued to pound his hull. "It's been a while since anyone's seen a Dipsa class warship at full power. Now would be a good time to remind them what they can do!"

Gris's fleet launched what fighters they had and opened fire on the OSEC ships. In addition to their fighters, each ship boasted a compliment of a dozen enhanced Ardalan fusion cannons, as well as nuclear missiles and other weapons; and, unlike the rogue Kealt ships fighting with OSEC, Gris's ships could fire their main guns while shielded.

With such overwhelming firepower it wasn't long before OSEC was on the defensive. After losing over half their ships, including all five Kealt ships, they prepared to flee into hyperspace. As they were leaving, Jasper exclaimed, "One of those ships is broadcasting Brawn's transponder signal!"

"Isolate it and disable it!" commanded Aden.

The *Garm* came about and began firing on the ship carrying Brawn. Just as it appeared it

would escape with the other OSEC ships, a
bright blue beam lanced out and destroyed it.

Chapter XXII

"**D**amn it Abby!" exclaimed Aden. "I wanted them alive!"

"You're welcome!" she replied ironically. "I overestimated the strength of their shields. The *Garm* must have inflicted more damage than I anticipated, considering your ship's antiquated nature."

"Antiquated!"

While they were arguing, an ensign shouted, "The EA vessels are training their weapons on the zon!"

"Abby!" exclaimed Aden. "The zon have taken their weapons off line and their shields are down! They're defenseless!"

"They're zon, they eat us!"

"I won't let you to fire on defenseless ships, especially when they've intervened on behalf of our allies. I will at least hear them out!"

When one of the EA ships powered its weapons despite his warning, Aden ordered the *Garm* to fire a blast across its bow.

"The next one is at your bridge!" he bellowed.

While the *Garm* was no match for a front-line EA warship, he gambled they would be reluctant to fire on an ally, especially one who was the King of Kealt and backed by fifteen of the most fearsome warships ever built. He had guessed correctly, and breathed a sigh of relief when the EA ships stood down. He hailed the zon and waited. When they didn't respond he hailed them again. Just when he was about to hail them a third time, they responded.

He put them on his vidscreen and was surprised to see a type of zon he'd never seen before. It wasn't as big and awkward as a queen, but it was much larger than a drone. Like a queen it was gray, had hands, and was covered with something between fur and feathers. It also appeared to possess a set of functional wings, something queens lacked.

Aden couldn't tell if the one facing the vidscreen had three eyes like the other zon forms he was familiar with. However, based on the similarity of its head to queens he had seen, to include a hanging proboscis designed to draw blood out of its victims, and its opaque, nearly transparent nature, he assumed it did.

When the creature continued to face the vidscreen mutely, Aden said, "I appreciate your assistance. You have been gone a long time. What could possibly bring you back to Laima?"

While zon did not possess vocal cords, they could communicate telepathically if the being on the receiving end had been exposed to their neural fluid, something that typically happened during the feeding process. Absent that ability, they used technology to convert the vibrations they sometimes used to communicate with other zon to the spoken word.

In a harsh, artificial sounding voice, the zon replied, "We desire what all things desire: To exist."

"I don't understand."

"Your allies, whom you call the Earth Alliance, have hunted us mercilessly across two galaxies. We continue to survive only in small, isolated groups. Our society is in ruins. Soon we will cease to exist altogether. We are here to surrender to you unconditionally. We have followed recent events in this solar system. We were aware of OSEC's plot to dominate it. We destroyed their ships when they attempted to thwart your own plans. It was we who provided the Earth Alliance the antidote to the weapon that devours their ships, and it was we who prevented the slaughter of your other allies, the taal. We throw ourselves on your mercy."

Before Aden could answer, Abby exclaimed, "What do zon know of mercy! To you we are nothing more than sustenance, to be discarded like refuse when you're done with us!

You've destroyed millions of human lives and families. You deserve no mercy!"

"From your perspective, that is true," replied the zon, "but there is another perspective."

The zon then invited Aden and a representative from the EA to come to his ship to continue the discussion face to face. When Aden quickly agreed, Abby did as well. She thought Aden had gone mad, but wasn't going to allow him to risk his life alone.

When they beamed over to the zon flagship, two unarmed drones met them. They said nothing, but gestured for the humans to follow them. As they made their way through the ship, they were surprised by the number of different species they observed, most of whom they had never before encountered.

It was well known that zon frequently employed other species to help them operate and maintain their technology. Drones, the most common form of zon, had pincers instead of hands, and were incapable of performing many of the functions required of a ship's crew. In addition, they were unintelligent and not capable of creative thought. Queens, and presumably the new zon form Aden had seen on the vidscreen, controlled drones telepathically. One queen could manage many drones at the same time, and over great distances.

To their surprise, the non-zon members of the crew did not appear to be working under duress. As they proceeded down a labyrinth of narrow corridors, they took note of a number of unusual features, including several rooms that contained small, reptile-like life forms in a series of cages. Eventually the drones brought them to what seemed to be a zon version of a conference room. Before long the zon who had answered his hail joined them, along with a pair of humanoid aliens belonging to a species Aden did not recognize.

"Thank you for honoring us with your presence, Your Highness," said the zon. "And you as well Captain Watanabe." He waved a hand and added, "Please have a seat." Once they were comfortable, he said, "I am the Supreme Commander of this fleet, which is essentially all that's left to us of any significance. We understand the animosity that exists between your people and ours. In violation of our most sacred tenants, we have inflicted great harm on your race. If it weren't for the power of the EA, even to this day some of us would still be feasting on you."

If the creature noticed the look of hatred on Abby's face, he ignored it.

"And yet you ask us for mercy?" replied Aden. "We're not suicidal, nor are we insane. What could possibly compel us to forget what you've done—what you are—and prevent the EA from finishing what you started?"

"Our thirst for human blood has been as destructive to us as it has to you...even more so. Those of us that remain understand that profoundly."

"You mean because it provoked the EA to destroy you!" spat Abby.

"No, our destruction began before that," answered the zon.

He explained that when they first became aware of humans from an ancient probe they found floating in space, they were excited they had discovered another sentient species from so far away. They planned to initiate first contact and establish trade relations, as they had with dozens of other species.

When their scientists began cataloging the various mementos of the human race carried by the probe, they discovered a sample of human blood. Curious, they tested it and found that, not only was it compatible as a food source, it would have a unique and pleasurable effect on the zon nervous system.

Against their strictest societal norms, a senior scientist synthesized the blood and ingested it. As anticipated, it caused a euphoria and sense of wellbeing well beyond the effect of any known drug or food source. With his encouragement, several other scientists also tried it.

Before long there was a surging black market in synthesized human blood on Krax, the zon home world. While the government and most of zon society were appalled that zon were ingesting the blood of another sentient species and enjoying it, its consumption spread rapidly.

However, they quickly discovered human blood had another side effect: It was highly addictive to them, and over time impaired their mental faculties. As its use and availability spread, the government became desperate to stop it. They began a campaign to destroy labs where the blood was being synthesized in the hope that if they choked off the supply, the demand would decrease as well.

Sadly, they underestimated the appeal of the new, intoxicating food source. Their society began to splinter into two camps, one which opposed the consumption of synthesized human blood, the other rationalizing it. Before long an armed conflict broke out. Several queens and soldiers that had become addicted produced hordes of drones to protect their supply of the blood, or take it by force from rivals. Queens opposed to consuming the blood of a sentient species, even in synthesized form, produced armies of their own.

The resulting population explosion put a strain on the zons' traditional food source, a primitive, blood rich creature called a druzag. When the druzag population sank too low to sustain the increase in drones, and there wasn't enough synthesized human blood to fill the gap, millions of zon headed to the Milky Way, and its promise of billions of humans to feed on.

Along the way they discovered Kealt and Ardala, and their millions of humans. While they were too well armed to defeat militarily without sustaining huge loses, they had many less well-defended colonies. The zon used these colonies to provide sustenance for their long voyage, and eventually set up way stations to resupply and repair their ships.

They also set to work undermining each world by capturing and controlling certain key officials by means of their neural fluid. They gained other allies, such as Abeg Mar's nephew Kux, and King Edris's chief aide, Tock Horat, by playing on their natural cowardice and self-interest.

With Krax depleted of the zon's natural food supply, most of the remaining zon fled to their various colonies. When the EA began to push back on the zon invasion, they made no distinction between zon who consumed human blood and those that didn't. They chased them all the way back to Krax, where they destroyed the entire remaining zon population.

What little was left of their society settled on obscure colonies so well concealed even the EA couldn't find them. With their remaining allies serving as their eyes and ears, they watched from the shadows as OSEC plotted to destroy Kealt and Ardala.

When OSEC's plans for dominating Laima were foiled, the zon suspected they would take their fury out on the taal for their role in it. Unlike Kealt and Ardala, they had no technology with which to defend themselves and would be an easy target. The zon were ready when OSEC came, and now hoped their support of another, seemingly defenseless, sentient species would open the door to a peaceful settlement that would allow what was left of them to return to Krax. There they would attempt to rebuild their society and eventually rejoin the galactic community.

When he was finished, Aden said, "You are a soldier?"

"Yes. There are five classes of zon. Queens rule what you might describe as a 'hive.' Each queen has a number of loyal soldiers, such as myself, who control large numbers of drones, which are unintelligent, but perform most of the labor. Soldiers also provide the seed necessary for our propagation. Another class of zon is similar to the soldiers, but is dedicated to learning and improving our society. They are scientists, teachers, and what you would call bureaucrats. They ensure that the work of our species is productive and creative.

"The last group looks very different from the rest of us. They are limbless, immobile creatures who lack the normal senses, but have extraordinary telepathic powers. It is through them we are able to communicate with each other over vast stretches of space."

"And those cages we passed on our way here…those were…druzag?

"Yes."

"If we do as you ask, what would stop you from following the path that led you here?" asked Aden.

Abby leapt to her feet and shouted, "Enough! You can't possibly be considering their request? If you do, you're insane! I will have no part in this!"

"Abby, genocide is wrong. They are beaten. With a united EA, Ardala, and Kealt, it will be many generations, if ever, before they can threaten us again."

"You are a monster Aden Cade!" she hissed. "I never knew you!" With that, she beamed back to her ship.

Aden turned his attention back to the zon. "I'll not apologize for her," he said. "Many of us share her sentiment. You chose the wrong species to become addicted to."

"That is abundantly obvious, Your Highness. To reinforce your thought, while our queens can replenish our numbers rapidly, the availability of our natural food supply will limit our reproduction until it reestablishes itself on Krax and builds up its own numbers. Additionally, the war has ravished our infrastructure. As you correctly noted, we will be hard pressed to maintain our few remaining assets, let alone build a force sufficient to threaten other worlds."

"I can't unilaterally guarantee your safety."

"No, but you are quite persuasive. And the taal will make it a requirement for regaining access to their natural resources."

"The taal?" asked Aden. "What role are they playing in this?"

"We have been in communication with them. We have a certain telepathic affinity."

"Of course you do," he thought to himself.

When the parlay eventually ended, Aden told the zon he would support their request to return to Krax unmolested, provided they agreed to abide by certain, yet to be identified conditions. When he beamed back to the *Garm*, Jasper told him the EA ships had departed without an explanation. Aden prayed he hadn't made yet another potentially homicidal enemy.

Before leaving orbit, the *Garm* scanned Seti's surface using information provided by Bang to find OSEC's base. When Aden was satisfied it was abandoned, the *Garm* destroyed what remained of it and he ordered Jasper to set course for home.

Upon returning to Kealt, the surviving members of the Council of Elders insisted Aden receive a proper coronation. He agreed, as long as it was private and attended by a small group of family and friends.

Despite his most fervent desires, the event turned into a national celebration, highlighted by one of Kealt's famous palace balls. Disappointed Abby wasn't in attendance, he eventually excused himself and strolled through the royal gardens until he reached the goliathan tree. Finding himself in a pensive mood, he sat down, closed his eyes, leaned back, and inhaled the cool night air.

"There you are, Your Highness. Someone told me you had left, and I thought this as likely a place as any to find you. May I join you?"

It was Aija, although Aden barely recognized her in her formal attire and perfectly coifed hair. When he nodded affirmatively, she sat next to him.

"Major, even when you were separating me from my fingernails, I have to confess I thought you were beautiful; but seeing you now…you are truly stunning. I'm glad you've recovered from your injuries."

"You are so kind!" she replied, her cheeks reddening noticeably. "I never had a chance to thank you for accepting my account of what I did to you without question or reprimand. Any other man would have had me locked up until I was an old woman—or skinned!"

"Not so Aija, you took the only avenue open to you to save me. As painful as it was, I have to say it was quite clever. For that, I am much appreciative. Still, I am disappointed you didn't trust me enough to reveal yourself earlier."

"It was important for you to truly revile me. If either of us gave even the slightest indication that I wasn't who Brawn thought I was, we'd all be dead."

"A good strategy, under the circumstances you were faced with," he grudgingly admitted.

"This tree is spectacular," Aija said. "You know, Brawn ordered me to cut it down and sell off the splinters to raise funds for his war effort. It's another thing I never got around to."

"The man never did have any taste! Beyond that, I am beginning to sense a pattern: You, dear major, are not very good at following orders."

Aija laughed gently. "Actually, that's why I'm here. Besides Jaak, and now that your father's gone, there is no one I trust more than you. I want you to know that I will always follow your commands faithfully, without question, to the best of my ability."

"I appreciate that Aija, but you've done more than your part for Kealt. I will endeavor to make no further demands of you. To the contrary, if there is ever anything I can do for you or your husband, it is you who should seek me out."

"If I may," she replied, "how is your friend Abby? I was hoping I'd see her tonight so I could apologize to her as well."

"Well, you're Ku Assa, not me. I was hoping you could tell me. Last I heard, she was on Ardala serving as acting ambassador."

"Ah, I have intruded onto a sore subject; my apologies, Your Highness."

"Please, call me Aden; you *and* Jaak."

Aija stood up. "Thank you again," she said. "I hope you find peace—for all of us!"

Before she left, he asked, "On the OSEC ship, would you really have made love to me?"

"I knew you'd decline, although I admit I was taken aback by your overly evocative language. You really know how to hurt a girl!"

"That is not an answer," replied Aden with a smirk.

She smiled stiffly. "Well then, I guess neither of us will ever know."

"You know, next time you have me at your mercy you could give *me* a kiss. I would much prefer that to having my fingernails removed with a hammer and a piece of wood!"

"Your High…I'm sorry, Aden," she replied coyly. "Shame on you! I'm a married woman!"

"I don't envy Jaak; you must be quite a handful!"

"You have no idea!" she retorted brightly, as she walked away.

"Oh, I think I do!" he muttered under his breath.

Chapter XXIII

Furious at Aden for acceding to the zons' request, the EA ships broke orbit and, except for Abby, set course for their nearest base. She proceeded to Ardala, where she had been ordered to serve as the EA's acting ambassador until the actual ambassador, Niles Larr, returned from business on Earth. When she landed, a driver from the EA Embassy met her on the tarmac.

"Hello Ambassador Watanabe," said the young man. "Your luggage will take a while. If you wish, I can take you to your quarters and we can bring it later."

Feeling tired, dirty, and depressed, she readily agreed. She said little as the car sped through Dilax. Watching the city flash past her window, she felt lost for the first time since Aden had come back into her life. While they had parted before, this time there was a sense of finality to it.

Eventually the car came to a stop in front of the ambassador's residence. Her driver helped her carry the luggage she had brought with her into the residence and up the stairs to her quarters. After he left, she took a long, hot shower and ordered dinner.

While she ate alone in her room, she thought about the way she and Aden parted. She told herself she should have told him the truth long ago. If she had, he never would have allowed her to go to the zon ship, and perhaps they'd still be friends, or whatever it was they were. Now, after witnessing him cooperate with them, she didn't see how that was possible anymore.

After dinner, she found a bottle of Ardalan wine and poured herself a glass. Before she knew it, the bottle was empty. Disappointed, she got up and went to the bathroom to get ready for bed. She took off her clothes, stood in front of the mirror, and studied her naked body. She briefly rested her hands on her taut stomach, put on a clean t-shirt and went to bed.

Not long after she fell asleep, the familiar nightmare returned. When she woke up crying, she got up and went to the small bar on the first floor and poured herself a glass of the bourbon Trent had so enjoyed. It tasted like poison to her and she nearly gagged, but she made herself drink enough of it so she could fall back asleep without having to worry about dreaming again. After a while she staggered back to her room and fell onto the bed. Her head spinning, she found the relief she was looking for and passed out.

When she woke up the next day, her head felt like it was going to explode. After she cleaned up, she went down to the dining room where the ambassador's cook had breakfast waiting. She picked at it unenthusiastically, before pushing it away half eaten.

Hoping it would take her mind off recent events, she went to her office and sat down to review her correspondence. Along with the usual diplomatic taskings were several notes from Aden and a couple from Dandridge on Aden's behalf. He was persistent, she thought. Her head still splitting from the night before, she was about to go off in search of something to relieve the pain when a servant caught up to her.

"Sorry to bother you ambassador, but someone is here to see you."

"Please, tell whomever it is I'm indisposed," she replied. When the servant stayed where she was with an unhappy look on her face, she asked her what was wrong.

"I'm sorry ma'am, but it's the high princess. She is usually…foul tempered…when she doesn't get her way."

Understanding the servant's reluctance to tell Celesta to come back another day, Abby shook off the pain and told her to bring her into her office. She was sitting behind the massive desk pretending to be busy when the servant introduced her.

Abby got up and walked around to greet her. To her surprise, she was smiling. Taken aback by her uncharacteristically cheery disposition, Abby forced herself to smile back despite the construction workers trying to jackhammer their way through her head.

Still self-conscious about her appearance, Abby said, "I'm sorry if I look a little disheveled, but I just got in yesterday and I haven't unpacked all my...supplies."

"Nonsense!" she replied brightly. "You look gorgeous!"

"Your Highness," she answered firmly, thinking Celesta had come to torment her, "I'm really not up to trading barbs with you today. Is there something I can do for you?"

"I'm sorry, it was rude of me to stop by without an appointment. Please forgive me—and stop calling me 'Your Highness!' I came to invite you to dinner with my family tomorrow night."

"Dinner?" replied Abby, as the concept fought to take hold in her aching brain. "With your family?"

"Yes. Sarin and I were talking, and we realized you've been to our planet many times, but we've never seen each other in an informal setting. It is an oversight we would like to remedy."

Realizing she was serious, Abby said, "You do know you're talking to Abby Watanabe? Or am I mistaken in thinking I've been addressing Celesta Mar?"

"I know who you are!" she replied, smiling again. "A friend to whom we owe a great debt. Please consider dinner a small installment."

Once she secured Abby's commitment, Celesta bid her goodbye and found her own way out, as Abby stared after her. Not knowing what to make of the unexpected invitation, she went back to work.

The next day she was still catching up when she noticed the time. Determined to prove to Celesta that she took pride in her appearance, she took extra care getting ready, and even applied some makeup she borrowed from an aide. When the car came to pick her up, she took one last look in the mirror to ensure everything was in place. She picked a stray piece of lint off her shoulder, and stepped out to the car.

Later, when it pulled up to the front entrance of the royal family's residence, a feeling of nervousness swept over her. While she was well acquainted with Celesta, Polis, and the rest of the Ardalan royal family through her diplomatic duties, Celesta had correctly noted her dealings with them had been strictly professional in nature. This was a personal venue, and promised to be uncomfortable at best.

Celesta was waiting for her as she stepped out of the car. She looked her up and down and said, "You are stunning, ambassador. Thank you so much for coming."

"You're very kind, Celesta. Coming from you that means a lot."

"I appreciate that you came tonight," she replied, taking her arm as she led her up the steps. "I know this must be a little awkward for you, but I think you'll find we're not that bad."

When they reached the massive entrance to the royal palace, Celesta escorted her through the equally cavernous foyer into a surprisingly cozy drawing room. There, Ivege, Sarin, Polis, and a handful of other guests she didn't recognize were discussing sports, smoking cigars, and drinking brandy.

"Hello Abby!" exclaimed Sarin when she came into the room. "Thank you for coming!" She left the guest she'd been talking to, went over to her and embraced her heartily. "You know," she said, "I feel like I've known you forever, but I don't think we've ever had a proper conversation!"

After Sarin introduced her to everyone, she pulled her off to the side. Abby stared at her as though seeing her for the first time. She was as tall as Sia, and still stunning midway through her fifth decade. Her naturally pale blond hair had not yet begun to gray, and her blue eyes had a youthful exuberance to them. Abby had always enjoyed a positive relationship with her, but today she was smiling at her in a way she never had before.

"I'm sorry Your Highness," replied Abby when she realized she was staring at her. "Please don't take this the wrong way, but I wasn't expecting everyone to be so…friendly!"

"Well, that's our fault. I'll admit when I first saw you at the ball for Aden and my daughter, I didn't know what to think of you. You were pretending to be a doltish refugee and spent most of the night dancing with my future son-in-law. Sia didn't know whether to be pleased he was leaving her alone or jealous he was dancing with such a beautiful woman."

Thinking Sarin was upset with her, she said, "Your Highness, I can assure you, Sia was all he ever wanted. I was merely a diversion, someone he killed time with."

"My name is Sarin! And that is unfair to both of you!" she rebuked her gently. "You've been a great friend to him and us. Bang also speaks highly of you."

"Bang?" repeated Abby.

"We got to know each other quite well when we were stranded on Kealt. She was worried about you and Aden. You know she considers him her son."

"That man has more mothers than anyone I know," replied Abby. "Between his birth mother, the Queen of Kealt, you, and Bang the man has an abundance of them!"

Sarin laughed. "He is one of kind, for sure!"

"Mother, I do believe you are monopolizing our guest!" chastised Celesta. "I promised her this would be fun!"

"Please forgive me!" replied Sarin sheepishly. "I love to talk!"

Celesta had to pry Abby away from her. Once they were out of earshot she said, "I love my in laws, but they can be very intense at times." When she saw Abby looking at her quizzically, she admitted, "OK, I can be too! I need to look in on my children. Would you like to meet them?"

"I'd love to!" replied Abby truthfully.

After she and Celesta took leave from the other guests, Abby followed her up the stairs to the nursery.

"I hope you don't mind," Celesta said. "It's a little stuffy down there for my tastes and I still don't have much interest in Ardalan sports teams, I'm afraid! Besides that, I'm nursing and need to avoid smoke and alcohol. The smoke is easy, but I do miss a drink now and then!"

When she got to the nursery, she opened the door slowly in order to avoid disturbing the children in the event they were asleep. It was an unnecessary precaution—when they stepped inside, they were both wide-awake. The toddler ran up to Celesta and gave her a big hug.

"My goodness Gabo, I think you're trying to crush me! Please say 'hi' to Miss Watanabe."

He greeted her formally, which made both women laugh. Celesta sent him back to the game he was playing with a servant, then led Abby over to the crib.

Abby looked down on the smiling infant and said, "She's beautiful Celesta, both of them are."

"We named her Sia. Would you like to hold her?"

"Would you mind? It's been so long since I've held a baby, I think I've forgotten what they're like!"

Celesta glanced at her curiously, before picking up the child and gently placing her in her arms.

Abby held her close and inhaled her scent. "I love the way babies smell!" she said.

"You look like you've had quite a lot of experience with them," observed Celesta.

"Oh yes!" she agreed. "My first assignment was on a large, deep space survey ship that allowed families. There were quite a few children onboard, including some who were born during the mission."

"I'll bet that was fun."

"Oh, it was!"

"What was the ship's name?"

Abby kissed little Sia, hugged her tightly, and reluctantly handed her back. "Thank you so much for letting me meet your kids. They are truly beautiful. You and Polis are very blessed. I don't want to be rude, but shouldn't we head back down?"

Much to Abby's surprise, once she got used to everyone, dinner was fun. She had half-expected it would turn into some kind of grand family "intervention" to get her and Aden back together. Instead, their wide-ranging conversation covered just about everything but him. When it got late, she found she was reluctant to leave. While Celesta was walking her out to her car, she paused suddenly and faced her.

"Abby," she said, "in case you don't know it, Aden is on his way to Ardala on official business. I know you and he didn't part under the best of circumstances. His decision to help the zon is controversial to say the least. You know they've fed on me and tried to turn me into a drone. Honestly, if they blinked out of existence tomorrow, I wouldn't mourn them.

And that might be the worst thing they've done to us: Compromise our humanity. Right or wrong, by helping them Aden is reminding us of who we are. We shouldn't hate him for it."

Not sure how to respond, Abby stood there mutely.

"Listen," Celesta continued, "what goes on between the two of you is your business; but if you allow his humanity to be a wedge between you, the zon have won."

Abby hugged her. "Thank you," she said. "You are very wise."

Chapter XXIV

Upon taking the throne, Aden kept his word and put the wheels in motion for turning the government back to the Council of Commons. The council itself was quickly reconstituted on an interim basis with acting members, under Abeg Mar, who had recovered from his latest ordeal. Abeg made reconstruction the council's first priority, ensuring that all provinces were treated equally, including Harma, which had been devastated by Brawn's war.

With peace again the order of the day, the taal reopened Seti and returned their ambassadors to Kealt and Ardala. It also wasn't long before Kealt's acute xanide shortage was a thing of the past.

Although Aden was looking forward to being free of his official duties, the Council of Commons asked him to travel to Ardala to patch up relations with them and negotiate a new treaty for their mutual defense. As gesture of good will, Kealt also would present Ardala ten of their new Dipsa class warships, which was five more than Ardala had been expecting when it agreed to help build them.

When he reached Ardala and stepped off the ship onto the tarmac, he closed his eyes and breathed deeply. Sia had once told him she believed Ardala smelled sweeter than any place she'd ever been, and that the first thing she did whenever she returned home was savor the air.

"You still miss her, don't you?"

Startled, Aden's eyes flew open and he saw Celesta standing in front of him. His subsequent, enthusiastic embrace threatened to swallow her petite body.

"Please!" she gasped, "I'm not as young as I used to be!"

Aden released her and laughed. "Forgive my fervor!" he replied. "It seems that every time we say goodbye the circumstances are dire and the entire universe is in jeopardy. It's good, for once, to enjoy a peaceful reunion!"

As if to mock him, he heard the sound of weapons rattling. Eight soldiers had surrounded them, and had their guns trained on him.

"What are you doing!" exclaimed Celesta. "Don't you recognize the King of Kealt?"

"I'm sorry, Your Highnesses!" replied the sergeant in charge. "We have standing orders to arrest him on sight."

"You will release him now!" commanded Celesta, her eyes beginning to smoke.

The soldiers' commitment to their task began to crumble rapidly.

"Sergeant," said one soldier, "we're at peace, maybe we should just let him go."

"Peace or not," insisted the sergeant, "orders are orders."

Seeing Celesta was on the verge of exploding, another soldier said, in a trembling voice, "She's Ku Assa sir, and she's getting really pissed! We all saw what she did to those zon and Minister Sin's men."

"My wife just had a baby!" whined another. "She'll kill us all!"

"What's the matter with you?" exclaimed the sergeant. "There are eight of us and we have energy weapons trained on them. She can't weigh much over a hundred pounds. What are you so afraid of?"

"Sir," replied another soldier, "didn't you see the vidcap? She'll pull our guts out and feed them to us! Or each other!"

Aden saw that several soldiers were so scared they wet themselves. When Celesta stepped forward aggressively, he put a hand on her shoulder. "It's OK Celesta. Sergeant, you're right to follow orders. I consider myself under arrest."

"What in God's name is going on!" bellowed Polis, who had walked up to the group with his young son in tow. "I take my son to the bathroom and I come back to find you've arrested the king of Kealt, one of our most valued allies! And you're threatening my wife, the future queen of Ardala! Sergeant, you better have a damn good explanation for this insanity!"

"Your Highness!" he replied, all but throwing himself on the ground in supplication. "We were merely following standing orders to arrest Aden Cade should he be found on Ardala."

"That's ridiculous! Whose orders are those?"

"Uhh, yours, sir."

"Consider that order rescinded! And consider yourself downgraded two ranks!"

"Your Highness," interrupted Aden, "if I may be so bold. If the sergeant was in fact following a valid order, I commend him for it."

"Sergeant!" barked Polis. "You and your men better get out of here before I lose my sense of humor!" Before they had taken a step, he noticed their soiled clothing. "Did you men piss your pants?" When several soldiers nodded sheepishly, he said, "It's OK. Before I got to know her, I almost did it once or twice myself!"

As the soldiers shuffled past, they thanked him under their breath.

The three royals had all they could do to keep from laughing until they were out of earshot. "My dear wife," said a guffawing Polis, "you have once again confirmed what I have known all along: You are the most terrifying creature in the universe. I know several of those men; they're brave soldiers who fought admirably against the zon. Nevertheless, faced with your wrath they become incontinent! To be honest, I know exactly how they feel!"

Celesta tried to look cross, but failed miserably.

"Why were you so calm?" she asked Aden. "You act like you get arrested all the time!"

"Lately I do!" he replied, which reignited their laughter.

Later that night, over dinner, Celesta told Aden about her experience with Abby. "That woman has a dark side," she said. "I suspect whatever is going on with her isn't about you."

"Sia once described Laima as a 'system of secrets,'" he replied. "Apparently that applies to everyone in Laima, even if they're from the Milky Way."

"Ironically," answered Polis, "as far as I know, Sia was one of the few people who didn't have any, at least of the whopping big variety."

Aden refilled their glasses and held his aloft. "Here's to Sia! May she always be close to our hearts."

As their glasses clinked, Celesta added, "May we honor her spirit."

"Polis," said Aden, while cutting a large chunk off the slab of meat on his plate, "when your mother was returned to you, that must have felt like a miracle. I can only imagine how your father felt."

"It did," he agreed. "Losing Sarin and Sia so close together nearly drove father mad with rage. I don't know how he did it, but somehow he kept a clear head. If I had been the monarch, I'm afraid to say the outcome might have been very different."

"You underestimate yourself, my brother. You will make a worthy king one day," Aden assured him.

"Coming from a king that's quite a compliment," said Polis. "I hope that, at least for a while, Laima will enjoy the peace we've paid so dearly for."

"I hope so too," replied Celesta wanly.

Over the next few weeks, Aden successfully negotiated a new treaty with Ardala. The gift of the warships ensured there were no last-minute hitches or complications, and dispelled whatever lingering hostilities remained.

While diplomatic functions normally bored him, he went to every event on Ardala in the vain hope Abby would attend at least one of them. As much as he wanted to, he didn't try to contact her directly even though Celesta urged him to. Abby knew he wanted to talk to her, he thought. When she was ready, she would—or she wouldn't. Either way, it was beyond his control.

He stayed on Ardala longer than he should have, ostensibly because he couldn't bear to leave his niece and nephew, which wasn't altogether untrue, but primarily because he was reluctant to admit he and Abby were finally through. When he had run out of excuses to stay, he visited Celesta to say goodbye.

"Where to now, my brother?" she asked, while pouring him a cup of coffee, which, like French wine, was catching on rapidly in the Laima System.

"Back to Kealt to file my report," he replied, picking his cup up off the low table in front of him. "Then I will officially retire and take a vacation on Seti."

"Seti?" she repeated with a laugh, as she poured a cup for herself and sat down next to him. "No one goes there on vacation!"

"Well then, I guess I'll be the first."

"Don't forget to come back, like Abby once did. You're too young and have too much to offer."

Aden shifted uncomfortably in his seat. "I know you two were never the best of friends," he said, "but I miss her. She's a very…complicated…woman. Unfortunately, by now she's probably headed back to Earth, or will be soon."

"Actually, I've grown to like her," answered Celesta, "but that doesn't matter. All that matters is you do. And I don't think she's complicated at all. All you have to do is find the key to her heart."

"Oh?" he replied dryly, between sips. "Is that all?"

"I get the feeling she's like a dam holding back a deluge of emotions. I don't know what happened to her out there, but it was something terrible. She needs someone to break through her defenses."

"She won't even talk to me!"

"Keep trying."

Aden laughed.

"What's so funny?" asked Celesta.

"That's exactly what a selkie once said to me."

"A selkie? You mean one of those living ships?"

"Yes."

"Is there anything you can't befriend?"

"Never had much luck with a bolba tree." Aden finished his coffee and stood up. "Time for me to go. Please say goodbye to Polis and your in laws for me, and give your kids a big hug. I promise I'll be back soon."

Celesta later confirmed that Abby had indeed left Ardala. With her gone, she thought it was time to invite Ambassador Larr to lunch. She eventually bent their conversation toward Abby. Curious about her evasiveness when discussing her first space assignment, she told Larr about their dinner together. She said, "Celesta told me she once served on a survey ship that allowed families. We don't have anything like that here. I forgot the name of the ship and it's driving me crazy. Do you know it?"

"Abby told you about her assignment on the *Beagle*?" he replied, with a shocked look. "As far as I know, she's never spoken to anyone about it."

"Why not?"

Larr was a bright man, and quickly realized Celesta was trying to manipulate him. He smiled and said, "I think I've already told you more than I should have. You need to talk to Abby herself if you want to know the rest."

After lunch, Celesta rushed home. She sat in front of a computer terminal and pulled up the database the EA had provided on the Milky Way. She typed in: *"Deep Space Ship Beagle."* When the search came back with numerous results, she accessed one at random. Halfway through the first paragraph she gasped, put her hand to her mouth, and exclaimed, "Oh my God!"

Chapter XXV

When Aden returned to Kealt, he planned to stay just long enough to pay his respects to his family's resting place and arrange for travel to Seti, where there was one last thing he needed to do before he could get on with the rest of his life. The day he was to leave, a servant approached him and told him he had a visitor—it was Abby! He was surprised, having assumed she was either still on Ardala or on her way back to Earth. Regardless, he was sure he'd finally seen the last of her. After a moment of hesitation, he went down to greet her.

"Hello Abby, it's nice to see you," he said awkwardly. "I didn't know you were on Kealt."

"Not for long. After our regular ambassador returned to Ardala, I came back in an unofficial capacity to help Jeff out. He's caught up now and I really don't feel like going back to the dig, so I have no more reason to stay. I'm heading back to Earth tomorrow."

"I've been trying to reach you. You've been ignoring me. What made you come here now?"

She smiled wanly. "After what we've been through, I couldn't leave without at least saying goodbye." She noted Aden's own packed luggage. "I see you're traveling as well." She went over to a bag that had a sheathed sword sitting on top of it. She picked it up, pulled it out of its sheath and hefted it. "This is beautiful," she said. "I'm glad you finally got rid of that worn out piece of steel you picked up on Seti."

"You know, that's the same sword. I got curious and took it to an expert in old weapons. He told me it was close to five hundred years old and most likely forged for King Daniel Cade, an ancestor. How it ended up on Seti, where they were using it as a pry bar, is a mystery. Anyway, when I realized its significance, I had it restored."

"How did you manage to hold on to it?"

"A long story best saved for another day," he answered with a smile.

"Well, there's only one place I know of where this is necessary. And from the looks of all this luggage, you're not coming back for a long time."

"I'm a distraction on Kealt," he replied. "We need to get back on our feet. The Council of Commons deserves a chance to do its job without having the media wondering what I would do."

Abby deliberately re-sheathed the sword and gently laid it down where she found it. "Perhaps that's true, but that's not why you're leaving is it?"

"No. I have unfinished business there."

"Sia once accused me of hiding in the jungle because I didn't want to face certain things. I denied it, but she was right. So I'm speaking from experience when I accuse you of doing the same thing."

Aden grinned and rested his hands on her shoulders. "It's a shame life only happens once. I've been such a fool. I'd do anything to be able to start over with you."

Abby surprised him with a hug. "I'm the fool!" she said. "Other than say some really, really stupid things from time to time, you've been wonderful to me. If even the zon can start over, why can't we?"

"I'm going to Seti and you're going to Earth, for one thing."

"I'd rather go to Seti with you, if you'd let me."

Aden stepped back from her. "You would? After what happened onboard the zon ship? I was pretty sure that was the last time I'd ever see you."

"I said some things I didn't mean and weren't true. It's taken me a while to understand this, but you are who you are, no matter the circumstances. And that's what's so wonderful about you—you will not be compromised."

"Won't they miss you on Earth?"

"A week, a month, a year, what's the difference? The world doesn't revolve around me like it does you."

For a moment Aden thought she was serious, and then he saw her lip quivering. He also tried to keep a straight face, but failed miserably. As they dissolved into laughter, he hugged her back and said, "For me it does! I'd be honored if you'd come with me."

Aden found her a berth on the transport taking him to Seti. When they arrived a few days later, Arvid met them at the spaceport. Aden was pleased to see things were beginning to return to normal. Most mines were back on line, and Kuste was coming back to life. Kealt and Ardala had quickly put the events of the past behind them and, with the consent of the taal, were picking up where they'd left off.

"Welcome back high prin…I mean king!" exclaimed Arvid. "I think Borg has finally gotten over your adventure in the jungle. Will you be staying long?"

"As long as it takes."

"For what?" he asked. When Aden didn't answer, he shrugged his shoulders and loaded their bags onto a utility vehicle. "Where to, boss?"

"Any idea if the old lodge is still fit for human habitation?" he asked.

"Sure is!" confirmed Arvid. "Before the latest troubles, the Council of Commons, in agreement with Ardala, designated it an historical site. They've taken steps to preserve it, and it's in the best condition I can ever remember. When Abeg Mar made the dedication speech, he said it's where he realized democracy was the way of the future, and that he should lead it."

"Ah, humble as always! Under the circumstances, are we allowed to stay there?"

"Of course. It still belongs to your family, only you don't have to pay to take care of it anymore!" Later, as he drove toward the lodge, he said, "We've cleared the road and cleaned the place up; I think you'll like it. You're on your own though, we can't spare anyone to assist you."

"That's fine, as long as it's properly provisioned."

"I don't believe it is, but if you provide me a list of necessities, I will have them delivered by nightfall."

"Excellent!" replied Aden. "We'll probably only stay a day or two, or as long as Abby can stand it, then take up residence at your fine hotel!" What he left unsaid was he hadn't been back since Edris and Sia died and didn't know how he'd feel about the old place. The last time he was there he, Celesta, Sia, Edris, and Abeg had made their stand against Abeg's ambitious nephew Kux, who, having chosen the wrong side in the war with the zon, attempted a coup.

When they arrived at the lodge, Aden was impressed. It was indeed in better shape than he'd ever seen it. It even had a strangely lived in feel, but Arvid assured him no one had stayed there since the last time Edris was there.

He helped him take the luggage they needed into the lodge, and agreed to take the rest ahead to the hotel. Before he left, he handed Aden a pad and a pencil and asked him to note the items they needed. After ensuring Abby was satisfied as well, he handed the pad back. "Oh, Arvid," he said, "one more thing before you leave…"

"Yes?"

"Tomorrow I'll have need of a small shielded ship."

"Tomorrow? A shielded ship?"

"Yes. I know it's short notice. I don't want to inconvenience anyone, so it doesn't have to be anything special."

"Shielded ships are in short supply right now," answered Arvid, "but I'm sure we can scare one up for a king, as long as you're not too picky."

"I understand," replied Aden, before sending him on his way.

While he was pleased with the lodge's condition, Abby was less impressed. After he shut the door behind them, she looked around at the aged wooden furniture, the dusty and corroded hunting implements hanging from one wall, the heads of evil-looking creatures hanging from another, the worn, unfinished wooden floor, and the generally rustic nature of place.

"This place has been…restored?" she asked dubiously.

"Partially, at least."

"I can only imagine what it looked like before."

Aden laughed. "Yes, I could never get Sia to stay here."

"But it's good enough for me?" she replied, pretending to be offended.

"Abby, there is no place in the universe that would do your beauty justice." He bowed for emphasis. "Please accept my apologies for the condition of my humble family estate."

"Well," she replied, "I've slept in worse places."

"You have?"

"Now that you mention it, perhaps not."

Contrary to Arvid's assurances, the requested supplies never arrived. It was getting late, and it had been a while since they'd eaten, so Aden scoured the cabinets hoping to find something to tide them over. To his surprise, he found enough preserved food to cobble together a decent meal. When they finished, he cleaned up the kitchen, then picked up Abby's luggage and showed her to her room. While he wanted desperately to make love to her, he was afraid any such overture would only end badly.

He offered her the best guest room, which was large, bare, rough, and substantial looking, with large, exposed roof beams and paneled walls. It did have carpeting, a concession his father had made for the comfort of the rare guest who stayed the night. He rummaged through a linen closet in the hallway, and was pleased to find bed covers that seemed freshly laundered. The bathroom also was well stocked and clean. Aden silently thanked Arvid—clearly he had prepared the place for him when he learned he was coming to Seti.

After ensuring Abby had what she needed, he said, "I'm not in the master bedroom, I'm staying in my own room, which is at the end of the hall. If you have need of anything, don't hesitate to ask."

As he turned to leave, she asked, "Is it safe here?"

"Well, yes. While we're close to the jungle, the grounds are shielded and monitored by a security team in Kuste on a 24-hour basis."

"That sounds reassuring," replied Abby, "but it didn't stop Abeg Mar's demon kin from storming this place during his little coup attempt, did it?"

Aden grinned wryly. "I didn't know you knew about that! Yes, the system isn't full proof; its reliability is subject to the natural ebb and flow of the xanide field that brackets this place. However, I also believe the taal are watching it."

"Is that good or bad?"

"Good question," he answered with a chuckle. When he saw her frown, he hoped she was sufficiently concerned to invite him into her bed. Instead, she shrugged her shoulders and said, "I guess we'll find out," and stood by the door until he left.

Later that evening, the sound of his bedroom door opening jolted him awake. Abby stepped inside wrapped in a bathrobe and whispered, "Aden! I hear something downstairs!"

Remembering her ploy to get into his bed during a thunderstorm not long after he met her, he threw aside the covers and said, "Come on, there's room here for two!"

"No, you idiot!" she hissed. "Someone's moving around down there!"

Suddenly alarmed, Aden leapt from his bed, unsheathed his sword, and, wearing only his underwear, crept into the hallway with Abby following closely. When he reached the top of the stairs, he realized she was right: Someone was moving around furtively in the kitchen. He told her to stay where she was and went down to find the source of the commotion. He peeked around the doorway to the kitchen and saw a figure moving around in the dark. Holding his sword in front of him, he flipped on the light switch, jumped into the room and let out a war whoop.

Arvid screamed and dropped the bags he was holding. "Don't do that!" he shouted, covering his chest with his hands. "Do you know how wrong it is to scare someone like that on Seti! This place is frightening enough without nearly naked men jumping out of doorways screaming!"

Realizing he was talking to a king, he quickly apologized. "I'm very sorry Your Highness! I tasked my men to get you the supplies you ordered, and when I discovered they'd never gotten around to it, I took it upon myself, as I should have from the beginning. It's late, I was hoping to drop the stuff off without disturbing you. Please, forgive me."

When the brief tableau gave way to unbridled laughter, Abby came down the stairs. "What's going on?" she asked, as the two men picked up the spilled groceries.

"Well, our supplies are here!" replied Aden. "It was late, so my good friend Arvid was hoping to drop them off without disturbing us."

"I'd say he failed miserably," answered Abby, obviously shaken up.

Seeing Arvid's chagrinned expression, Aden said, "I'm sorry you were disturbed, but I can assure you this isn't his fault."

When he asked Arvid to stay for a drink despite the late hour, he accepted, but only after Aden assured him, he meant it—it wasn't every day a king asked someone in his position to share a drink. Aden was surprised when Abby asked if she could join them as well.

After they donned more appropriate clothing, they went down to the lodge's great room. While Arvid prepared something for them to eat, Aden deposited a booty of wine, whiskey, and ale in the middle of the large, cracked wooden table. He pointed to the alcohol and exclaimed, "This more than makes up for disturbing our slumber! You have outdone yourself, my friend!"

When Arvid finished preparing their meal, he brought the food into the room and took a seat. Aden poured them all some wine, held his glass aloft and said, "To old friends!"

"To your father!" replied Arvid.

"To Sia and Trent," countered Abby.

Before long Arvid was regaling them with tales of Aden's youth and his adventures on Seti, some of which Aden thought even held a grain of truth. Laughter filled the room deep into the early morning, until Aden poured out the last of the alcohol. When he offered to get more, Arvid said, "Thank you for your boundless hospitality, Your Highness; however, I don't wish to wear out my welcome. With your permission, I'll be on my way."

"Aden, he can't drive after all this!" protested Abby.

"It's quite all right," replied Arvid. "The vehicle is automated and can return me on its own. I'll be fine."

"You're more than welcome to stay, old friend."

"Thank you, but I have to get up early to ensure a proper ship is available per your request, assuming you still want to do whatever it is you want to do tomorrow. Anyway, you know the old expression: A bicycle only needs two wheels."

Abby blanched at his crude meaning, but it was lost on the exceedingly drunk Aden, who helped him to his car and sent him on his way. When he came back into the house Abby had returned to her room, safe behind an undoubtedly bolted door.

The next day, as promised, Arvid showed up early—too early for their tastes—and drove them to the spaceport. Abby noticed that Aden carried a small bag over his shoulder when they prepared to board the ship, which looked as old and dilapidated as the lodge. Unlike the time he and Sia ended up marooned in the jungle, he packed very little gear. He was confident he wouldn't need it this time.

Once they were aboard and secured for takeoff, Aden said, "Abby, are you sure you want to come? I'm afraid I won't be very good company."

"Do you want me to?"

"Yes."

"Then it's settled."

When the ship landed without incident in the now familiar clearing, Aden threw the bag over shoulder and up picked the ax, machete, and other implements he'd asked Arvid to load, and headed to the wrecked ship. Without saying anything, he began to hack at the vegetation covering the cargo hatch. Abby picked up the ax and helped him. It was slow going—the jungle had taken firm hold of the ship and returned it grudgingly. When the hatch was sufficiently clear, he pulled it open and went inside.

Other than a musty smell, the cargo bay had somehow thwarted the advances of Seti's ravenous flora and fauna. He saw the remains of the bandages and the cut pant leg that had resulted from his run in with the nearby bolba tree. He went over to the seat where Sia had carefully folded and laid the pretty dress she'd been wearing after she'd changed into clothing more suitable for a trek through the wilderness.

While Abby watched, he hesitated as though he was afraid to touch it, then he picked it up, held it up to his face, and inhaled deeply. He knew it had to be his imagination, but he was sure he could still smell her scent on it. When he was satisfied, he put it back on the seat, careful it was in the same position in which he'd found it.

Then he picked up the bag, pulled open the zipper, and reached inside. When he withdrew his hand, he was holding his wedding sash, the one Abby saw him throw to the ground while renouncing his and Sia's arranged marriage, and later wore at their wedding. She didn't know it, but Sia had cherished the sash as a symbol of Aden's love for her. He looked at it closely, as though to memorize every thread, color, and feature, then he folded it neatly and gently laid it on top of the dress. When he sat down in an empty seat, wiping tears from his eyes, Abby sat next to him and held his hand.

"She was a wonderful woman Aden. I know you loved each other very much. I'm sure she's never left your side."

"Yes," he answered, as he regained his composure.

"Why did you come here?"

"I never told anyone this," he said, "but when I was in a coma and Sia and my son were still alive, the taal brought us all here—in spirit, anyway—so we could say goodbye properly. They could have brought us anywhere, but they chose here. It took me a while to figure it out, but now I think I know why: If it weren't for this place, we never would have gotten to know each other. We didn't fall in love here, but it's where we learned to trust each other. I think that's even harder than falling in love. It wasn't easy to get into her heart, but once I did…"

They sat quietly for a while until Aden broke the silence. "Thanks for coming Abby. I really need you here; but you've always been there for me." She didn't answer, but rested her head on his shoulder. "And now it's time for me to be there for you. I know you've been carrying your own burden. It's time you shared it with someone."

When she didn't immediately respond, he thought she would carry on stoically as she always did. To his surprise, she said, "I wasn't always an EA officer. I started out as a civilian xenobiologist onboard a deep space exploration ship called the *Beagle*. It was on a four-year mission to survey a part of the Milky Way home to previously unstudied stellar phenomena, as well as several potentially Earth-like planets.

"I took the assignment with my husband, Ken. He was a very kind, gentle, and thoughtful man! I met him when we were in school. We quickly fell madly in love, and were married before we even graduated. Our parents were furious! We had our first child, Jordan—we called him Jordy—three years before our assignment on the *Beagle*. A few months before we left, we found out I was pregnant with our second child. She was born onboard the *Beagle* and we named her Drusilla—now you know why I chose to impersonate Drusa Prine.

"Near the end of our mission, on my birthday, I returned to our quarters after a long day. I opened the door and it was dark except for a birthday cake with one small candle on top. I could see the three of them hiding in the shadows trying not to laugh. I turned to flip on the light, and when I turned back, they jumped out of their hiding place and sang 'happy birthday.' I'll never forget the look on Jordy and Drusa's faces!

"I reached down to cut the cake, and just as the knife touched the icing, something rocked the ship and the cake fell on the floor. Alarms were going off and my kids began to cry. I was the duty officer in our section, so I left them with Ken and ran to the bridge. We were under attack from vessels belonging to a species we'd never seen before. We were a science ship and had no way to defend ourselves. We quickly surrendered, after sending out a distress call.

"As it turned out, we'd run into the leading edge of the zon invasion of the Milky Way. They boarded the ship and went room to room looking for crewmembers. They fed on the weaker ones, like the children, and took the stronger ones to the cargo holds, where they could watch over them until they were ready to feed on them. When Ken and the children weren't among the group I was with, I feared the worst.

"Two days later, before they got to me, an EA battle group commanded by Trent showed up and freed us. They tried to stop me, but I went to my quarters as fast as I could. When I went inside Ken and both of my children had been…had been…!" She wept bitterly, unable to finish.

Speechless and shocked at her revelation, Aden reached over and hugged her. While he stroked her hair gently, she said, her voice breaking, "Later, I went back and looked at our personal logs to see what had happened to my family. When the zon reached our quarters, Ken fought furiously and killed one of the things before they killed him. The children were small and it was over quickly for them, although Jordy tried to defend his sister. They were all so brave. Ken was nothing like you—he was small and slender, and had no idea how to fight. Yet he killed one of them and held them off as long as he could.

"Trent later offered me a commission with the EA Expeditionary Service. He became a dear friend and mentor. I miss him badly as well.

"I will not debate your moral objections to genocide, but perhaps now you can understand why I have no interest in making peace with those things, regardless of how convincing their story. I've had too many nightmares that ended with the desiccated bodies of my husband and children lying on the floor of our quarters."

"Abby I…I…you've been carrying that around inside you for years," said Aden. "Sia tried to tell me. I'm sorry I didn't listen to her. I should have been there for you long before today."

"I didn't want any help. Literally, until this moment, I've never discussed what happened with anyone beyond what was required in connection with my official duties."

"I see now why you've been reserved toward me," said Aden. "You're not mad I've been callous, you're afraid if you fall in love with me, I'll be taken away from you too."

"Yes," she agreed with a wan smile, "even if you are nearly invincible!"

Aden looked at his chronometer. "It's getting late, and I don't wish to worry Arvid. If you don't mind, I have one more thing to do before we leave."

When Abby nodded, he got up and she followed him outside the ship. Aden carefully cleaned the seal around the hatch and secured it. With Abby by his side, he walked out into the clearing between the ship and the bolba tree. Seemingly to the air he said, "Bang, if you're out there, I need to know you're all right."

After what seemed an interminable delay, they felt the ground quivering and off in the distance saw treetops waving without any wind. On Seti that could be an ominous sign, but the warm feeling that coursed through their bodies let them know they had nothing to fear. When Bang finally burst into the clearing, they were pleased to see she had regained her previous, robust condition.

"I'm here my children," they heard in their minds. "As you can see, I'm fine. I'm pleased to see you are as well."

"Thanks for your help," replied Aden. "I assume it was the taal who ensured there was hardly any xanide on OSEC's bomb. That's why they were able to cloak it, wasn't it?" When she didn't answer, he added, "Taal also saved the crewmen of the *Vaden* from those vampris birds that attacked them, didn't they? I'm a good shot, but I couldn't have hit two invisible creatures at that distance at that time of day without help.

"Oh, and then there was the cave full of xanide. I was lost until I had that 'spontaneous' revelation. Thanks to you, OSEC has shown its hand and been dealt a bloody nose. They will be less inclined to meddle with us in the future."

"Perhaps, my son, but they are avaricious and soulless—don't think they'll walk away from such a prize so easily."

"Did the zon tell us the truth about themselves?" he asked.

"Their version of it, but yes. It would be wise to keep them at arms' length. Once addicted they crave human blood as much as OSEC craves xanide. While they have a conscience of sorts, that will never change."

"We have to go now Bang. Please come back to Kealt soon. I have much to learn from you."

She turned and headed back into the jungle. As she disappeared from sight, she snorted and thought, "You do indeed!"

The two said little on their flight back to Kuste. They had a polite dinner that night at the lodge and enjoyed a few drinks. By the end of the evening, neither had spoken of the day's events. They eventually headed up to their respective rooms and said a formal 'goodnight' to each other. Aden had barely fallen asleep when Abby was again in his room shaking him.

"Aden!" she whispered insistently, "I just heard the door open. You're not expecting Arvid again, are you?"

"No," he answered, throwing his legs over the edge of the bed. He pulled his pants on, then found his sword and yanked it out of its sheath. "Abby, hide!"

"I will not!"

Before he could reply, light filled the room and a dozen armed men stormed into it. Aden saw they were carrying old style projectile weapons, the only kind that worked reliably on Seti. Although it was futile, he stood in front of Abby and brandished his sword. The tableau held until another man arrived and pushed the armed men out of the way...

Chapter XXVI

"**G**ross!" exclaimed Aden, when he came into view. "We saw your ship blow up!"

"Yes," he replied, feigning a disappointed sigh. "That damned Brawn eventually revived after I accidentally beamed him onto my mothership. Before anyone knew what was happening, he made his way to engineering and manually interrupted the coolant to the engine core. Next thing we knew, BOOM!" He threw up his arms for emphasis.

"Thankfully someone had the foresight to equip the ship with cloaked and well stocked escape pods, although, as far as I know, these poor fellows and I are the only ones who made it off in one piece. We've actually been living here on and off while we've tried to find a way out of this figurative and literal hellhole.

"We were foraging for food when you arrived. We're a disciplined bunch and cleanup after ourselves; otherwise, you might have been spooked. Anyway, when we returned and saw that someone else had moved in, we decided to lay low until we could figure out who it was.

Imagine our surprise when we saw you and your girlfriend!

"When you left this morning without your luggage, we knew you'd be back. We decided to wait until you returned to make our move. Which brings up a good point: Why are you in separate rooms?" He smirked at Abby, who was wearing nothing but a nearly sheer t-shirt and panties. "Against my better judgment, will someone get her some decent clothes? She's too distracting and I can't have you all gawking at her!"

One of his men left and quickly returned with her luggage. After he dropped it at her feet, he held up a small, shiny object and said, "Look what I found! One of those fancy EA scanners!"

"Excellent!" replied Gross, while taking it from him. "We lost our own inferior version some time ago." When he saw Abby was still in her underwear, he waved it at her and added, "Don't stand there, get dressed!"

Suddenly aware of her near-nakedness in the presence of so many men, she covered her breasts with one arm, yanked open a bag with the other, and pulled out her uniform. With everyone watching, she turned her back to them and got dressed. When she was finished, she asked if she could have her boots.

Gross nodded to one of his men, who retrieved them from her room. Then he picked up the shirt Aden had worn the day before and tossed it to him. "Here, I guess you deserve a little dignity too. Put on your own clothes! And drop your sword; I'm afraid it might embolden you to do something stupid!"

Per Gross's instructions, he dropped the sword on his bed and pulled on the rest of his clothing. While he was tying his boots he said, "You've been living here and the taal have tolerated your presence after you attempted to obliterate them?"

Gross pointed to the armbands he and his men were wearing. "See this?" he asked. "When we're wearing these, they can't hear our minds. That's why we were confident we could safely build the weapon on Seti. They wouldn't know we were here, and no one would think to look for it here."

"How did that work out?" asked Aden sarcastically.

"Well, to be honest, not as well as I'd hoped!" was his equally sarcastic response.

"Not that it's unprecedented at this point," said Aden, "but how did you even know about this place, let alone manage to circumvent the security around it?"

"Some time before he met his demise," answered Gross, "your old friend Tock mentioned that your family had a lodge located in an isolated area outside of Kuste that no one besides you and Edris ever stayed at. Realizing it might come in handy one day, I asked him to tell me what he knew about it.

"Based on his information it was easy to disable the force field and cut off communications without alerting what passes for security around here. You know, you should be pleased the late, unlamented Mr. Horat is no longer extant—that man must have collected every secret in the history of Kealt, and was well on his way to amassing a new set at our expense. Again, fortunately for us, when they refurbished the place they neglected to upgrade the security systems."

"What now?" asked Aden. "I assume you're not going to kill us, at least not yet, or you would have already."

"Very good, my muscular friend. Thanks to you, we finally have a way out of here. Your little sex toy is going to stay here with half of my men, while the rest of us are going to take you to your ship in our cloaked pod. Once we're in orbit I'll beam up the rest of my crew, send you home, and be on our way.

"Now, if either of you attempts to interfere, we will not hesitate to kill the other. Of course, my horny friends won't let the delectable Ms. Watanabe go to waste before it comes to that. A very circular plan, wouldn't you agree, Your Highness?"

"Why didn't you send out a distress call from your escape pod and wait for someone to pick you up?" asked Aden.

"We tried, but we were too close to the planet and the xanide radiation blocked our coms. Since the pod had limited power, we had to land. We need something a little more sustainable to try again."

"Your plan's all very well and good Gross, except that I don't have a ship. We arrived on a commercial transport."

"We don't need a ride home," answered Gross, "only far enough away from this abomination of a planet so the ambient radiation won't block a distress call. You're still a freaking king, aren't you? I'm sure you could manage that without too much trouble? I mean, there are only two of you in the entire solar system."

"You'll release us once you get the ship?" he asked. He knew Gross was going to kill them both regardless of the outcome, but he was playing for time.

"Yes, damn it, we'll let you go once we're off this place." Of course, he thought, it will be out an airlock.

"OK, Gross," replied Aden, "we'll play it your way."

"Good." He nodded to the rest of his men. "Come on boys, we're going…!"

A bloodcurdling scream interrupted him, as one of his men disappeared down the throat of a huge, serpent-like creature rising above the doorway. Before they could react, a second man was fighting to escape from the tentacles that wreathed the creature's neck.

While the rest of Gross's began firing their weapons wildly at the slavering beast, Aden took advantage of the confusion by grabbing his sword and fleeing with Abby through a back door that led to a second story deck.

While they scrambled down the steps leading to the ground, one of the men fired wildly in their direction in an attempt to stop them. When they finally succeeded in killing the creature in the doorway without losing any more men, Gross ordered several of them to follow Aden and Abby out the back, while he took the rest out front door in the event they chose that way to make their escape.

"Son of a bitch!" he cursed, seeing no sign of them.

"Sir," said a man named Blair, "Yu says he found blood on the steps—it looks like we clipped one of them."

"Well, let's take a look," replied Gross. He went around to the back of the lodge and pulled out the hand scanner. He aimed it where Yu was pointing. "Human blood all right." He waved the scanner and added, "As long as they don't get

341

too far ahead, we ought to be able to track them with this, radiation or not!" He looked back down at the scanner. "Sure enough! I've got the two of them moving southward about a kilometer from here. I have no idea how they got that far already, but hurry up, grab your gear and let's get moving!"

"Southward sir? That's away from Kuste. According to Horat, there's some bad stuff in that direction. The moon's not up yet, so it's pitch-black in there. We have flashlights, but all they'll do is let them know where we are and attract things like the one we just killed. They'll never get out of that jungle alive without any real weapons. Maybe we should just let them go!"

"I'm done underestimating his royal pain in the ass and his buxom sidekick!" he replied sharply. "I won't rest until my heel is stepping on his warm, recently beating heart! Anyway, he's our ride out of here! Keep your flashlights off. We'll move out in single file. They'll probably assume they've lost us and double back anyway. When they do, we'll be waiting."

The remaining men looked at each other nervously before gearing up, forming a line, and following the path Aden and Abby had taken. It seemed with every step the jungle grew louder…

Chapter XXVII

Aden ran into the jungle as fast as he could without leaving Abby behind. Once inside he continued his breakneck pace, despite the thick foliage and poor visibility. Abby knew he was trying to put as much distance between them and Gross's men as he could, but it was dark, she wasn't familiar with the terrain, and was terrified of what might lie in wait for them.

Aden obviously knew the area well, but even he needed to see where he was going. It was only a matter of time before they stumbled over a rock or a tree root, fell into a hole, or were snatched by one of the countless voracious creatures that lived on the ground, in the trees, or in the air.

"Aden, stop!" she insisted, after nearly losing her balance. "We're far enough away they can't possibly find us, especially in the dark. We're pushing our luck. We're making so much noise and we're such easy targets, I can't believe something hasn't tried to eat us already!"

Aden pointed to the rising quarter moon. "It's not as dark as it used to be, but I get your point. Regardless, if he uses your scanner, they may not be as far behind as you think; but even with it I doubt they'll be able to move as fast as we can. I know this place well; my father and I hunted here frequently when I was a child. There is a tall cliff not far from here. I know a way up, they don't. We can take shelter in one of several shallow caves and we'll be able to defend ourselves by throwing rocks if we have to! Also, there are other raw materials we can use."

"For what?"

"Come on, we're almost there!"

Against her better judgment they began running again, albeit more deliberately. Just as they settled into a pace she was more comfortable with, something wrapped around her legs and dragged her to the ground.

"Aden, help!" she screamed.

He stopped and ran back to help her, but couldn't find her.

"Where are you!" he bellowed.

"I'm over here! Hurry!"

He followed her voice until he found her in the clutches of a creature similar to the one that had devoured Gross's man. It was smaller, but equally capable of swallowing a man—or a woman—whole.

It was so focused on dragging Abby into its throat it paid no attention to Aden as he got behind it, raised his sword, and swung down on its neck. Even in death, its tentacles continued to pull Abby toward it. Aden swung his sword again, severing them with one blow. Abby jumped up and threw the lifeless remains away from her.

"Goddamn it!" she cursed at him. "I told you this would happen!"

"I'm sorry. Are you all right?"

"I...I think so," she answered uncertainly, as she ran her hands over her body. "Where are those damn Ku Assa? You're the king, aren't they supposed to be watching over you?"

"I ordered them not to. There aren't very many of them, and I felt their services would be better used elsewhere."

"I don't see what better use they could serve than to protect their king from getting eaten!" she replied gruffly.

"Under the present circumstances I'm forced to agree with you. Come on, we're almost there."

As Aden noted, with the rising of the quarter moon it was getting brighter. When they reached a small clearing, Abby could see it bordered a massive escarpment, as Aden had promised.

"I don't think 'cliff' does this justice," she observed. "How big is this?"

"In places it's almost two hundred meters high. It goes forty kilometers in either direction. To the east, it terminates at an inland sea. To the west, it continues until it hits a mountain range. All in all, a most effective barrier against the beasts living on the other side, which are among the largest and hungriest on Seti."

"It didn't do much to keep that snake creature from devouring Gross's man—or attacking me!"

"It's called a hoggorm. Believe it or not, it's related to the bolba tree. While they're capable of scaling the cliff, they mostly live on this side—we're treading on one of their major breeding grounds."

"You've got to be kidding me!"

"Afraid not," he replied wryly. "On the bright side, this is the end of their reproductive cycle. The females are dormant and the males are generally lethargic, although they won't turn down a meal if one happens upon their doorstep. That will work in our favor."

"How could that possibly help us?" she asked incredulously.

"We left a pile of fresh meat on the same trail Gross and his men are on," replied Aden. "What do you think happens to fresh meat on Seti?"

"You're hoping they stumble across it while these monsters are fighting over it! Couldn't we have just killed something small and left it? Did you need to use me as bait?"

Aden laughed. "I didn't use you as bait, but had I thought about it…" He stopped suddenly, his attention drawn to a number of trees that bordered the field. While Abby watched, he began hacking off small, straight branches with his sword and collecting them in a pile. Next, he cut down a few small saplings, trimmed them down, and flexed each one until he found one that met his requirements. When he was ready, he carried his collection to the base of the escarpment, took off his shirt, and began filling it with rocks chosen in the same meticulous fashion he used to select the tree limbs.

"Aden!" gasped Abby. "You're wounded!"

"Yes, a projectile nicked my shoulder when we were escaping the lodge."

"Let me look at it!"

"No time!" he insisted, and continued filling his shirt.

"You will stop long enough to allow me to bandage it and stop the bleeding. Among other things, it will undoubtedly attract more large carnivores."

When he reluctantly agreed, she pulled down her uniform and lifted off her t-shirt. She was braless, and her bare breasts brushed him as she used the t-shirt to cover the wound and staunch the bleeding. When she was done, he gawked at her and said, "Abby, you are beautiful!"

"I don't believe it!" she exclaimed, as she tugged her uniform back over her shoulders and zipped it up. "We're virtually unarmed in the most dangerous jungle in the universe, with a homicidal madman and his henchmen right behind us, and all you can think about is your penis?"

"It has nothing to do with my penis. You *are* beautiful." When she didn't reply, he added, "I've noticed you wear a beat-up old cross. Is it just a relic, or are you a Christian?"

"I found it near the generational ship. I took it as a sign. At this point, it's pretty clear there will never be peace without help from above. Now, what were you doing?"

He went to a group of ferns and pulled off several large fronds. Then he handed Abby the pile of sticks and the fronds, picked up his rock-laden shirt with one hand, his sword with the other, and began walking toward the cliff. When he came to a break that was virtually invisible, he led her up a steep, rocky path until he came to a narrow ledge just below the top of the cliff. He stepped onto it and she followed him until they reached one of the caves he had mentioned earlier. Once inside he sorted his booty into piles.

"Are we safe in here?" she asked doubtfully.

"Yes, this cave doesn't go back that far. If anything was in here, it would have introduced itself by now."

"That's comforting! What on Earth are you going to do with this mess?" she asked with bemusement.

"Ever hear of a bow and arrow?"

"What are you going to use for a bowstring and to lash your arrows together?"

He pulled off his belt and held it out. "This is woven from weep hog wool. So are my socks. It's some of the toughest stuff around. It should do the trick."

"And I suppose those leaves will serve as feathers and the rocks as arrowheads?"

"These fronds are tough and stiff; they'll work well enough." He held up a rock and added, "This is flint; with any luck I'll be able to make a passable arrowhead."

"Why do I have the feeling you've done this before?"

"When I was a child my father made it a point to teach me how to survive here with nothing but my wits. I'm glad I paid attention!"

Abby watched him work and was impressed with the speed at which he was fashioning a makeshift weapon. While he was hafting a roughhewn arrowhead she said, "Your shoulder is injured in the same place that thug stabbed you the time you took me to the refugee camp I was living in. Do you remember?"

"Yes," he replied absently, throwing a completed arrow onto a growing pile. "How could I ever forget those shoes you insisted on retrieving? They almost got me killed!"

"I was supposed to be an objective observer for the EA. When I realized I was becoming infatuated with you, I tried to push you away, albeit halfheartedly. I was sure if I acted dopy enough, you'd quickly lose interest in me. Instead, you took pity on a poor refugee and brought me to your home with no expectations.

"I remember thinking how foolish Sia was for spurning you. I know now why things happened the way they did, but I have to admit, for a time I was quite envious of her." When he didn't answer she said, "Tell the truth, was I ever anything more than a good time to you?"

Satisfied he had enough arrows, Aden had begun working on turning the sapling into a bow. At Abby's question, he paused. "I have to admit," he said, "at first you weren't much more than that, but you were at least partly to blame, pretending to be someone you weren't. That said, over time I sensed there was a lot more to you than you revealed. As I have gotten to know the real you better, you have certainly grown on me, Abby Watanabe…" He paused as screams rent the air, followed by an explosion of weapons fire.

"Sounds like your theory was correct!" she said.

"They're close!" he replied. "As I said, they're probably tracking us with your hand scanner. Hopefully this cave will provide us some protection from it, but I'm not counting on it."

As gunfire continued to ring out, Abby asked, "Are they shooting at us, or something else? If we're lucky maybe Seti will take care of them for us."

When a projectile hit the cave wall next to Aden, he yanked her to the ground with him. "Maybe it will!" he exclaimed. "But I wouldn't count on it!" With that he stood up, strung his makeshift bow, and leaned out over the ledge outside the cave.

"Are you crazy?" she whispered. "They'll see you!"

"I doubt it, it's still too dark. While the scanner will tell them where we are, they have to aim their weapons manually. It would be the greatest stroke of luck—bad luck—if they managed to hit us up here. Besides, I'm pretty sure they still want to take us alive in order to get at a ship."

"Doesn't the same apply to you? I mean, the part about it being too dark to see?"

"When they fire their weapons, I can target the flash. They have nothing to cue on—watch!"

Aden stood near the edge of the cave, notched an arrow, and drew back the bowstring. He shouted, "Gross, we're up here!" When he saw a muzzle flash, he let the arrow fly.

"What the hell was that?" exclaimed one of Gross's men when an arrow thwacked into a tree next to his head.

"Son of a bitch!" cursed another man. "The bastard got me in the arm!"

"Mr. King!" shouted Gross. "That's a clever little weapon you've fashioned from bark and tree roots. We don't want to hurt you; we were just trying to get your attention. We can stay here forever, or at least until the sun comes up and we get a good look at your hideout. I'm guessing you have no food or water. Eventually you'll have to come down. If you do it now, the deal we offered back at the lodge still applies. If you don't, well…"

While he was talking, Aden looked in the direction of his voice, hoping his eyes had adjusted enough to the gradually lifting gloom to allow him to discern the figures of Gross and his men. "There you are!" he muttered under his breath, and loosed another arrow.

"Ahhhh!" screamed one of the figures. "My goddamn leg!"

Before they could react, Aden fired again, hitting a man in the neck.

"Fall back!" yelled Gross. "Get behind a damn tree, any damn tree!"

When they were safely hidden from Aden's barrage, Gross hissed, "I thought you were the best-trained men in OSEC! That freaking caveman is turning us into human voodoo dolls with nothing more than sticks and rocks!" When no one answered, he ordered his senior officer, a man named Burke, to take a headcount.

"Well," replied Burke quietly, so Aden couldn't target his voice, "Johnson got eaten back at the lodge by that snake thing; Yu and Blair were carried off by those bird things; Karl here has a bad arm courtesy of His Royal Highness; Evans ate an arrow; and we left Dow back there with an arrow in his leg…" just then a scream issued from their former location, accompanied by the sounds of creatures fighting. "…I think we can count Dow out now. That leaves seven of us, counting you, unless you still want to count Yu and Blair, in case they're still alive."

"We've been here for weeks you idiot! Have you ever seen anything get carried off and live?"

"I don't know, Evans got grabbed by that tree thing a while back and we managed to save him; of course, he's dead now, I think. I mean, he was pinned to a tree and wasn't moving when we fell back here."

"Shut up! How much ammo do we have left?" When his remaining men reported they had less than two full magazines apiece, he said, "We can't afford to waste anymore ammo on these two! They got up the cliff, so can we! Karl, Kline, and Lewis, I want you three to find a way up there; the rest of us will wait here until you reach them, or until morning comes."

"Sir!" whined the one named Karl, "I can't climb with this arm! Anyway, he's still up there playing Cowboys and Indians."

"Stop complaining! We weren't that far behind him, how many arrows could he have made? Anyway, he got us with lucky shots—no one could intentionally shoot a half-ass bow that accurately. Get moving!"

Reluctantly the men stepped out into the clearing. A burst from a projectile weapon immediately dropped them. Gross looked at his scanner and exclaimed, "The bastard isn't on the cliff anymore, he's less than forty meters away in that direction! He must have picked up one of our weapons!"

"What now Gross? This guy is freaking everywhere!"

"No he's not!" insisted Gross. He pointed and added, "He's over there, which, according to the scanner, means his blowup-doll girlfriend is still up there somewhere in their love nest—big mistake your kingness!"

"How does that help us?" asked Burke.

"The rest of you spread out and keep him occupied," replied Gross. "Try not to kill him if you can help it, he's our ride out of here! And try not to get killed! While he's busy down here, I'll make my way up to her. If we're lucky, with her under control he'll quit trying to chop us up!"

"OK," replied Burke doubtfully, "but how are you going to find your way up there?"

"The same way we've followed them this far: The scanner recorded their path. I'll follow it right up to her."

"If you take the scanner, we won't know where he is down here!"

"Are you guys professionals or what? There are still three of you! Deal with this." He checked his scanner and pointed again. "He's still over there somewhere. The sun's starting to rise, it will be harder for him to hide."

He checked his weapon, walked away from where the scanner said Aden was, and doubled back to catch his trail up to the cave. When it led him to what seemed to be a solid cliff-face, he cursed under his breath. Realizing there had to be a way up, he studied the cliff carefully, and eventually found the break.

Abby hadn't agreed with Aden's plan to go after Gross's men, especially since they could track his every move. However, from the sounds drifting up from below, it was evident it was working. After a while it was quiet, except for the sounds of the jungle. Unsure of Aden's fate, she picked up the sword and the bow and arrows he had left her and went back in the cave as far as she could. When she heard footsteps coming toward the entrance she rejoiced. Aden was back! She rushed to greet him and almost ran into the barrel of Gross's weapon.

"Easy sweetheart, I know you're happy to see me, but I promise there will be plenty of time for that later." He looked past her to the bow and arrows lying on the cave floor. Keeping an eye on her, he walked over to them, picked up an arrow, and shook it at her. "You gotta be kidding me! *This* is what he was using for archery practice? Next time I'll have to pick my men more carefully."

"It won't make any difference Gross! Let go of your weapon and raise your hands!"

He turned and saw Aden standing at the cave entrance, aiming a projectile weapon at him. As he complied with Aden's demands, he exclaimed, "I can't believe it! According to the scanner you got every goddamn one of my men—at least, the ones Seti didn't get—and except for that nick on your shoulder, you're spotless! You're a goddamn killing machine! It must run in the family. How would you like to work for OSEC? We'll pay you double whatever a king gets. Hell, we'll even give you another planet to rule over if you want."

"You killed Sia and my son," replied Aden grimly. "You nearly succeeded in destroying every inhabited world in this solar system. The only reason I haven't killed you already is because I'm struggling to think of a punishment fitting the barbarity of your crimes!"

"You make it sound so personal!" whined Gross. "It was only business; and you better get used to it, because now that we're here, we're not going anywhere! So this may be your last chance. Put down your weapon, take me to a ship and, I promise, we'll go easy on you."

While he was talking, Abby saw a shadow from the newly risen sun creep over Aden, followed by the head of a hoggorm.

"Aden, look out!"

Before he could react, the creature lashed out with its tentacles and pulled him up and out of sight. With Gross's attention riveted to the scene unfolding at the front of the cave, Abby picked up the sword Aden had left her and slammed the hilt into Gross's neck, driving him to the ground. Then she grabbed the bow and remaining arrows and went after Aden.

She scrambled up the short path to the top of the cliff and found him close to the cliff's edge. He had fired the few remaining rounds of his weapon into the creature, and now was using it to keep it from pulling him into its jaws. Abby dropped the sword and hastily notched an arrow. She fired it at the monster's midsection, which caused it to flinch, but it refused to relinquish its prize. When her last arrow hit it in the neck, it dropped Aden and turned toward her.

Aden scrambled to his feet, ran over to Abby and picked up the sword. He pushed her behind him and prepared to defend her when a huge form moved with an almost unnatural quickness and latched onto the back of the creature's neck. The battle ended quickly, with a blood-smeared taal standing over its still-twitching victim.

"Thank you taal!" said Aden. "Do I know you?"

When the creature ignored him and shambled back the way it came, he shouted, "Why must you all be so…enigmatic! It was a simple question!"

The creature took another step before pausing. It turned around and in their minds they heard it say, "We find communicating with humans…irritating!"

"What? Why?" asked Aden.

"Taal have no words. We communicate with each other with perfect clarity, passing our exact thoughts to one another with ease and without misunderstanding. Your minds are far less developed. While we can hear your thoughts, we cannot reply in kind, except in the form of basic emotions and feelings. To communicate with your species on a higher level, we must translate our responses into words so that you can understand us with specificity. That is extremely tiresome."

"I understand; but I'm afraid I must ask another question: Why is it you've chosen to intervene on our behalf now, and not earlier when Gross's men were threatening us?"

"We prefer not to get involved in human affairs, except when such affairs directly threaten Seti. We left him in your more than capable hands."

"But he fired on you—tried to kill you."

"We understood his intentions from the beginning and responded accordingly."

"Yes, Bang told me they don't have the ability to block you from manipulating their minds. In fact, it is you who ensured they had that misperception in the first place, isn't it? And why Gross still thinks they can."

"Very good Your Highness; we were never in any danger from them."

"You've intervened in recent events quite a bit more than you're letting on, haven't you?" When the taal remained mute, he asked, "Where is Gross now?"

"In Seti's hands."

The taal turned and headed back to the jungle. The last thing he said was, "I am River. Be warned human! Not all taal share Bang's enthusiasm for you."

"Well, that was unsettling!" remarked Abby, as the taal disappeared from sight. "Apparently you were correct: They've been watching us. I'm trying to understand why what he said makes sense to me."

"Because he wants it to," advised Aden. "Suffice it to say, they've been in control the entire time. We've seen and thought only what they've wanted us too."

"Gross didn't kill any of them with his attack?"

"No. Not one."

"Their relationship with the zon troubles me."

"So it should," responded Aden somberly, "especially if they can manipulate them like they have us. It raises questions about their ultimate role in all this—including the Zon War—I'm not sure anyone wants answers to."

"You don't trust them either."

Aden smiled. "Think about it: Kealt and Ardala once again at each other's throats and both of us banned from Seti. That's how the taal have played this game for the last 10,000 years. We could easily blame it on OSEC, because that's also how they operate, but they certainly make a convenient villain."

"And what about Bang?" replied Abby. "The leader of the taal has the most powerful and influential human in this solar system thinking he's her son and she's his mother. That also fits into their modus operandi. And not that I feel good about this, but I fooled you too, when I played the part of Drusa Prine. You have a soft heart Aden. It will be your undoing."

"When they play the games they do, it's hard to tell up from down," he observed. "To be honest, I've thought of what you said; but we have to have faith in something. I have faith in her. As for you, you only hid your identity from me. You stood up for us, and me, when you needed to. I make no error in judgment when it comes to you."

"In this solar system," she answered, "I only have faith in one person, and that's you! Not to be overly dramatic, but if it weren't for you, I'm not sure the taal wouldn't have let OSEC's plan succeed. You may have thwarted not only their plans, but the taals' as well. You better watch your back."

They returned to the cave, now armed just with Aden's sword. When they reached it, as they expected, Gross was gone.

"Where did he go?" asked Abby.

"I don't know, but if he still has the scanner, he'll use it to return to the lodge. He'll be no worse off than he was before, except that he won't have his henchman."

"He's still armed," she reminded him.

"At this point all he wants to do is get to the safety of the lodge. He's a coward, after all. We'll be fine."

Abby followed him down the side of the cliff and into the clearing. Despite the carnage that had just taken place, there was little sign of it—Seti was an efficient housekeeper. Aden picked up a discarded weapon, ensured it was loaded, and led Abby back the way they came. They hadn't gone far, when off in the distance they heard someone screaming: "Help me! Help me please!"

They ran as fast as they could toward the sound. When they got there, they found Gross in the grip of a bolba tree. The lower half of his body had already disappeared into its trunk, and the rest of him was sliding into it slowly. When he saw them, he begged them to help him. In response, Aden turned and walked away.

"You can't just leave me here!" Gross pleaded. "I'm a human being! Please, I'm begging you, help me! I promise, I'll make it worth your while!"

In response, Aden walked back toward the bolba tree. "Gross," he said, "after what you did to my family and countless others, I'd be justified in leaving you to your fate. Still, I couldn't sleep if I did."

"Oh, thank you, thank you! I knew I could count on you! You've got Abby anyway, who needs Sia?"

Aden pointed his weapon at him. "The last time I saw my wife, she was being ingested by a bolba tree. You're not worthy to share the same fate."

"What are you doing? No, no, no!" Gross begged, when he realized Aden's intention.

Aden replied, "Consider it, 'A Taste of Sia.'"

Abby looked away. She heard the weapon's report, and then silence. Aden took her arm and they continued back to the lodge. When they reached it, he called for security. While they were waiting, Abby asked, "Would you have killed him if he hadn't mentioned Sia? Not that anyone could blame you; he more than had it coming."

Aden grinned mirthlessly. "The cruelest thing I could have done would have been to allow the bolba tree to finish its work. He didn't know it, but by the time we'd reached him, he was past the point of no return—it had already begun digesting him. Had I let him be, he would have suffered the most excruciating death imaginable.

"A bolba tree prefers fresh food, so it keeps its prey alive until the very end. It would have dissolved his skin and sucked on his oozing fluids slowly enough to ensure he'd survive for hours. So, believe me when I say that, more than anything, I wanted to just walk away from him."

"I'm sorry I asked," replied Abby.

He caressed her shoulders. "I'll bet you're also sorry you came."

"Not in the least," she replied, smiling. "Sure beats being stuck behind a desk like Dandridge! I'll say this about you, Your Majesty, you know how to show a girl a good time!"

"Please, don't ever call me that again. We've been through too much together."

They were interrupted by the sound of multiple vehicles coming to a stop in front of the lodge. As they discharged dozens of armed men, the leader came up to Aden and introduced himself as Constable Amos Cludge.

"Are you all right?" he asked.

Aden touched his wounded shoulder. "I need to get this looked at, but otherwise I think we're fine."

"I understand you were accosted by a group of armed men. Are they still in the vicinity?"

"They're part of Seti now, constable, and I mean that quite literally."

Cludge shuddered at his meaning. "If I may sir, at some point would you mind if I sat with you and got a detailed account of your ordeal? This place is supposed to be safe. I'd like to know what went wrong so it doesn't happen again."

"Very prudent. I'll be more than happy to go over it in detail once everything has settled down. Now, if you don't mind, could someone bring us to the hotel?"

Chapter XXVIII

A t the hotel, under Abby's watchful eye, a medic cleaned and patched Aden's wound. After he closed the last stitch, they went to the now-crowded bar, where she bought a bottle of French wine and filled their glasses.

"I guess you can find this stuff anywhere these days!" she observed.

"Yes, but not the company," he replied.

Abby held up her glass. "Thank you, Aden. I'll second that!"

"Tell me about your family."

"Please, it would bore you to death!" When Aden insisted, she finished her wine and refilled their glasses.

"Well, I warned you!" she said. "Jordy was the rambunctious one, always getting into trouble. He would always beg us to go on away missions, but most required environmental suits and the ship didn't even have one his size. So, one day Ken made one for him. It wasn't real of course, but it was very convincing.

"They put on their suits and walked down to hydroponics. Ken told Jordy to close his eyes, and they went inside. Jordy wasn't fooled, but he thought it was hilarious his father had tried to trick him into thinking they had beamed down to a planet! I'm convinced he would have been an explorer had he…had he…"

"Tell me about Drusa."

"Drusa was beautiful! She was very affectionate and fun. She was the more social of the two and had lots of friends. Everyone wanted to be near her. I'll never forget coming back to our quarters and seeing her and several other little girls talking seriously about fashion, with Ken moderating. He was really good with kids."

"Do you have pictures of them?"

"I do!" she replied. "Here, let me show you…" She pulled out her communicator, touched the screen a few times, and handed it to him. He took his time as he scrolled through them. When he reached the last one, he handed it back to her and said, "You had a beautiful family. Thanks for sharing them with me."

"You know," she answered, trying to keep from crying, "I never talked to either of our families about what happened." As tears began to flow freely down her cheeks, she sobbed, "I miss them all so much…so very much!"

Aden reached across the table and held her hands. "I'm sorry," he said, afraid to say anything more.

They eventually had an enjoyable dinner together, despite the melancholy mood that had settled over them. Once Aden got Abby talking about her family again, it was as though a dam had broken. For the next hour and a half, he did little but listen as she talked about her childhood, her parents, her siblings, and other things she hadn't talked to anyone about in a very long time. By the end of the evening they were both exhausted. When Aden walked her up to her room, she hugged him and said goodnight.

He returned to his own room, which was actually a large suite. It counted among its amenities multiple bedrooms, a large living room and dining area, and a hot tub. After he took a shower, he tried as best he could to catch up on his duties. He waded halfheartedly through a daunting backlog of messages until he came across one marked, "Call me—urgent!" from Celesta.

He walked over to the com panel and called her, as instructed. When she appeared on the vidscreen she said, "There you are! You aren't the easiest person to get a hold of, are you?"

"I've had quite an adventure," he replied. "What is so urgent I have to call you immediately?"

"I thought you would like to know: Abby had a family. They were killed by the zon."

"I know."

"What? How?"

"She came with me to Seti. She told me about it. All part of the adventure."

"Aden, it was horrible—her husband and children were devoured by those…those monsters! No wonder she wanted no part of your negotiations with them."

"I wish I had known," he answered. "I would have been more tactful with her. Thankfully, I think we're both finally ready to move ahead."

Aden went on to tell her about his 'adventure' and near brush with death. When she got over her dismay that he had again put his life at risk, they said goodbye.

After reviewing about a tenth of his remaining messages, he decided to turn in. As he was about to climb into bed, he heard a knock on the door. When he opened it, Abby was standing there wearing just a bathrobe. Speechless, he stared at her, noting that she smelled as irresistible as she did the night on the *Hyperion* when she teased him mercilessly. When he didn't move, she put her hand on his chest and pushed her way into the room.

After she shut the door, she walked past him, and with her back to him, removed her robe. Now fully naked, she glanced coyly over her shoulder and walked toward his bedroom. He followed her, and when he started to say something, she told him to shut up and warned him not to ruin the mood.

When they reached his bed, she pushed him onto it, climbed on top of him and began removing his clothes. She did things to him that night even Drusa hadn't, and he thought she'd done everything.

When they finally fell asleep, Abby found herself back on the *Beagle*. It was her birthday. She had just gotten off duty after a long day, and was on her way back to her quarters. When she opened the door it was dark, except for a single, small candle stuck in the middle of a cake.

In the darkness she could make out three shadowy figures and heard one of them giggle. She turned to flip on the light, and when she turned back, Ken, Jordy, and Drusa were singing their own joyful, cacophonous version of happy birthday. She felt tears forming in her eyes as they ran over to hug her. She couldn't stop kissing them.

After a while, she stood up and smiled at Ken. He hugged her tightly. "We love you Abby," he said. "We'll never leave you. But it's time to let us go."

"I know. I love you Ken."

"I love you too."

She gathered her family to her and hugged them. She kissed them one more time, then turned and left the room.

She woke with a start. It was only a dream, but she was sure she could still smell her children. She grasped the old cross, smiled, and whispered, "Thank you," and went back to sleep, knowing her bad dream would never return.

The next morning Aden got up first and ordered room service. Abby arose when the door chime sounded, put on a robe and went into the suite's dining area. Aden had already retrieved the room service cart and wheeled it over to the dining table. When he saw her, he greeted her enthusiastically.

"Welcome to the day, my morning star!" he exclaimed. "I hope you slept well!"

"Very well, thank you," she replied crossly. "Please, must you be so enthusiastic so early in the morning? I'm not ready to be shouted at!"

"I'm sorry," he responded in a lower tone. "It's just that every day I wake up and find you're with me is cause for celebration! I will attempt to rein in my enthusiasm."

Seeing his chastised expression, she went over to him and gave him a hug and a kiss. "You absolutely will not!" she insisted. "Your ardor for even the simplest things is what I love most about you. I promise I'm done complaining for the day!"

"In that case," he said, relieved he hadn't put her in a bad mood, "I've ordered a little bit of everything. I don't know what you're in the mood for, but if you retain dear Drusa's tastes, I'm sure you'll find something here you will enjoy."

Abby went over to the cart and marveled at the bounty Aden had procured. She picked up a plate and merely stared at it.

"What's the matter? You don't like anything?"

Abby smiled. "I like everything! I don't know where to begin. Do you think you left any food for the other guests? You even found some coffee!"

"Kuste has come a long way," he assured her. "There's more than enough."

With that, they both began filling their plates. After they sat down to enjoy their repast, Abby said, between eager bites, "I have to say, it's been a long time since I've enjoyed a breakfast this much!"

"Well, I'm sure having survived another near-death experience is at least partly to blame for our heightened senses, but I agree, it is uncommonly good. I'll have to thank the chef before we leave."

After finishing a piece of bacon, Abby said, "I can't believe your father used to take you hunting here! How did either of you make it to adulthood!"

"He was a resourceful man," answered Aden, "literally and figuratively larger than life."

"You hunted those…hoggorms?"

"Not typically. That slice of jungle is full of tasty game animals, as well as prized trophy animals, many of whose heads adorn the walls of the lodge."

"I have to say, I didn't look at them too closely during my brief stay. Even in death they terrified me! Some of them looked even more frightening than the hoggorm, or even the bolba tree!"

"Fortunately, they aren't all there at the same time," said Aden. "Many are migratory and follow their natural prey. Now is a rather poor time to hunt. That is probably why the hoggorm goes dormant this time of year."

"I remember you said they were dormant," she replied. "As it was, we almost got eaten by three of them! I can't imagine what it's like when they're fully awake and the jungle is crowded with those other beasts!"

"That's the best time to hunt! Humans aren't the natural or even preferred prey of any of Seti's creatures. They'll eat us if we're careless, but most of the time they're too busy eating or being eaten by each other to notice us."

"Which reminds me—how did the hoggorm get into the lodge? I thought that place was shielded?"

"It is. In all the excitement, I guess one of Gross's men forgot to raise it after they came in."

Abby poured herself more coffee and nibbled on another piece of bacon. "This is good! I'm almost afraid to ask, but does it come from a pig?"

"Yes," he answered, "but based on the records you recovered from the generational ship, after 10,000 years they bear little resemblance to the ones you're used to, assuming they haven't evolved as well."

"Either way it is delicious!" When Aden merely nodded, she added, "Your father was a great man. I didn't know him well, but I was always surprised by how gentle and kind he was. I doubt we would have even met if he hadn't opened up that ball for you and Sia to refugees. You know, he also provided us with proper clothing. You must miss him badly."

Aden paused from digging into his second plate. "In fact, the longer he's gone, the more I appreciate him and what he stood for. Every man, even the worst tyrant, wants peace, but usually only if it's on their own terms. For him peace was paramount to almost everything else.

"There was a time when we could have crushed Ardala, and many thought—wrongly— we would have been justified in doing so. Even after he lost two sons to them, he didn't waiver.

In fact, that made him more resolute than ever. His greatness was in his willingness to see the good in everyone, no matter how deeply buried."

"Well," she replied with a grin, "It seems he passed at least one trait down to his surviving son."

Aden smiled crookedly and continued with his breakfast.

When the meal ended, they took off the little clothing they had on and stepped into the hot tub. After all they'd been through, the hot, bubbling water was a welcome tonic.

"Ahhhh," sighed Abby, as she eased into the nearly scalding water. "I may never get out! This is quite a room you have here. I guess in any galaxy it's nice to be king!"

"I'll stay in as long as you do!" Aden assured her. "My body's been through quite a lot recently. It will do me good to linger awhile." When she merely smiled at him suggestively, he asked her what was on her mind.

"Well, Your Majesty, this has been quite a ride. What's next?"

"I thought I asked you not to call me that!"

"You're stalling."

"What do you mean?"

"You know what I mean," she said coyly.

"You want to talk about this now?" he asked. "I was hoping for a more romantic setting."

"Why not?" she replied. "Your own beloved wife once told me, more or less, we should say what we need to say when we can, because if we wait for the perfect time, it may never come."

Aden cleared his throat dramatically. "OK, well, here goes: Abby I love you. I've loved you for a long time. It seems like we've always been there for each other. Well, at least, you've been there for me. I can't imagine my life without you, I really can't. Please don't go back to Earth; stay with me."

"Not good enough," she said with a scowl. "Except for the 'love' part, you might as well be talking to your friend Arvid!"

"Arvid? Really?"

When she continued to scowl at him, he reached across the water and took her hands. "Abby Watanabe, the brilliant jewel of two galaxies—you are love, passion, and compassion unequaled in the universe; no man is worthy of you, least of all me; yet I dare to ask, will you…will you marry me?"

"Don't you have to marry a princess or something?"

"A yes or no would suffice!" he replied sharply. "Anyway, I'm a king! I can *make* you a princess if I want to!"

"Wow, that's not very romantic!"

"Why do I feel like I'm talking to an OSEC officer?"

When they both stopped laughing, she said, "Of course I'll marry you. You should have asked me a long time ago, you idiot!"

"Now *that's* not very romantic!"

She slid over to him and gave him a deep, tongue-twisting kiss.

"How's that?"

"I think you have to do it again!"

After she kissed him again with equal passion, Aden hugged her tightly. He said, "Abby, I love you unconditionally. Still, if we are married…"

"Yes?" she replied, when he hesitated. "What is it?"

"I…I'm afraid I'm about to ask you something stupid or insensitive again, although, with all my heart, that is not my intention."

"It's OK, just say it!" she insisted.

"I understand the depth of your loss. I would understand it if you say no; but are you open to the possibility of additional children?"

"Yes, of course. Are you?"

"Having children with you is my most fervent desire, next to marrying you."

"Why, Your Majesty! That is the most romantic thing I've ever heard you say!"

"You called me that again…it is?"

"Yes. It certainly took a while, but I think you're finally beginning to understand me!"

"I doubt that. But if you'll let me, I'll spend the rest of my life trying!"

She didn't answer, but kissed him again. And that was all the answer he needed.

The End

About the Author

M.B. Smith, the oldest of eight children, was born in Kingston, NY, and raised just outside of Woodstock. He has lived, worked, and gone to school on the East Coast, in the Midwest, and in Southern California. He is a graduate of the Ulster County Community College, Bradley University, and the Pepperdine University School of Law. He currently resides in Ashburn, VA, where he and his wife of nearly three decades raised their four daughters. If you enjoyed this book, you might also like his other books: *Chancy, Queen of Ashes*; *Love, or a Safe, Sterile Life*; *System of Secrets*; *Purity*; *The Children of Kalothia*; and *The Secret of Hawk's Talon House*. Mr. Smith would very much like to hear from you at mmbkbc@verizon.net